The Reckoning of Rance

Best re

D0912341

A

Roger Browning Novel

REECER
CREEK

Reecer Creek Publishing
Ellensburg, Washington

DEDICATION

To Keely for bringing inspired meaning to our way in this world.

ACKNOWLEDGMENTS

The Reckoning of Rance is a work of fiction. Any resemblance of the characters to actual persons is purely coincidental. I would, however, like to acknowledge certain individuals for their encouragement, love, and support through this process: Jim, Mark, Lisa, Brant, Garrett, Colleen and their families. A special thanks to photographer Jonna Parr for her patience and good humor with a grumpy old rancher.

1

TIME HOLDS NO STOP

Rance made his way through the catch pen gate, leading his big roan in a cooling walk before allowing him to water. The big round trough was splitting the fence of the holding pen and the feed barn lot, where water flowed over its side endlessly, while the windmill above spun slowly under the midday breeze. "Whoa, Yank, yer shore a goodun," he said while patting the lathered neck of the hot gelding. "Not yet, old son, goanna hafta cool ya down a little more... I'll wait with ya," Rance said out loud, as he was as dry as the worn out old cow horse was. A grasshopper made its fluttering hop from the barnyard grass and over into the water tank where that would be the end of him. He would soon meet with others before him at the bottom of the open top water tank's graveyard with its layer upon layer of grasshoppers and West Texas dirt. The time had been enough, so Rance loosened his girth, led Yank over to the trough and dropped his reins, where he took in water in long sucking gulps. Rance did as well, but, instead, from the well pipe that supplied water to the trough.

A lonely yellow jacket wasp swept in, agitated from Rance taking his spot at the spout. Without his mouth leaving the flow, he swatted him with his felt hat, never missing a swallow. The wasp joined the grasshopper in the cool pool. With hat still in his left hand, he raised up and looked out over the backs of the boney stand of lotted cattle as they raised the dust of the pens. He wiped the sweat coming down his leathery face with a forearm swipe that left a streak of mud upon him. The sweat mixed with the West Texas dirt that he had acquired in his behind hoof travel of another grouping of bunched up cattle heading to the pens. "What a beautiful land," he said. The roan looked up at him, water dripping from his quivering lower lip back into the trough, then went back at it to finish his drink. Beautiful is one word to describe it, but that was only if you were raised in it and had known nothing else. Looking around, short dead hackberry trees dotted the horizon, scarcely 15 feet in height for the more mature ones. The dry had always been there and although Rance ignored them, now dead, some would wonder just how they had gotten that big in the first place in the endless dry. The mesquites managed their way successfully, as neither wet nor dry could kill them. They were survivors, as was Rance and his weathered ancestors that had settled this ranch before him. He stood and listened. It was quiet. A different quiet to him. The rustling of the lotted cows, with their occasional wanting, bawling, call for their separated calves that were just one pen over in their containment was keeping time with the accompanied random stomping of the big roan's hooves to the pack dirt where he stood, keeping rhythm to a bothersome horsefly he was trying to rid in his stomping; the hungry fly thus being the timely conductor of Rance's afternoon symphony.

Rance stood there completely silent in thought. "How did it git this way?" He asked himself quietly, while looking out over the top rail of the pipe lot fence toward the dry grass pastures that lay beyond it. A group of buzzards flew high above, circling in on the scent of a dead wild hog, that Rance had shot and lost, two days prior, ending its destruction of another rolled round bale, left pastured to make up for the summer and winter grazing lost. He had been unable to locate the spot where the big boar had dropped, but now was able, as the soaring group above it, had found it below them, for him. Rance saw them and realized their find, but his mind just wasn't there. He was alone now and truly felt it, even though he had a good friend again with him and his dependable steed leaning into him, he still felt very much alone.

"Hello Bingo. What's goin oan with yew today? And how did we ever git this far into another Century?" he asked his old dog, while reaching down and giving his trusting friend a firm pat on the head. His dog was a good friend. He was always there no matter what, and wanted to be. He never judged as many had – even in times of Rance's passing him by and ignoring him while in heavy thought of the day ahead. The old dog never held it against him and never lost love for his old master, regardless. Rance thought about that in the moment and short of pulling his hand back from his pat given, stopped in it and joined that hand with the other and briskly rubbed the shoulders of his old friend with them both. Bingo came alive in the gesture and it almost looked as if a smile formed on his face. His tongue lay out of the left side of his mouth and his eyes rolled back in his head. He had only one good eye, as the other was glazed over from some past injury. Rance had not known the cause. The glazed blind eye seemed to dance uncontrollably in its socket in Rance's patting, as the old dog relished the moment.

He was not your average ranch dog as he was pitbull bred. Abandoned as a pup, he latched onto Rance's kindness toward him and built a lifelong bond – a bond built over a leftover water-sopped pack of bologna and half a gallon of sour milk from Rance's truck bed ice chest, in his fending. The pup was weak and starving and Rance just couldn't see it staying that way, so he picked up the exhausted pup from the parking lot of his home at the Lonestar Motel. Rance had just moved into it himself, and had witnessed the young pup several times in his moving, taking handouts of old scrap sandwiches, leftover fries and chips from the occasional morning checkout guest that would toss them his way. It needed the strangers' food in passing to survive. Sometimes that old motel would go days without offerings and his ribs shown it plainly. Rance could see that the pup was alone, as he was, and he needed the pup as much as the scrawny little pup needed him, but unbeknownst to Rance, he would be taking in a pitbull breed, as he looked nothing like one at the time. He was starved down and floating in fleas and ticks and reflected the look much more of that of a coonhound. Rance had never really been around any other kinds than that of the hound and the cow dog that was common to his lifestyle. The pup would not be Rance's first choice but it wouldn't have been his last choice either after feeling the pup's smile in his taking. Even familiar with his true nature – and society's fear – he wouldn't have put much thought in the doing of it. He was out of place in the life Rance lived, but Rance was himself out of place too, and in his learning of his new friend, there would be no equal to him, in comparison of the cow dogs he would come up against and those of Rance's past. Other dogs in his dealings were just tools, like the cow bred mounts the cowboys rode, to be used and discarded when their time came. No time for relationship made, and only necessary means to get the job done. But for this old one-eyed pitbull-bred cow dog Rance was giving the well-needed shoulder rub to, it was more than that. He was proven. He was as true a friend as ever, and even in comparison to the species of Rance's own he appreciated the old dog for his value in it.

Rance was no longer young, but he was not what could be considered old either. He was stuck in the middle of it, knowing his prime had passed him and wondering if his future was done. He often wondered if he should have built more to his own instead of hiring out so much to others. In his own building, was it enough? Had his prime been a waste? Who and what would he build up for anyway? Questions the old cowboy routinely ran through his head. He was a tall man. In his youth felt he had the strength of a bull and he feared nothing, but that was then. It was odd to him, because his mind's eye of the present presented to him the solid image of the young man. The picture of him at his peak. It was always there, stuck in his mind unchanged until the reality of chance reflection at his present day mirror, would remind him in its correcting. It wasn't that he saw the self of his youth, but only the boss he once was. The solid man of his prime, with speed of reflex and hardened frame, thick skin of bronze tone. The Rance with the 6'5" frame and hard blue eyes to match it. The Rance that when strangers encountered, would just move out of his way allowing him the path of free rein in his walking. The man that had a steadiness about him and sometimes cast wrongful impressions that were fully felt by reaction given, as his outward appearance did not meet the real man inside. His outward self had projected in ways that set him up for isolation, as his awkward bulk and quiet way gave way to wrongful impression, that he was a man to be left alone. But how he was, was just how he was.

His want to mingle and conduct small talk led him to a nervousness and sometimes inward panic that would lead him to the avoidance of most gathering places, which most often left him out and falsely read as a man to be left alone. He found his true friends were the ones who took the time. The ones that carried him, like the old dog he was happily patting on the head. He felt that it must be a subconscious choice, to avoid what was truly there. Maybe evolution had placed it there in mind like a halting point, for not setting limitations on the true self as means of survival in the end. Did everyone experience it the same, or only he? Either way he avoided the truth until his reflection met. His dark hair turned white, his mustache the same. A slump to his shoulders, with almost an inch of his height forever lost over the rough saddle-spent years of his life. The acquired limp to his gait, his shoulders stretched and torn haven't been as broad and he missed their slowing loss of strength. There was a change to his skin texture and tone that arrived to a man in his mid-life and Rance would not be left out of that rule. He noticed it and was reminded of his truth when the light readied him for his morning shave and forced him to accept the appearance peering back at him from his reflection mirror. But afterward, and light turned out, his mind reverted back to the picture of the Rance when everyone moved from his direction met gait. Thoughts came to him at times, brought back in moments of his youth when on occasion the chance encounters with men of his current age he took in without notice. The passing "Howdy," said to each in normal greeting. He remembered some his age, some much older, as they would pause, in their moment's need for just a bit more conversation, than the juvenile Rance would want to give. He remembered back on his thoughts of that time, wondering "just how did somebody git that damned old in the first place and what good were they for it?" Not in a mean tone of his memory, just misunderstanding their worth as if he himself could ever reach it.

He also remembered the question that followed the first, that long-time ago, "Why would anybody want to?" Even though both thoughts were from a boy of his time, it would be clear and registering to him now, just how short the gap in time filled, where he still hadn't reached the answer to that question of "Why?" He would see it the same of the young boys of his town, as with his glance, boyish grins with quick talk suddenly halted, along with coming to quick stop when sidewalk met. "How ya doin sir?" sounds respectful from the lips of each young man in their passing, but just as quickly after the awkward meeting pass, each re-engaged from quiet pause back to youthful gait and rejoicing vigor. It would happen with such speed in moment fleeting, that there would be no time for Rance's reply of "All right, how boutchew?" No time needed for the response of Rance's recognition, their memory and notice of him already forgotten. Rance remembered the old man plainly, in those meetings of his own time and recognized the method, but his mind would not picture the same thing happening to him as it would only allow him to see the young men and still perceived himself to be just like them. Ready to join in as if he were of their time, but with reality brought home in a single reflection glance in a sidewalk store front window. That would be all he needed for true reflection, in both senses of the word. It would be all it took, in that moment, for him to be brought back to reality of the way that he hadn't been stopped and asked to join in as if he were the same as they. He would see what they saw; a man stuck in time, and in the wonder of the need for the reasons time past had left him.

Rance led the horse back through the lot gate, past the holding pen of calves, held for their weaning, where the barn door housed the coffee can of welcome oats, readied for Yank. The old Ford truck sat idle, waiting, with stock trailer attached, for the roan to finish licking up every morsel of quick nourishment of rolled oats from the ground where Rance had tossed them. The old truck had brought them there as it had done so many times before, but struggled in its starting as did Bingo with his jump to clear the bed of it, in his way to load up for his much anticipated ride home. After two attempts, Rance helped the old dog with a shove to his hind quarters and he finally made it there and managed his way over to curl up in his tool box spot under new found shade. He walked Yank around to the end of the worn-down rig's trailer and loaded him into the already-open left side gate. The old horse, like Bingo, was more than ready. With a forced lunging hop, he almost caught Rance's high-back cantle on the trailer's ribbed top before he landed, four feet flat, and slid to his spot in the center of it. Rance closed the gate with heavy squawk of dry hinges and a dropping clack of the rod pin latch to its pocket, then slid in place its locking bolt. He walked up the side, reached in where the horse stood ready and pulled the reins from his neck then wrapped them over the side of the top rail. The old horse calmed to it, as this was his sign; it was time for quitting and the ride back to more feed and free time rest.

Rance looked around again. In his surveying of the ranch, he caught sight of the lonely old ranch house sitting on its lonesome ridge overlooking the valley below it, the old oak lots, the unused garden spot now covered in tall weeds, and the broken-down chicken coop that sat beside it, just barely, as if any storm front passing might take the whole thing down. "Had it come to this? Is this real or is it only in my mind? Am I dreaming?" If he was dreaming, something needed to wake him up right then. It was not a dream to him, but a nightmare that his waking couldn't change. The time that was and the feeling of being stuck there without forward motion was just the time that it was and no good emotion for it. He was lost to it, and this would be the year and season he would never forget. A new time for some, but a forever changing time to him. The year was 2009 and the season was fall, and Rance felt it in the literal sense of the spoken word.

2

RECOLLECTIONS NOT SO UPSIDE DOWN

August 1967. Rance hung from the tall oak tree limb, held in place with just the bend of his legs. With the feeling of the blood rushing to his hanging upside down head, the world looked differently to him. His young strength was the only thing keeping him there from the ten or so feet drop to his possible neck-snapping death.

It was hot and the ranch family was scattered about doing what they wanted, or nothing, whatever suited them in their mid-work-day break. That is the way it is done in the blistering summer heat under the Texas sun. Work started early and finished late, to be sure to take advantage of both cools, with the heat break starting just about the time the cattle showed stress and the horses' sweat began to lather. A needed break for all, quickly to end when cool enough to finish the day. Routine rotations happened when the men, like the other beasts under the wave of heat, felt it just like they did. The oak trees that rimmed the yard of that Clay County ranch house on the ridge overlooking the valley provided the much needed buffer from the heavy, wet hot coming down. Rance righted himself as the rise and falling song of the chattering locust broke the silence of an otherwise quiet and lazy afternoon. All a mirage to him, as he quickly righted himself in that old oak tree. But just as he was righting himself now in memory, he once again caught himself back in real-time from another day dream visit, when a moment, an object or a place would provoke his need for recollection. This time it would be the view of that lonely old oak, along with the rest, that circled the lonely old abandoned home on the ridge overlooking the valley.

His thoughts went back to his Aunt Lukey. Long gone now, and the old home left to ruin in decay, by the strangers allowed to take her place. It had been the home of his grandfather and grandmother. Then only his grandmother, then uncle, then Rance's own father, before Lukey felt the need to take it over and sell it for its now abandonment for all and Rance to see. It had been built from private loss, on government money gained by the uncle Rance never knew. Killed in a long ago war somewhere on the beach of Anzio, buried under a hero's white cross there, and never to be seen again by the mother who bore him. The ranch, along with the headquarter house, had always been handed down to the next in line for operations since its start. In Rance's time, it would be his grandfather, then lastly his father. That was where it would end for the house on the ridge and the ninety plus acres that surrounded it – forever centered in the vastness of the Backed ЯB. Rance had lived there, but that chance was given only until the event of his father's passing and that would be Rance's first picture of family greed. The Backed ЯB was generational and worked and hard earned for, up and through that point, by the ones of the line that had earned their rights to it. It had been from the land conquered then lost, first by the large beasts that roamed it, then by the nomadic tribes that forced them to their extinction. Wars had been fought in its claim. No one truly owned it – the land watching the passing of its stewards like the small grains of dust forever shifting around on it until its relevance in the time of Rance. The short history of the Abernathy clan Rance would be privileged by – built there through the Comanche wars and the extremes of overburden rains and drought times that followed with not much ease in between – with all of the struggles to hold onto it and the constant fight of it all.

The ones in the line, deserving, were left to hold it. The ones not in the line had their rights of it bought out and forever relinquished of any hold to it, along with their memory of ever being titled to it. Settled in the early 1800s, there had been many more bought out than those that were willing in its fight to work it – and the life it took to hold it. That was all to change though.

Back in 1965, Rance's father couldn't handle the guilt that his sister, Rance's Aunt Lukey, had been left out of the will. He unknowingly changed the dynamic for all in the years to follow. He, along with his brother, Rance's only surviving uncle, thought it best to give their sister her own piece. So the house and a little over ninety workable acres outside its yard fence, would be cut out for her to hold. One hundred acres, removed from the center of the Backed ЯB, with the ranch continually moving solidly around it. His father's belief at the time – she being the youngest – that it would eventually go to the running of it by her anyway, and it would ease her in thought that one day she would. The days of the ranch as a whole ended with that decision. Precedent placed, it broke the mold forever of the right to hold it by reason and the will to work it, and the rights to buy out those that hadn't was replaced with thoughts of entitlement. Little did his father know, that as soon as that decision was set in legal document and forever recorded, his brother Jade, who lived there, would pass, preceded by all of the earned ancestors before them, leaving his father with the need to take his turn.

They did not live on the ranch, instead they lived forty-five miles away, in the small dust blown Texas town known as Archer City. It was an oil boom town with prevalent salt washes and large ranch expanses that seemed to surround the town like the Comanches of old had surrounded the region's settler wagons. They fought to stay there, unsuccessfully, in their protection of their own place in time, just like the small boom town was losing its hold to the salty washes and dying oil boom that was settling in on it. It was his father's turn, and the house in Archer City was quickly sold and the move commenced forty-five miles down the highway to the old ranch homestead on the ridge.

Rance's aunt had other plans at the time and allowed the move to happen. His father would find she was no longer the sister he had known. She had married into a family of wealth and quickly learned how to look down her nose as if she wasn't born in one room of the original two room house that sat atop the ridge overlooking the valley below – the small squatter's shack they all once called home before a war allowed the building of the one that took its place. She was born in depression times, yet only a tip of the rattler's tail of it. She had not pulled the cotton, or fought the war that had taken the brother she barely knew in it, or the two outside of it directly, but still as a result of it. She only knew the rise from it – the Phoenix of the new government that rose out of it. She had forgotten the short time spent of no goods to be bought or sold and the hardship of bartered life. She had been afforded prosperity and change that her brothers had not; they had been worn and aged.

Instead, Lukey went off to college where she would meet her husband Claude, whose family had managed to buy his way out of ever seeing combat, but smoothly carried an officer's rank and status shoreside. Rance's Uncle Claude had been a good teacher in many ways; how to raise privileged spoiled children and how to grab onto an opportunity and hold it at all cost, once in hand. So after the death of her brother Jade, she was already primed and set to handle the ranch house acquisition and was moving on it with speed endorsed by Uncle Claude. One fact she neglected, was even though owned and filed, there was one stipulation in the recorded deed. It was only hers to possess when the next in line of succession neglected to accept the job as boss of the Backed ЯВ.

Still, she stood there blocking the entrance to the screened in porch, leading to the main door of the ranch house, steadily pushing well-rehearsed and well-prepared eviction papers at Rance's father. He was steadily carrying one box of household wares at a time in his forcing way past her in his ignoring and silent way. She couldn't stop him for the stipulation, but she could charge him monthly rent. That wasn't even thought about in his father and uncle's agreement when arranging for the place to be given to her in the first place. His father was forced to agree to that, not knowing that his family would feel the strain of it just nine short years later, when a diseased heart finally proved the postponed eviction to be. Rance had worked the ranch alongside his father and his brother Hadd. His mother had never wanted to be there, as she enjoyed the city ease in living and the excitement that came with it. She fit in more with the designer cateye glasses, stirrup pants, high heels and pearls that went along with preferred lifestyle lived. But she did love the father and made best of what had to be.

Rance had one sister, Lindy, who spent her time assured that she was safe doing as little as possible around the household, much less any ranch work required. She did what she wanted, when she wanted. His mother saw to it that it would be that way, as she was her only daughter and the baby of the family to boot. Rance's father turned a blind eye to her spoiling and had provided an awkward hand in it as well, because of his need to relate to her and his reality of not knowing just how. Rance had two older brothers; Plover, the eldest at ten years his senior, and Hadd, the one he respected and was closer to.

Hadd was eight years his senior himself, but seemed as though they had been born of the same time. Both thought and acted out things as one, maybe Hadd was less than his years, maybe Rance more. The only telling in it was society's gap in time, as the world wielded its intent in actual regard to true years spent in each skin, no matter the maturity felt in reality. In 1969, the U.S. Navy and its gunboats on the rivers of Vietnam would be Hadd's decider of true ages split, but on the ranch it was if they had been born twins. Plover, being the first born, enjoyed his mother's attention, and Lindy carried the same effect. Hadd and Rance, on the other hand, could not remember even a simple hug from her, or the sound of the words, "I love you" as far back as each could recall. Both had clearly known that they would spend a lifetime seeking recognition from her of their worth. Their father had noticed the differences as well, oftentimes assuring them that it was just their mother's way, and that she had the same love for them that she had with Plover and Lindy. Rance and Hadd listened to their father's attempts to cushion them from the truth, but always realized their separation differences, as well as knowing their father had seen them, too.

In the seven years before his father's passing, Rance witnessed the teachings of his Aunt Lukey and Uncle Claude's greed adopted by Plover's self-absorbing tendencies wanted and learned. In Plover's own way he felt as if he was Claude's best friend – Rance believed he admired him even more than his own father. Plover followed what he felt was success and Claude oozed it to him while his own father didn't. Their father's wealth couldn't be measured or spent as he was humble in monetary gain, but he was honest and respected, neither trait did Claude or Lukey have. The truth in it was that Claude had blown through his inherited wealth by the time Rance's father had passed and he needed Lukey's inheritance to sustain their wealthy showing, however false it may well be. And they used Plover in its finality. Claude was living day-to-day, off of anybody that he could tell a good story to and Plover fell right into it; he would spend the rest of his life in it, worthless and using in it the same. He was lazy and Rance's sister was simply entitled. Neither would prove their worth and neither would earn their place, but times were different. More different from any generational change before, from the Comanche wars to the Great Depression. There would be no money for buyout as fate would dictate, as their birth ages separated in such gap, made it that way. Rance often thought that had he been born to the ranch in Plover's place, and Plover in his, things might have been completely different. It was timing he thought. Wrong timing, maybe. Or possibly the right timing. Was it supposed to play out the way that it had? Only God would know the answer to that. One thing Rance had known for sure was that he didn't have it. There would be no money for the fifteen year old Rance to buy his brother's rights to the ranch. Not a single banker would take him serious when he walked through their doors – and he had done just that. Timing and age in the decade of the Seventies would prove different than that of a much earlier time, when a man was valued on accomplishment alone. When trail bosses barely past the age of sixteen ran rough shod over five thousand head of ornery Texas longhorns and controlled the pay of fifty hands or more at the end of a one thousand mile drive to the Kansas stockyard pens.

Rance's time would not be that of his great grandfathers, but a time of limit-setting laws that placed all into one category, likened expectation with date stamped like an ear tag, or brand upon a piece of paper with listed birthdate. All released for grouped peoples of legal established recognized readiness to be turned out through the alley gate in great herds, as if each were the same as the other, until a single longhorn lead steer raced out ahead of the others and determined he was better suited to lead the rest. That was how Rance saw it all; endured castration with the use of the legal paper knife, and all placed into a single category for controlled outcome of the rest. Rance had already known that the time set the rules, and bankers did not.

He was better than the rest and ready before the paper endorsed his release of the accepted general perception to be sure. He knew as well as most that he was better than his brother, but there was no money to be had for him to cull the waste from the herd. His father gone, he was left with orders given but unrecognized in his age. There was no one left to keep things straight. Hadd long gone to a war that no one knew and was himself forgotten for it. Rance's mother was the matriarch given for decisions, but without so much as one made, or at least one that was based in reality. She believed the old rule invalid and that equal quarter should be guaranteed. Truth was she not only felt it, but would rather have been given the opportunity of

Hadd and Rance not being there for the division in the first place. If they hadn't been there, Rance assumed that it would have been much easier on her. He sensed her perception of them always one step out front in the blocking of Plover's and Lindy's place. It was true. Her perception was correct, but it wasn't from spite they were there, rather out of necessity. Just as a fence is placed to hold in the cattle, the blocks would be there in prevention of the ranch's ruin.

Between Hadd and Rance, there was another child born, but not to be known about, just ignored of ever being – lost in childbirth on January 19, 1959. Rance wondered if the loss of him had been the reason of lost expressions of love toward him and Hadd. He had always felt, possibly from intuition, that maybe their mother held a form of resentment for their surviving over the loss, a son. A son that was never given a chance, much less a name at a proper burial spot. A son who never even made his eternal sleep in the ancestorial burial plots centering the ranch. He instead lay nameless, in a pauper's grave, outside of the brush covered, unkempt pasture, location unknown, unfounded and never marked place adjoining the Olney, Texas, hospital where he never took his first breath. "Maybe it was just as simple as that," Rance thought. Her resentment simple; a loss felt, never to see again and unknowing where his vessel lay, with no place to visit and mourn his loss. It was Rance's father's decision to leave him there. The boy born to be unrecognized was why his mother held resentment for the two, especially toward Rance, and it would follow him for a lifetime. Unbeknownst to Rance, in the proof he was missing, he was correct in his assumption that she did hold resentment for them both. Their father wanted them to know everything, so they were both told of the loss of the brother between them. Maybe he felt, as Rance had, that it may have been the difference that both boys needed to have understanding with. His grave was not marked. There was no name written, but his father had love for the child lost. He had always regretted his decision to place him there, but it was his way to cope in the moment. His hopes were to protect his wife in her heartache. It would be a decision made that would follow him for the rest of his life, too. His stillborn son's name was to be Paul Abernathy, and his father wanted it known to Rance. In the telling, he knew his father's love for the child. And in his telling he also knew his mother was witness to the name his father had given. He thought of himself and his brother Hadd, and on what side of his mother's fence they might have been – or even if there would have been a fence at all – if Paul had lived that day so long ago. Never forgotten, however, as January 19 was always a day set aside from work each year.

3

THE DAY THE EARTH LOST ITS SUN

May, 1975. A bad month to all that lived in the ranch house surrounded by new leaf oak blossom, on the ridge overlooking the valley. Rance's father, the patriarch and the tie that bound civility to the family, was tired and worn and would pass away in a mechanical bed, far away from the place he was brought into life. Dying in a plain stale room, in a place he would never want to pass from. His last place would be so opposite of everything he ever was; a city-held hospital. The city he would only visit a few times, mainly in his business forced, where such uncomfortable times had left him with even more reason to avoid it as much as possible. Witchita Falls was not the place for him; to him busy with contradiction and as confining as a jailhouse cell. He welcomed the open country surrounding it and had known every connecting farm market road circling its way outside of it, taking the way that would bring him past it, on to his way to where he wanted to be. He welcomed those open drives and small connecting towns that lie between, over the avoided race of the city where he was so confined. Rance remembered his non-trusting wariness of the crowds the city housed, and their own visible confinement worn by them, leaving him feeling the same. Rance remembered his father greeting them with the tip of his hat or the silent raise of his index finger through his truck's windshield glass and how it bothered him, when his gesture was unreciprocated in his passing, opposite the tradition of the less traveled country roads. He did not know how to live there and Rance was sure he didn't know how to die there. Yet, on May 19 of that year, he did just that.

Rance was there. His father needed to see him. So, with unknowing and misunderstanding, he made his way to his father's bedside rail. In his standing there, he watched the nurse adjust his pillow in jaded formality, showing order to comfort the one incapable of comfort. She checked his vital signs with sideways glance to the overly large watch strapped to her small wrist, while the monotone tick of the industrial clock on the wall sounded its heavy beats, echoing about the silent room. A vase with a simple, single, flower held – that of an early season Indian paintbrush – sat the table beside the bed. It was an early bloom that must have known to be there, as it was his father's favorite wild flower, even over that of the blue bonnet – both prevalent in their world. It had been found, and his mother stopped the car to pick it from the roadside on her way, in hopes to brighten such a dreary room and lonely time. It had gone without notice, as his father could not see the beauty of it at the time. He hadn't even known it was there. It stood slumped and wilted in the drinking glass that his father had not had the strength to use. Its head bent, and seemed a sorrowful sight, as it mirrored Rance in the long day they were to endure, as it was then that the heavy sound of the ticking clock was erased from his ears. His father's heart had ceased of its timed beat, and Rance heard nothing after that.

4

NEW BOSS COMING

That day in May, 1975, at his age of fifteen, would be the day that would build Rance, and the day that would be the beginning of his breaking down. He had made a promise, quietly, to his father. A promise that no other was asked to make that grievous morning in Wichita County. Rance had agreed to the promise to take care of his mother and, moreover, his younger sibling Lindy at the time – a serious promise Rance had not weighed under the circumstance presented. A promise in the moment to honor, that he welcomed, but unknowingly a promise of the fight that would create burning sores that would fester into an unfulfilling way to keep it. His promise and action on it led only to dissension from the ones left out of his father's asking. Only Hadd understood, but even he felt his being left out at times. Rance believed if the Navy and his battle time in Vietnam hadn't had its hold on Hadd, his father would have skipped over him and asked it of Hadd. Rance often felt things might have been much different if he had. Hadd recognized his father's meaning though, as Rance was there and he was not, and it was really the only choice available to be made. War time draft, and Navy enlistment, ensured that he would not be asked and he understood. He took the opportunity as his own, too, and backed his father's request to his younger brother. Once promise was given, he backed his brother to make right of it.

Plover spent his time for his own, living off of what everyone else brought to the table. Lindy, with all needs insured by Rance, didn't see the need to grow up in the moment and recognize him in his efforts, only despise him for them and show absolutely no appreciation for him. To the contrary, she hated Rance just for the chance given as the chosen one for receiving the request by her father. Her hatred would only build, as new time went on, of Rance being given that role and his title of boss to go with it. Her jealousy of him gained with each decision Rance made that concerned her, as well as the others, without any input by her in Rance's casting. He knew the ranch and the day-to-day operations of it and had come by it hard. He didn't leave her out of the operations out of spite; it was that she knew nothing and hadn't tried to learn. So it was just how it was. From that moment of her father's death and request of Rance to run the ranch, Lindy never lifted a hand to work or earn her rights to it, but lived as if she owned it all. She felt entitled, and could not see or want the need to assist Rance in his protection of it, even if it was protection for her also. Plover's deceiving plans to hold it put Lindy and himself into joint contract of greed. Rance's disallowing them both the privilege of input in the ranch's operations left them both to undermine every decision he made, confirmed by ill-warranted lies told to their mother in their efforts to increase hold at Rance's expense. He had tried in earlier times to leave some of the decisions up to his siblings, but found, in short order, that neither was equipped to handle them and were most often times too indecisive and inept to handle the job. Eventually, Rance was forced, along with Hadd's backing, to wean them both. Born out of necessity, it would be the process necessary, but it only enhanced Lindy's hatred toward him that much more.

It would be the vision of the wilted Indian paintbrush Rance would last remember while leaving the room numbered 219, as his world closed up around him. He met the cold wind of the day, as winter still held slight grasp in its faltering reign. The grass shown of green, but grow it didn't that day in the adjoining county of Clay. Or maybe it just seemed it should be that way to Rance.

The silence of the sanitized building was broken, when the wind whistled at its exit doors corners, when Rance opened them outward, in his need for breath. It seemed as though even the birds fell silent, possibly from the charging drive of the chilled wind. Or maybe because of the setting sun ending its time while closing its day upon a decent and very good man. Rance felt the sorrow of it. And as the sun's rays drew in, he broke to it, like a new spring colt when its life had forever changed with the new bit between its teeth. He lost his one true friend, the only true friend he had known to that point, and he sobbed. Rance knelt by the last step of the sterile lifeless building, just at the curb. Tears moved from the corners of his eyes. He wiped them, stood tall, then turned back into the corridor entry, back into the fire, to comfort as best he could his mom, his sister who didn't quite feel it, and prepare for the journey they would now be on.

5

DEVOLUTION

That first year would be a rough one in their change. Rance's aunt had decided, after her brother's death, that it was her turn as the last living member of that generation to spend her days in the ranch house with the oaks above the valley. She served the very familiar words, written on new paper, that his father had torn up just a few years before. Words that she, with the help of his Uncle Claude, handed to his mother, who didn't do the same with them that his father had done. Unable to pay the new rent hike presented, the family was given thirty days to leave. His mother, worn in the moment of life from profound change, gave in to the letter. With the ranch's running and her husband's death and Lukey's force, there just wasn't enough left from their meager checks to sustain it. She set a date to move. Plover watched it all unfold before him, and rather than step in and confront the decision and push it back, decided it would favor him in the long run if he did not, so in cowardly form, he allowed it. In his thinking, siding with his aunt and uncle, would be better for him in the long run. He just sat there and smiled, hoping that they would remember him along the way. They didn't.; false promises from false prophets.

Before his passing, Rance's father struggled with the fact that he had not prepared for his family in the event of his not being there. He was correct in his belief of it, as his end was nearer to him than he would know, or that he had prepared for. He had started in a new direction; with a precious few of his own cattle sold, he had managed to drill a water well high on a hill. A place that was his. A place that Rance's aunt had no say in, or ability to stop his drilling, even though the ranch hadn't been fully broken up at that point. It was a place on a barren hill that stood in sight of the ranch house that stood with its surrounding oaks, but also far enough away to not be bothered by inheritance loss, though within view of his sister. He chose it, in fact, so that one day he would be able to look down on his sister – her and his accomplishment plan. He never succeeded in that pleasure, but had started the process of it nonetheless, and Rance hoped that he had found satisfaction at least for that, in its start. The money was thin and the water well was covered in cost only, by the few boney head sold to initiate its drilling. There would be just enough left over to set the power pole needed for its pumping. A private endeavor, he could not use the ranch's earnings to facilitate his build as there was still divided interest with his sister until separation by inheritance – slowed by a will, held up in a probate by Rance's deceased Uncle Jade.

The well sat beside the lonely pole high on the "Green Place" hill, until his father found more reason to cull his own herd. The well with the pole was soon to be joined by a small single open room house, once he managed enough additional funds and barter in day work trade. The trade for labor finalized, he managed to move the little shack, once used for storing feed, by borrowed trailer and paid workers with the needed expertise to accomplish its setting. Four more old boney cows gone and six hundred bucks later, the cramped little shack sat ready for forced living if it came to the need. One open room, with two windows in the front and a single door to enter that sat between them. In spare time, he managed to provide running water, install a refrigerator he bought brand new at Sears and Roebuck and a slightly used toilet (found discarded at the local county landfill), along with a sink and an overhead cabinet to match. Roughly 320 square feet, he managed a small kitchen and a bed area, quartered off by a hanging curtain. Enough room for his wife and daughter to comfortably live, if the need arose.

There was no money for septic, but he cut a wide ditch facing out and down toward what would be his sister's view and if he were to be up there, and she watching from below, he wanted her very much to see the beautiful view.

He had always felt the boys would be men, and a bedroom and dry place found would suit them until alternate means could be met. In his plans, he had been given an old run down house from a nearby community town that was condemned and destined to be torn down. The giver saw his need and offered it, in chance it could be moved. It hadn't been lived in for forty years at that point. Two bedrooms and a kitchen. It had been built in the day that it required an exit to the outhouse that sat in wait out behind it. It lacked modern wiring and its only plumbing was a single cut pipe that had supplied water to the tap from the windmill tower that sat beside it. It would be a start, and with six hundred more he was able to get a mover to bring it down the red dirt backroads, the eight miles needed for its new second chance in life. He started its transformation but only managed the cleaning and gutting needed. That was February and May was quickly approaching, like a demon fever coming down. He would never see its finish. He had planned with more hope than promise.

His expectation of Plover, his eldest son, to provide had failed him. He could see it in his active restraint to its readying. Rance figured that was the telling he needed for him to ask Rance his promise. Plover had proven his lackluster in the preparation and his father had doubts in his ability or want, but still held optimism for a forced reality; that he would come into the role even though he had dealt Rance the question for promise. Plover only worried about where the next meal would come from and completely lacked the drive or the skill to work the ranch or even to be seen as a hand, to be hired by a rancher for outside work. The country had known him all along and had already formed their own opinions. There were no jobs for him, even if wanted. Everything had to be easy for him or it wasn't worth it. His only care centered on himself even with joining of Lindy later on. They both played on each other as if each were holding the winning hand. Plover was the holder of big dreams that never materialized. His only worth was unfulfilled grand ideals that, for some reason, only he could see the value in. Never accomplished, yet something in his own mind allowed him to wear them as if successful and medallions to be worn. A falseness to life he would spend a lifetime in. He ate, slept and took what little monies that had been accumulated and squandered them away. So, along with Lindy and their mother, Plover would happily move into the little shack at a ripe age of twenty-five years – right there sandwiched between his eleven-year-old sister and his momma.

Meanwhile Rance spent his time working, then coming home to an army cot bed at the end of it. A bed that would see the absolute heat of the long hot summers and the contrasting confining cold of the five-blanket winters that seemed to follow, with no spring or fall between. That cot lay inside the airy unfinished house that sat beside the little shack on the hill. Rance and his father had planted a fingerling ponderosa pine beside that little well, and from Rance's cot he could see the seasons changing around its steadily-shown green. Personally, he felt he had it better than just anybody around and especially anyone else on that hill. At ten years his brother's junior he had already taken on the role of provider and was the only one there that was earning the way.

Rance's jobs ran the gambit, and he worked himself in the way of three men his senior. Any job and every job was not turned down that came his way. A paycheck was needed and his promise was made. A job as a janitor on an after school work program, set up for the student in need of assistance to provide hardship income, would be two hours each day spent in it, while his peers enjoyed their sports-related workouts that his job replaced. He worked the local ranches as a daywork hand in the footsteps of his father. Most created work for him, not out of necessity in its giving, but knowing Rance would not receive handouts but would prefer a check with valued work given for it. Work ranged from feeding cattle, hauling square bale hay and the unloading of cottonseed hulls by hand, and piling it high in the neighboring Mayfield ranch barn for the nickel a bag pay for every eighty-pound bag tossed and stacked. He mowed lawns and plowed pastures, no job too small for him and he was admired for it. He rode and worked alongside the best and became one of the best in his catching and doctoring the rogue brush-bound and river bottom cattle that ran the breaks to their cover, like wild herds of deer. He would earn 25 hard dollars for every head caught in the chance given. Rance was given approval in taking the last period off from school to finish his work early, so to be able to get to each job called upon. He earned the paychecks needed to pay the bills and still managed the time to work the ranch and meet the needs that any adult in the business would envy. He did it without help of his brother, his sister or his mother and he kept it from Hadd, who had enough to worry about with deeply etched and painful memories of riverbed skirmishes with the Viet Cong, and his continuing U.S. Navy service.

He continued to support his older brother, mother and sister who enjoyed, as did her older brother, the easier life it brought them. Rance was bitter with the watching of Plover and Lindy and their expectations of his need to continue to reinforce their mother's meager monthly government supplement. It wasn't the bitterness of the work; he actually relaxed to it. It was their expectation of his earnings, without the offer of a thank you for goods bought by it.

6

PLOVER'S FOLLY

Plover eventually tired of the washtub baths and confined space, but in his ways of doing something about it, enticed his mother into a deal with the devil in asking their Aunt Lukey and Claude for a loan to finish the house that sat beside the shack on the hill. He got it mostly done, but not without the placing of his father's hill as collateral in guarantee to get it. The house was finished and Rance switched places to the shack, but it would be Rance's paychecks expected to pay against the new debt owed. The chain had been secured to his ankle and the ball grew to the shape of an anchor's hold to Rance, as he fought to keep that portion of land sovereign over the ranch and to never let it fall to his aunt's want. Plover gladly moved into the partially finished home and continued his ease in life, when most his age would have been embarrassed of the prospect. He hadn't realized yet, that in his efforts to support that ease, his days because of it were numbered there. Within four years of their father's death, the place looked invitingly in need of completion – and chivalry prevailed to do so.

Its savior would be in the form of the lonely rancher on the first section joining the northwest corner fence. His mother's short dating arrangement led to marriage bliss – or convenience – however one might interpret the reason, and many that lived that community of ranchers had done just that. His mother was not willing to move in her agreement terms, leaving the rancher to reside at the house by the single ponderosa pine planted on the hill. The rancher moved in and completed the house and encouraged Plover, in his time, to depart. This time the mother didn't block the given order.

Plover knew better and he was on a desperate race to find his new meal ticket. After his convincing he found one homely girl. How he'd met her, Rance had never known. He dated her once, then through her, met her mother, who must have been quite a bit easier than the daughter. Saddle worn, seventeen years his senior, and soon to be his mother wife. Two women. Two dates. That would be the accumulation of his entire experience with the ladies in the three county wide area he never left. Within the month spent to know them both, his accomplishment would be the marrying of the latter of the two. He had his new mother to take the old one's place. His hardship was gone for the moment.

7

BURDENS TO BEAR FOR THE TAKING

Time moved on, taking its toll on their mother's second husband as it had the first, and Rance carried the load of the ranch. Hadd returned and assisted Rance in the trap of supporting his mother and sister. Between Hadd and Rance, the ranch would be held with loan paid in full, denying his aunt the prize she was set for. Plover was denied in coming back, as Hadd made it plain it'd be better for him to just stay established somewhere else. With Rance in it from the start and Hadd being gone, Hadd never endured the brunt of the other two. All upset and displeasure was always directed toward Rance. He had spent his time working the land, with no choice, he worked it because it was there and he expected to work it; his pride could not allow it to fold – not in his time. Not because of him. He worked it solid and hard, and watched the brother who should have earned it fail in big misguided dreams.

He watched his sister rush to marry the first outsider who looked her way, who might carry her from her torment. It would need to be a stranger to take her – someone who hadn't the privilege of her ways. Her new husband was a bible thumper who volunteered his services to the church, the youth league, and to any single woman who laid down for his secrets kept. He fathered three worthless sons by her, none of which he wanted. For, and in spite of, them he continued to hold his place in the church as upstanding to all of the rest of the congregation that needed to be seen like him.

Rance would remember the ceremony insisted by Lindy. The most expensive dress along with the gold plated reception, bought and paid for by the new stepfather before his passing. She wholeheartedly expected it and allowed him to take the place of her father with grand ease, because his money was better than that the lesser amount known of her father. She never thought twice about her own money after her mother's marriage to the one that agreed to buy her anything. During the wedding, Rance watched her soon-to-be husband, Brick, standing in wait with disinterest at best. His brother, the preacher, in long winded speech, eventually got to the part of the significance of the ring and what it represented. How it represented a never ending circle, unbroken line, forever. Brick was too busy staring at the maid of honor's breasts and missed that part completely. He must have, because that circle wouldn't interfere with his chasing of tail. Brick would eventually be leaving Lindy for his best friend's wife after the two shared more than just coaching of the church's Christian Youth League in basketball.

Lindy proudly kept his name, believing it spited his new bride by doing so. She did so completely ignorant of the fact that the new wife, Irene, felt his name was a badge of honor. He was the prize, and she relished the fact that Lindy would keep his brand, better now that she fully owned it and the one who branded her, too. She enjoyed the thought of Lindy needing to explain her relationship every time someone without the knowing recognized her last name and asked the question, "Are you Brick's wife?"

Lindy would wind up with the house and half of Brick's business profits for the following two years in the divorce settlement. She spent her second time around running. She would run all the way back to the little shack. The same little shack still sitting beside the new house, with the ponderosa pine behind it and the thirteen more planted a few years later that adorned the front. Rance had added one more transplanted young oak to the mix, from the old home place yard, to stand solidly with the pine that shaded it. There she chose to drag the boys as far as she was able, in her hold to prevent them from having anything to do with their father. That would be her only reason, and that reason would become the reason of her sad life. It would be for the spite of it, but again misreading Brick's perception of her intent. Brick in reality was enjoying his new found freedom; more enhanced by the distance gap. Lindy stayed "wallered" in her self-pity and spite, and in short order managed to spend down the small fortune bestowed by the judge. With the money gone for her in Clay County, and the boys seeing the gain their father had retained, one by one, as law would have it each when at the arrived age of fourteen, left by court ordered choice back to where the money was. There, with their father and the woman he chose over their own (now gladly referred to as "Mom"), they left Lindy even more to fester over than just Rance. It was good riddance for Rance as their mother, out busy playing, had no time for them. They were a burden in lack of respect to their grandmother, who failed at her attempts to mother all three in Lindy's absence. And they were trained early on never to give even the time of day to Rance.

8

NEW DRAW ON A BETTER WAY

Rance stood in the tall ponderosa pine trees he had planted thirty-six years prior directly out front of the lonesome new ranch house on the hill. He looked down at the old ranch house of his past, his aunt long gone, along with his uncle Claude. The old house had been sold some years back to a retired city couple that were strangers to the area, and even stranger in demeanor. As he stood, he remembered the old white-washed structure that stood out before the old ranch house he once called home. It did sit straight southward, of his ranch house dwelling, just about eighty big steps in distance. There was the tree, standing there in leaning growth. So big around to him at the time, that his outstretched arms only guaranteed its girth when he hugged its rough base intended to climb. It looked so small to him now, although in a different place, the oak might have grown in a way to match his current outstretched arms. He looked and thought how he had hung from its sturdy outstretched limb. The same limb where he had built a three by four front deck, with straightened-out bent nails pulled from the old lumber he used, that had been borrowed from a once-neighbor's abandoned wind-blown barn. Rance had built that deck he called his tree house, even though there was no house to it and barely a floor to boot. One step in the wrong way coming up the rope to get into it might very well have had the climber with one leg fighting to swing over and the other hopelessly caught through a gap left in the floor, where he lacked materials to build it solid. Rance remembered the little white house that sat behind his tree. He remembered where it once had sat, and in his mind's eye could still picture it as if it were still there. But in that memory he would see it as it once was, before his Uncle Jade had painted it to match the new yard fence and the new cow lots that adjoined the feed barn.

Rance could see the weathered gray of the sun beaten wood siding and its split oak shingles that lay overlapping, some lifting in slight ways as their curl would turn upward in defiance to the hot Texas sun. It was the first house. The house of his father's and brother's birth. Rance held it in memory like a shrine. Hallowed ground, just as much as any grave laid in the ranch's long history of graves. Only a memory of what once was, fading, in some ways just as his father's had over life's time. Land and house ever widening the ranch, which began as a handed dowry to Rance's father's father, when the request for his grandmother's hand in marriage had been accepted by her father. The ridge and its valley contained the expanse of an already profound amount of acreage surrounding. It would be gifted as their starting point, by the Kerr clan of North Clay County. Rance remembered it how it once was and never again to be. Even though his mind had known the white-washed look of it, it would be the old look as it chose to relate to him. He believed he had been made that way.

He knew that change had been the reason he was there looking down, but he battled that within as he was not a great acceptor of it. Even though his current ways were vastly different from those before him, he still saw himself as being just as they had been. He was wrong to believe that, but simply could not make the distinction in himself. Silently, he imagined his grandmother making the little house on the ridge her home. The home of her grandfather. The home he had forged from the east fork creek timber, harvest oak, hand sawn. Four hundred-year-old oak cut from the banks of that creek that flowed in his time. The same once-flowing creek that ran a makeshift sawmill that force-spun the round blade used in ripping the smaller timber, leaving the larger logs to be sawn out by hand above and below from a southern pit dug especially for the lower sawyer to draw in a straight line – a pit that would later double as their fruit cellar. Each load was diligently hauled under harness mules, whose breeding carried back to the migrating clans reigning in the same name County of Clay, only back to the black dirt kind bred of Alabama. He thought of the challenge that house had presented to her. The daily milking at the old barn that once sat east of the house, now only there in memory, long ago taken away by one of the tornadoes that grew there as much as the ragweed plant of every spring spent in that region. Rance imagined his father's family, safely there, while their mother cooked the daily meals directly over the hearth fire, in the same old cast iron pot that hung from the pot hook that swiveled across the inside of the open sandrock fireplace; a hook hammered from what looked to be that of a long gun barrel. Likely that of a muzzle-loading musket, well better suited for its new place use, than its use at the time of its reappropriation.

He remembered his father's telling of how their clothes were washed there in the gathered water of the hand dug well – later outfitted with a pipe and lever pump that sat just outside the old house main entry. The pump still stood there, but it was far out of sight for him to see. Water boiled in a large cast iron pot set atop burning gathered firewood of mesquite and oak branches, set ablaze just beside that well. Rance thought about how the fire's flames might have lapped up the pot's sides, as his grandmother held and worked the large wooden paddle – working in the homemade lye soap, made from the very collected fire burned ash that heated the pot each time from past washings. The pot used in the washing of their clothes also doubled as the pot used to boil down the pig fat into lard – fat from the scraped hides of the pen raised bacon and hams that provided their sustenance year around. He pictured her gathering the cooking lard they provided and using portions of it to mix with the caustic ash from the cooking down fire. If the soap making was planned right, she would add in scented oils from her flower garden – for a fresh flower scent in its using. Rance remembered his father telling it, as to his memory they all smelled like lilac and bacon on wash day. "Both smelled pretty damn good ta me," he'd say with a laugh at his telling.

The old house was still standing in Rance's youth. Even in its leaning and decaying it had not looked much different then than it had in the time of his father fifty years earlier than Rance's notice of it. Of his memory, that would be the only way they both had known it. It was forbidden for Rance to enter it while living on that ridge. His father feared that his children would have a good chance – at any of the seasons there – to be bitten by one of the rattlers that lived below its rough laid rock foundation, or a possible few that might have made their way up inside of it. Or even some who might still have wintered between the loose stacked ends of the stored square bale hay then resting in the room where his grandfather and grandmother once had. Although the old home of memory had leaned a bit, and most likely always had, it was solid in its lean and Rance believed it had found its way to stand, as he had found his own way. Rance felt his imperfections just as that old house, but those imperfections were what was needed to cope, just like those binding bent beams had set against themselves in a moment of weakness, but firmly lodged together became the old structures strength. It was a haunting place as he recalled, but never foreboding, as it was home.

Rance once remembered seeing a strange ghostly image staring back at him through the blown glass panes that once let the light in, but held back the pervasive atmosphere left outside. The six pane windows graced the front of the old house just opposite the big tree of Rance's freedom-felt, bent leg hanging. He remembered the face there, and its stare, from his upside-down glance to its view, as if it were still that day. The haunting outline still registered fear in him, the same he felt that day. Rance stood there on the hill beside the house with the ponderosa pine, thinking about what he had spent many years ignoring, when it hit him suddenly. An epiphany; his realization of his ghost finally clear to him. It must have been with him all along, but the answer wasn't clear to him until this day. He had always seen the memory from a child's mind, and this was the first time he would analyze that perception. There had been no ghost, but he had witnessed one. He saw it when he was upside down peering into the window, and it was right side up peering back. With his looking back, the ghost wasn't right side up at all. Just as he was upside down, so was his reflection. It had always been that way – just his own blurred image in the wavy reflection of the old cylinder glass window panes. Rance laughed out loud, but to himself and at himself, for it taking fifty-two years for the truth of his ghost coming.

It had been a lifelong regret that he had not disobeyed his father and entered that old house as much as he wanted. He had missed the opportunity and wanted to study it. He regretted that he had not risked the whipping gained just to enter its hallowed rooms; to see for himself what it must have felt like to be there in the room his father and siblings had been conceived and then born. What must it have been like, where they had spent good years and bad years in their own way and time of living? Time spent feeding the hearth's glow and enduring its heat while the meal time supper cooked in the hottest of times of the summers, and the contradiction of its welcome radiation of close heat to warm them in the coldest of times. To have seen the pegged oak framing of the open rafters of the roof in its strongest form, sheltering them and smothering them all at the same time. Never personally witnessing the life himself, he thought back on the brutality of it, but forever knowing it not to be that way for them, since never living any other way. Their listening to the north wind howl its heavy way through the weathered slots of the hardwood window framing that held the then-rattling panes that were providing the view out, while protecting. Knowledge as well, of welcomed light needed to see by and brighten the dark rooms, while in their time and primitive design they seldom held back the blowing rain, the summer sun's heat, the wind-blown rain or the powdery blown snow, that not only left the dusting to the sill, but spread out into fan-shaped triangles only left to turn into water, if not caught early enough to be swept up and off the split oak floor. Rance had only vague memories of that old house, but especially missed the view as they would enter the curved drive leading up to the ranch house home, and see its west side. Standing proudly was the solid, wide, grand rock fireplace that dressed that side. Its finality was just the stepping stone to the great loss of that ridge where it all had begun.

In that moment of thinking back, Rance would have given just about anything to still be hanging there from the limb of that big oak. No thoughts, no worries, just hanging from that sheltering oak and wondering about the old house and its veiled, well absorbed secrets that were held, lingering with true ghost-like presence inside. Life once lived there, a presence alive and swirling around within its empty rooms. Rance was truly seeing that old house there with its once full, but now empty, rooms down to its final days of its long-lived spot on that ridge. It would only be a mirage, fading with his time and memory. It was long gone now to Rance and not even a distant memory to most still alive there. He doubted the others had even once thought about it, as if it was never brought up in conversation, not even by Hadd. He doubted Lindy was even old enough to have known about it. Certainly, she had no clue of why it was being there if she had. It had fallen into disrepair and new life's struggles would find it too expensive and not even practical to rebuild. It was that way for them as it was a part of time spent, and wouldn't have the historical significance to others later, who might see it differently. The ones that survived it had already moved on and it was just a familiar past to them, simply worthless to their betterment. It would be as low a priority and fading as new growth coming and dying out over time. No wanted relevance needed to anyone of age, but very much relevant for their descendants understanding.

In his father's final days of knowing just what he and his brother, Jade, had created in their sister by giving that single ridge over to her, he recognized somehow that it would never be a part of his life anymore. He also sensed that the old house would never be a part of anyone who had cared about it, anymore. Jade was gone now and he felt as if he was the only one left. So, on a single day in the summer of 1974, he chose to be the one to tear it all down. His thought was that he didn't want to give anyone else the opportunity to do it. Unbeknownst to Rance, his father did want the old house to stay there, but obviously knew that it couldn't; if anyone were to tear it down, it would be by his own hand. He would choose it as his only lasting control of the ridge overlooking the valley. It would be his way of removing his legacy there. His wish to himself was for the beginning place not to wind up in the hands of strangers.

Like his father, Rance played along that ridge in his childhood. He had run his hands down into the worn out bowls of the sandstone boulders that rimmed the slight rise. He roamed where the Comanche had ground their corn, and as he stood on the hill looking down, he felt what they felt when his ancestors pushed them out. "So many years ago," he thought. But really not that many. "Ashes to ashes. Dust to dust," and the world keeps revolving around all set claims. His father being the boss once more over the old ranch house spot, ran his truth in being there, as if he knew he was even closer than ever in riding the ways of the "Comanch," forever erased from the place that bore him. He was feeling the pressure and the uncontrollable knowing of being forced out. Rance tried to feel what he would have in that thought.

High upon the hill of their new headquarter location, Rance was still looking down. Changing his thoughts over the offset garage, still there and still in view. It sat its spot just east of the new house and had doubled for many a year as a feed storage barn, where the oak rail catch pen, tied into it on both east side corners. That pen had contained many a head of horned beef as they made their ways through the exit chute to new destined future.

Beside the main lot gate stood an old sycamore tree, high and broad with new summer leaves. In his looking, Rance recalled his grandmother's telling of "Zacchaeus the sinner," the collector of money through taxes – powerful in stature in his doing it, but short of stature in life. So small, he wouldn't be able to see over the large crowds that lined the roads to see Jesus in his passing by. Rance had heard the told story of the planting of that tree many times, and how it was a sycamore just like it that Zacchaeus had climbed up to eventually be forgiven of his sins. To the new owners, it would be just another tree, for to them they had not heard the story. He doubted his Aunt Lukey and Uncle Claude had told them of it. He knew that Lukey must have heard it as much as he had, as it was her mother who had told him.

Rance thought back to their visits while they lived in the ranch house above the ridge. He remembered their untimely visits as they would just show up unannounced for what he always felt was for home inspection and rent collection and his mother's home cooked meals. In tow were their high-browed kids, similar in age and split to that of Rance's families own. Spoiled in their ways, it was expected on their visits for Rance and Hadd to turn over their night beds when these visitors took the time to travel for overnight visits – a custom mainly of the age of his father's generation and not necessarily one of the times. It was believed to be something handed down from the wagon road days of travel, when longer periods of travel and rough hardships warranted the extra need of comfort and rest for their hard travel back home. Rance never got accustomed to giving up his bed to his cousins, especially the one who never claimed the wetting of it. He never actually accepted them as guests, for the simple reason of them being there to check things over and collect the rent.

There was one thing that he was okay with in their coming, and that was that it always led to a great time spent, for him, with his father. His father used an excuse each and every time they showed up, to design a plan. Always a place that he would need to be, for the whole day, every day they were there, spent in incessant work. Actually, it was just to be sure to get away from the overbearing blowhard Claude, and his annoying brags and throaty meaningless speeches. Those his father mostly ignored, but they were devoutly absorbed by Plover, who was completely impressed by the blowhard. Claude had a guaranteed audience of one with each visit made. Rance's mother entertained the rest, while Lindy pretended to be just like her cousins and began her entitlement learning along with them on those visits. Hadd was fighting in an unpopular war overseas, and Rance was horseback on a good horse while his best friend and mentor led the way up the trail just ahead and somewhere on the ranch, far away from the wearisome bunch back home.

...

Rance looked at the garage and remembered the readying of it, just a week or thereabouts after his father's dying. Claude, without permission asked, worked his way into it and was creating a large pile of his family's belongings and stored items from the garage that in protection had held. The pile built just out past the tilted up door. Items tossed onto the ground, without interest or care in just how their tossing took place. Hadd was back by leave and support of the Red Cross from his Navy duties. Still haunted by long months on a gunboat in Southeast Asia as part of the "brown water navy," and recently assigned to support the moving of the Vietnamese Navy to the Philippines, he was home for the mourning of his father, and to see him placed in earnest to the Texas red dirt home he'd earned so well. He was sad, and still sharp from the killing of those early tours on the rivers of Vietnam. He had lived a life of sleeplessness to the point of no expression, but his eyes told the story of what he had become. "Whater yew doing?" Hadd spoke quietly, but with an intensity as if it had been launched from a loudspeaker. It was an anger Rance had never witnessed from him – he had been changed. "Just cleaning out sum junk. Gitting it ready to git our thangs in," Claude stated boldly in his familiar irritating baritone way. "Well, yew kin just stop it rite there," Hadd informed his uncle. Rance watched his brother's stance, in a way that he had never experienced seeing before. "This is our stuff an yew can just put it back!" With pause, "Now!" Right now!" He finished with readied clinched fists that halted Claude right in his tracks, with his seeing. Plover started to say something, but cowered with Claude as he decided it best to not. The baritone seemed to leave the showboat uncle.

In truth, it was technically Claude and Lukey's home, but as far as the family and the timing, it wasn't yet. Hadd's father not yet cool in the ground and Claude's disrespect was more than Hadd was willing to handle. "This is our stuff and yew kin just put it rite back, just where ya found it, until we git ready to move it!" Hadd jolted at Claude, and his uncle recoiled in the intensity of the moment. After an assured short moment of calm, he reached out into the pile and made a grab at the old bird cage that rested on its side atop it. Feeling safe in his move to put it back, he made an under the breath comment, that was directed right back at Hadd. "Well one man's treasure, another man's trash," but not so silent enough, as Hadd heard it plain enough, then stepped toward his obnoxious uncle, who caught sight of his coming, almost falling over Plover in his retreat. "Maybe so, yew son of a bitch, but yew just be sure to put that treasure right back where ya found it! Yew hear me?" Claude had been so caught off guard he fell under the pressure understood and the fear he then felt. In cowardly tone, he submitted to Hadd and raced his way back into the garage answering to him, with, "Yes sir, Hadd, just a mistake that's all." Claude saw in the father's second eldest son, the father.

Hadd turned away and Rance witnessed the separation. It was clear to him as he watched his older brother, Plover, in his efforts to apologize to the hurrying uncle doing for Hadd just what he was ordered to do. Rance witnessed Hadd relay feeling on the matter that was his own, and Plover allowing Claude to violate the boundaries and respect that the family head deserved at all times – even in death – and Hadd force the respect back whether sincere or not. Rance saw one brother as a protector, fearless in the pursuit of the violation and the other as a fraud. He chose sides that day and Plover was not on his. Rance followed Hadd into the rental ranch house on the ridge that day, and firmly away from that side of the family forever. A new head of household was established that day, proven to Rance, and to Plover as well. Hadd made sure, at least on that day, it would be their home until they were ready to leave it.

9

THE STRAINING TIME

The Navy called him back, and Hadd was gone.

The running of the ranch was temporarily given, by indecision, to Plover. He was simply not cut out for the job. Rance, no matter how disciplined and structured for its running, was thought too young at the time of takeover, hindered by age. In time, he would pass those concerns and lean into the role of boss, but there was almost too much pause for Rance to come into it. Plover had almost driven the ranch into the ground, with bad deals made, and that would force him to turn over the reins to Rance.

Hadd finally gave into the yearning for his need to come back to his Texas ranch roots, foregoing reenlistment and the Navy that he both loved and hated. He came home and joined up with Rance, instead, as it seemed they had both finally caught up with each other as adults. It was the right combination needed to hold everything in check and keep the ranch together. If it weren't for the anchors of Plover and Lindy chained to both Rance's and Hadd's legs, the ranch could have been built upon even more and it could have thrived under joint effort, expanding into a powerhouse of a ranch. But for the personal greed and self-entitlement, it was halted in growth and straining just to sustain itself. The economy and drought were enough to deal it a closing blow, let alone having to continue in watch of Plover and Lindy. The large ranch sitting along the East Fork Creek in south Clay County was struggling, at best, to stay alive. No great plans could be enacted, no trust was there for cooperation. Plover, and especially Lindy, reeked of paranoia. Their growing problems had been brought out too many times, for Hadd and Rance to turn a blind eye. The profits were divided out at the end of each year by their mother, who, after all, was still head of the Abernathy clan. Monies shared out that just were not there. Those were lean years and every penny should have stayed in place for stability. There was not enough left in the pot for expenses and needed improvements, much less expansion. Plover's and Lindy's shares spent as quickly as given. Their mother the same. Rance and Hadd were only met with excuses when time came to pitch in. Profits split five ways, and three never did anything to earn it.

Shares were received on the backs of Rance and Hadd. Hadd was forced to pitch in extra and so was Rance. Hadd used his own outside monies earned to sustain himself, and forfeited his production profits from a private herd to put back into the ranch. Rance had done the same, with the added income of everything brought in for day work. Cash earned and labor traded for barter in supplies. A ranch could not work this way, but somehow it did. Rance saw its future in the dysfunction. It would be his generation that would be its undoing – something that he struggled with each and every working day and each and every sleepless night. Rance finished his thoughts, turned and looked out over the empty house, surrounded by pines and the single lone oak tree out front on the hill where he was standing. He wondered what the future might bring it, and if, like the ranch house below it, there was even one to be had there.

...

He remembered his brother Plover always the first to the table then sleeping through most of the day, while allowing his father left to perform the daily ranch chores. He was protected by his mother, and Rance's father had long accepted that it was just to be that way. Most of Plover's days spent would be planning in ways he could bleed as much as possible from his inheritance and he couldn't wait to get it. Even understanding the how and why it would come to him, he wished it to be in his control, no matter the reason. Rance had always felt their separation, even more than Hadd. He was reinforced in the feeling due to time spent with his ailing father, who leaned into Rance and Rance into him. Rance and their father became close, and seemed cut of the same cloth. Possibly that would be the reason Plover couldn't get past it.

For Lindy, the reason would be different and this is where he and his father differed. His father was instrumental in his sister turning out the way she was – or maybe not. Rance believed her spoiling by him, and it only being reinforced by his mother at her being the only daughter, was inherently justified. And it might have very well been genetically inherited as well. Either way nothing good could ever be expected from her. She was wanted by his father, but he understood that she would never be his namesake. She was born to take the name of another and expand *their* line. Loved, yes, but other than that nothing was ever expected for her. Rance understood that as well, as he had watched women take on the persona of their new family's line. No different than his grandmother, his aunt, his sister and his own mother. He believed, as his father did, it was to be expected. Maybe untrue for some, but not for the women in his world. She would one day be expendable in his father's view, where Rance had been groomed to carry the line on and for that he was not.

Rance believed he carried the hurt of resentment from Plover who despised his closeness and teaching by the father. He would have no control of how his father treated him, just as Plover didn't, but it made no difference. It was the way it was. His readying for the job would prove a burden to him. While others played and experienced teenage youth, Rance missed his time. He was always older than his years, and expected to be that way, and he came to terms with it. His mother, though, seemed to give into Plovers stance – years of coddling and one-sided views had been sufficient in her knowing what she was doing. She saw, but was blind to her design methods and her protection; blind to what she was forming and not just of him but of Lindy as well. His defense was so often by her, that she was unaware that others were denied it. It was her normalcy and was normal in the beginnings of the family's undeniable segregation. Unintentional, but it just was. Rance had witnessed his father many times in his trying to right the eldest into the position of his namesake, only to be derailed in his efforts by interference from his partner who didn't even realize how her interference set in motion Plover's lack of respect and need to listen to his father.

His father was caught between the woman he loved before his family, and the love for his children and their teaching. He didn't have the heart to set her right, but Rance believed he had regretted not doing so. Rance had watched it build and tear at his father in ways that he could never understand. He watched the man revered by most and feared by those few that crossed him, but respected by all in both factions. A man who was solid and firm in conviction, and decision, yet worn down by the dysfunction of his own family. It would be as out of control in his last days as the struggle in attaining his last breath – knowing to take it, but knowingly suffering the try and awaiting its outcome. He was afraid, and Rance saw it. Not of dying, but of leaving such ill-prepared dysfunction that he was denied the means to repair. Rance wished that he could ease him in that thought. Their dysfunction wasn't his to repair; it was the combining of the times, circumstances and things beyond his control in any way.

His father had watched a good woman change, absorbed in her own mind without sense of separate distinction between any of her children, and outwardly, without realizing, forever setting them apart. Even though she was blinded in seeing it happening, his father was not and he had taken opportunities given to explain the way his mother was to him and Hadd, hoping his explanations given would provide them the peace needed in understanding her ways. Rance had witnessed the good in his mother, but hadn't seen the love. She made sure her kids had the best that could be afforded and worked very hard in her own way in their raising, but he always thought it was more out of instinct than that of feeling. He could see the mechanics of it, but also the inability for her to feel love, much less show it. He felt it given from his father in a more balanced way, even within the differences with Lindy. But his mother, he believed, was incapable of empathy as if she had no way to conceive it to exist. A hot meal was always ready and day clothes clean for their wearing, and there was never neglect in respect to their care.

Rance, now in adulthood in his look back, never felt the love that had been witnessed so differently between his friends and their mothers. Then again, he had witnessed it time and again said or shown to Plover and Lindy. He was certain that there had been times as with them, but from the earliest recollection of his youth, he just couldn't recall it happening to him. The same he had witnessed of Hadd. His mother in those moments set two opposing defining differences between the two separate pairs of siblings in the family. They were housed under the same ranch house roof, but their shared lives would be the same and completely separate, never intertwining with Hadd and Rance, who somehow made it work. The mechanics of their physical raising was the same, but there was strained indifference to each other as if they were two totally separate families from different backgrounds. Two pairs of siblings, so different, being forced by the matriarch in the center of it all to get along without her ever knowing that she was the reason for them being so apart. No central dynamic or inclusion, but each treated so differently that it was a breeding ground for dissolution and false pretense for two, while the others were placed firmly in the trenches of reality.

It was quite opposite in the way of their father, as he seemed to allow them controlled reasoning to find their ways to earn their place. Time is what stopped him from testing their ways, as he died before the end of his teaching and the time needed for reining them back in. It was as if someone opened the lot gate and turned out the wild horses and no one gathered them back up and put them back in for their breaking. They were left to run wild, on their own, with no teaching. The same would happen to Rance, who first believed their differences to be in the genetics, as he saw in his sister the familiar characteristics of his aunt Lukey. But in the watching of his mother, he eventually realized her need to overprotect the chosen children was the cause. Then again maybe genetics *was* the design that warranted the behavior. The only truth was that his father might have struck harder on earlier influence, and then his not being there to fix the problem would not have mattered. The day his father left the earth – that day in May of 1975 – would be the day for him to finally find his peace. Rance would not be so lucky.

In the winter's end and the late days of spring of that year, in place of his father's finding peace, a burden was willed upon Rance. Because of it, for the years that followed, the promise made proved to drive its hardened wedge ever deeper, splitting the family even wider; no coming together, ever, but in certainty forever apart. The patriarch – the glue of the fabric not quite ever truly held together anyway – had perished, leaving Rance with the load. The load he would need to carry in a very lonesome time, and for a lifetime thereafter. In his father's last words he had asked Rance to do what he could no longer do – to take care of the family; hold them together and care for his mother and his sister. Rance did his best for it, but the rift was too deep. He failed his father. Deep down he had always known it wasn't his burden to carry, and deep down he had always known it wasn't his father's expectation to saddle him with it – or to even believe his youngest son would destroy himself in his trying – or he wouldn't have asked it. Rance had always known it was just his father, in life's last panic, reaching out to the only one there that he believed would hear the message. That was okay to Rance and he took pride in his father's fight to be thinking of someone other than himself. Rance admired him, and did not know if he could do the same, but as he watched his father fail in his efforts to straighten the path, he carried the guilt even more. He had never the feelings toward the others that a father would. He understood his father's pain in his inability to finish the job, but Rance had even more pain and blame for himself on his incompletion of it also. Maybe he was the reason – not his father – for the divide. Rance had watched the cloud drape around his father. The complication of the multiple strokes and his understanding of his father's nearly indistinguishable words. He understood everything left on the table that day, as clear as if they had been words written on paper. He heard him that day, even in his early age. Words unspoken or beaten and broken, but intensely felt, as if he were hearing him explain the growing cycle of the Sudan grass before its baling or the process in the need to give a young heifer more time before prompting the pulling of her newborn calf for its survival as well as her own. Rance understood him. This moment was no different, but in every way would be, for it would be the last conversation between them. His father's eyes welled up with tears. His hardened hand and sun wrought skin softly touched the forearm of his youngest son, in final desperation for Rance to hear his words. He heard them. And forever etched they would be. He promised that he would do his best.

10

THE TIMING FOR LINDY'S DESIGN

In winter of 1976, less than a year after her brother's passing, Aunt Lukey and Uncle Claude rushed the time they felt necessary, and carried on with their eviction. Hadd was still overseas, and Rance would be unable to stop the action, his not being quite the adult of recognized value, alone, and certainly not as boss by the legal limits set in that day and time. There would be no place readied for them to go, but his mother's acceptance of the paper ensured their going. His father, although a rancher living year to year on borrowed time and money, as did most in the life, had managed with old practices to keep things above board and running. There was no great wealth, even though hundreds of thousands of dollars moved through the ranch over the years. It was humbling, yet satisfying, to the life he chose, and above all else sustaining love of the life was all he had needed to carry forward. But without money left now that he was gone, there was no easy way for their new start.

Rance's Aunt had been born of poverty, but in all accounts had forgotten those times. She had been fortunate to marry money and her selfworth improved for it. It was odd to Rance, just how easily she had forgotten it, as he knew the life she came from well, though it was before his time. He listened at her talk of the times when growing up on the home place ranch, but in her stories there was transition from a very short time spent in poverty to the war time prosperities in her later years. Rance's father's story told was that of poverty complete to war time spent. It was only when Rance was grown that her stories made more sense to him as his interaction within his own family's dynamics had shown it. The time spent with their father was a different time spent for each. Plover and Hadd dealt with a man much younger and harder than the father he and Lindy had at his end. Through the aunt's telling, he realized the differences of life spent, and understandings changed, in perception of their father. It was as if there were two different representations of the man. Lukey had never endured the true hard times of her brothers. All of her hard times' rhetoric translated to just that. She had endured nothing. Her life had been much different. She lived a common way of life and never wanted for anything. She lived in what everyone else would know as never the need or want for anything. How could one know it was hard, if they had known nothing else? The only difference between his father and his aunt, was that his father and brothers starved and fought and died, where she had done none of it. His father and brothers were separated in age by thirteen years from their sister. They had experienced the time of the Great Depression and famine, which brought them eventually to the killing fields of the European

Theatre of war. Rance thought on it, and the times, and realized his aunt and her times were of war attrition, but mainly spent in the times of war prosperity – the exact opposite of that of his father.

Just like Lukey, Lindy hadn't experienced any time of difficulty either. Rance had. He was on the coming out end of it, but he certainly had the experiences, much more so than Lindy. Lindy had never worked a day – certainly never earned her place and, especially, the honest acquisition of it. She didn't earn it, but she sure felt that she had. One thing for sure she hadn't paid her dues, yet expected it to be handed to her just the same. Her mother made sure she was to get first choice, although Rance made sure that she wouldn't. He and Hadd, had earned the right over either of the other two. When the time came around, the only work Lindy put into the ranch was an underhanded crooked fight for control of it. Their mother was the pawn in her chess game. She wanted as much gain as she could possibly get and was willing to throw her own partner, Plover, under the bus to get it – along with her own mother. With lawyers and court cases, and no pooled money to fight back she would be sure to use the most inopportune time for the ranch, but the most opportune time and chance for her to strike.

11

PLOVER'S TRUTH

It was the drought summer of 2010. The estate was divided, but the rest of the working ranch for the operation left intact. A minor victory for Rance in the folding of the surrounding divided acres of the new house surrounded by the single oak and ponderosa pines on the hill. Plover breathed a sigh of relief in the division plots of his sister, because with Rance's win he would be covered in protection of his misguided and illegal business dealings. Unbeknownst to Rance or Hadd at the time, their mother, very much alive and involved, covered Plover in her same protection of not allowing anything to happen to him. In her protection and his asset hiding, he had put his share of the ranch and his royalties back into his mother's name, in the name of hiding it - mainly from the IRS and to stop bad debt collecting, placing liens, or the complete selling it off to cover bad debt. It worked, but by doing that he had tied up the ranch and everyone along with it, including Lindy. It had brought everyone into his lies as unwitting accessories in the covered crime, even though no one knew but Plover and his mother at the time of his conveyance. One full year later, it would be too late. It would be trouble because of the coverup and lack of ability to finance ranch programs and insure its smooth operation. Funding through Plover's portion wouldn't be there, and their mother wouldn't risk his loss under her care.

In order to keep the ranch from sell off and going belly up, Rance and Hadd were forced to operate the ranch and foot the bill on their own. Once Plover was out, Lindy decided she wouldn't have the need to help either. To offset their siblings' problems and mishandling of them, there would be a kink placed in Rances and Hadds ropes. To offset the loss of their own divisions, they were put in position for a fight, while the ones responsible for creating the mess just sat back and watched the show. Tensions grew as the pair watched the ranch's prospering, without so much as a dime's input into it by either of them – neither money nor decision-making. Yet by the books held, they would be dealt out an equal share of the annual production profits as if they had. Each year in succession, nothing would be put back into the kitty by them for the running of the next year's budget. The only budget set-aside would be that of Rance's and Hadd's input. Two shared the load of five.

Paranoia set in with Plover and Lindy; as privileged as they were to the ranch's operation, they were held out of the managing of it and were not privileged in the knowledge of the books, expenses and profit. They had to rely on Hadd or Rance to deal out their shares. They only saw the result sent to them by Rance, and had to accept and live with that result. Rance had known enough at that point to sink them both, and he and Hadd along with them. In her terms: stalemate. It had to be trusted, and even though Rance had reason to fix the books in his favor, he would have never chosen to do so. He would give no reason to be held crooked as they. Since they couldn't even trust themselves, they saw the lack of it toward anyone else. Both believed that they should be allowed to see the total breakdown of the operation. Rance realized early on the mistake in that, so he held them away with idle threat of outing their crooked dealings to others. All the while, he never would be put in that position, but always in the back of his mind, he wondered, if pushed to lose everything, would he resort to the use of his threat. He banked on their greed to cease their need to push it. Their possibility of losing it all for that time being, would be the factor in keeping that door closed. Rance refused, with Hadd's blessing, as they both knew that anything the two had touched in the past, would be what they were, and would be, dealing with in the present. Both Plover and Lindy eventually agreed to be left out of it and that was that. A confrontation in either financial situation would have proven out badly for the ranch and everyone involved in it. His mother's split favoritism had created the mess that Rance would need to dig their way out of.

It wasn't until years later he asked her out of frustration, just why she had sorted them out so differently. He asked her if she had even realized she had. She was then old and frail and it had appeared to Rance a good time to ask it. He saw in her that it must have been a good time for her to answer, as well. What Rance had thought she'd never seen in her doing, had not been that way at all. "I never had to worry boutchew 'n Hadd cause you've always bin good bout providence for yerselves – always have. Nothin ever seems ta work out for poor Plover, and that poor Lindy. It was just terrible tha way Brick left'er and them three boys that way. She just don't have the way ta make it like you have, an Plover tries, but the whole world's against him. Always has bin. Yew two I never had to worry about. No sir, not yew two," she rambled out. Rance had learned in that minute, that there had been a difference felt between her children. A feeling proved right he'd lived with all of his life. It was alright to him though; she was right in her thinking. They were better for it and had learned to earn their way.

But to his thinking, he and Hadd understood that difference the whole time coming up, and it long troubled him as to why. They were driven, maybe for and in spite of the facts she had quietly given him, but as he heard her telling, he felt no truth in her answer. Rance had felt the difference even as far back as he could remember; a small child that personally felt the variant. At that time in their young lives, how much could their mother have seen as able in that moment? After all, Plover and Lindy hadn't provided anything, other than trouble in their raising. Even Hadd felt the difference though close in age to that of Plover, but Rance was at the opposite end of the spectrum and he had felt the difference even before his sister Lindy had been born. In his mind that would have been nothing to compare him to, and how such an answer of comparison were to be made he could not comprehend in her answer, as anyone could see his and Hadds contribution and ethics, work and otherwise. That reason alone would have been more than enough reason for her favoritism to go the other way. Rance doubted his mother's answer. He felt she gave him one that he might believe, but he doubted it completely. He had always felt it had been much more than that. Nothing rang true about it. His understanding was more of what he had taken in routine nature of her actions. Kind of like a hawk pushing her weaker brood from the nest, only sadly this was the reasoning in reverse. He had sorrow for his mother and her inadequacy that she would turn a blind eye to their misgivings and just give them what she thought they needed. That was her way to mother and Rance had come to understand it. Her coddling even more shaped Plover and Lindy than it had him and Hadd. This was a question that had always haunted him, but it would continue to be that way for him. For him it seemed just as unanswered as it was before. His total memory of his distant childhood never brought to mind getting a hug from his mother or the soothing sound of an "I love you," with a smile to follow. He had never witnessed it with Hadd, either, and wanted to ask if he had felt the same way, but could never bring himself to do so.

12

The silence of the day had broken. The sound of the tires addressing the hot asphalt of the Farm Market Highway roared under load as the cattle hauler made its way toward Rance's homeplace working pens. The driver used the wound-up diesel's jake brake in his rapid slowing, disturbing the restless penned herd with its rumbling sound, causing them to move around the pen blindly looking for a way out from their containment behind the steel pipe wall. In their walk, random cry outs in their bellowing tones, raised the morning sound to match their own rising hoof dust.

Bingo raised his head in the excitement, but never enough to clear his view from the stacked rolls of barbed wire that lay upon the pickup's flatbed that also carried a high lift jack that kept the resting spare tire blocked from rolling off the half-used catch bag of cow cake it was holding down. Rance would have had to unload a hodgepodge of unused scrap that covered all of it, to grab the feed bag or change the random flat caused by the usual mesquite-tree-caught thorn he sometimes gathered in his rounds. The sack of cake, even in the dry conditions the ranch was enduring, had sat there long enough to gather mold, but Rance didn't give it a second thought. He just needed it for the tone it sounded in its shaking and the few scattered morsels sometimes needed to lure a cow or two that might need extra convincing that it was okay to go through the gate for their catching. The old dog just flopped his head back down and lay there sprawled out, as the cattle hauler rig clattered around him in its full turn through the entry gate, rumbling its way over the cattle guard and out away from the portable pen's chute.

Rance waved at the driver who was clocking his rapid turn into his well-rehearsed spot for loading. After finishing its circle turn, just as quick it vibrated to a full stop. He then hammered the old rig in reverse just as Rance had witnessed him doing many times before and brought the rig backward to the-two-inch-away, sliding stop centered to the loading chute gate. Rance signaled him in for the light closing touch. The door of the truck cab flew open and a short little man leapt down the steps on his way out to greet him. "Whatcha got for me taday Rance?" The round little man belted out in matching tone with the penned awaiting cattle. Rance looked out at him as he stood there in greeting. Quite the picture; deep bowed legs, britches that were held tightly under a pooched out, well-fed low-hanging belly. His pants held in place only by his taut hand-tooled dress leather suspenders. His hat was low brimmed, worn and held together by grease and black dirt. Rance had always known him to wear it, ignoring the ritual practice of white felt in the cool spring, straw for the dead heat of summer and the black he was accustomed to wearing in the event of a funeral, the occasional wedding and the frigid cold arctic blast-like winter that racked the plains of north Texas. His britches were tucked into his boot tops and his boot heels were run over to their outsides, accentuating an already extreme short legged bow, furthering his appearance that his legs were much shorter still than his long torso should have attached. Rance grinned, "Oh just what I can spare oan this go-roun, Hank," he answered, while the short, bowed man turned to remove his whip from the PVC pipe tube holder attached to the rear of his cab.

"Hank" was Hank Thompson, Rance's lifelong friend that he'd grown up and roamed the hills surrounding Clay County with, before the days of reaching adulthood changed their exploring childhood from ignored to just plain trespassing. He was also as close to being a brother as Hadd and was dependable in the support of Rance to a fault. Even though Hadd was older, they both, he and Rance, shared the same feelings toward Hank. He was part of their family even more than some born of the same blood. "I got twenty for ya, if ya count in that one-eyed ole boney over yonner, with tha lump jaw," Rance added. "Well they all look tha same ta me. Maybe yew oughta point tha one out yew thank is different so's I don't load tha wrong one," Hank bellowed out, followed by hoot, after a somewhat truthful but happy put down.

"Ya goin tonite Rance?" "Nah got plenty a work ta do here," Rance answered. "Whadaya mean? Whadayew got ta do here boy? Ya ain't got no pretty girls out here hid in tha barn er sumpthin, do ya?" "Nope. Like ta keep it that a way too. I don't make tha money yew haulers do. Now do I? Women don't come free and ain't got no time for'm anyhow!" Rance snapped back to an unfazed Hank, who had heard it all before. "Boy, I just Cain't figger ya. Yer always workin! Ya gotta play some, too. Life ain't all work. The Good Lord put them girls down here just for us ta try oan for size, an yew wudn't go agin tha Good Lord now, whudja?" The long-winded little bull hauler sermoned out. "Yew oughta be a preacher," Rance quietly answered while glancing back with head slightly dipped and one eyebrow curled, a clue to Hank to back off on his old friend.

Rance turned away from him on his way into the pen in his efforts to push the uneasy cattle on their way into the old bull haulers rig. Hank readied the gate and gave the go ahead for the restless bunched cattle into the chute. He was right. It was just that Rance didn't want to hear it. Women took time and money and most would want finer than what he could provide them. His future was uncertain at best and he wouldn't feel right hitching someone into that uncertainty along with him. It just wouldn't be the honorable thing, in his knowing his circumstance, for her or him either.

"Them girls are shore pretty. Ah daince with everyone ofe'm ah get a chaince to!" "Yea but that's all you do is daince, and they take yer money an drinks an smile atcha, the whole time they're doin it." "Well maybe it's worth my money 'n drinks an the smiles ah git. Ya ever thanka' that?" He blistered out at Rance, who knew his remark had hurt his buddy's feelings. Rance turned in his saying of it, checking with sideways glances hoping his remark, wouldn't be followed by a slice of that whip Hank was handling. After all, the hurtful remark to his old friend most certainly had warranted one if it came. "Don't mind me, Hank just gotta lot oan my mind these days. I know all them gals ain't after yer money. There's some that's goin for them good looks a yorn," he said facetiously. But his friend just grinned at him, his single gold rimmed tooth gleaming in response, as he never really caught onto Rance's sarcasm of the moment. "That's what ah'ma talkin about. Wontchew just humer me'n go ta tha daince? Ah git tired a sittin there all by myself." "Well, with all them pretty girls surroundin ya like Custers last stand, why oan earth would ja be by yer self?" "Ah come oan Rance. So maybe they ain't. Just never yew mind them. They ain't what ah'ma talkin about. I don't woantcher scabby old hide down there anyway. Yew'd probly scar'em all off! See if ah kear. Why don'tchew just let me git them last two sorry, no count, boney son of a bitches loaded so ah don't hafta deal with yew no more and no more a that smart ass talk yer always dishin out ta me. Ah doan't know why ah come out here anyway ta hep yer sorry ass out. Why dontchew git somebody else ta brang yer rejects into town? Ah'm embarrassed every time ah carry a load of these starved down, wore out, worthless hides into tha sale. Why, ah have ta cover my face all up just so's nobody recognizes me an who ah'm in associatin with…" Hank continued in his mad rambling all the way out to the middle of the boiling dust of the pens, where his constant mumble faded in with the bawling blasts of the stirred up cattle. Rance reached his objective as he turned with an ornery grin and went on about the task at hand. With the last one loaded, the rear gate slid down into its resting place with a clack. The movement of the repositioning shuffle of the loaded cattle rocked the trailer a few times before it settled.

"Ah'll be there," Rance said. "Ah knew yew'd change yer mind," Hank spurted after breaking the tension of his pout. He added a hop to his step on his way back to the step that led up to the seat of his rig. As the cab door slammed shut, the window began its rolling down and Hank yelled out, "Ah'll git these thangs up there Rance. You'll see my fee come outta yer check as always. An ah'll see ya at tha daince tanite. Try ta wear sumpthin presensible. Ah don't want ta be imbarrased by ya!" "I'll try ta suitcha," Rance answered. "Good. Ah'll see'ya there fer some cold beer and female entertainment," he hollered, followed by the toot of his horn, just before releasing the brakes and roaring his way out of the drive with each hammer of the throttle as each gear shifted into place.

Rance turned and looked at the empty lot. The dust still hung in the still morning air. What was left of its settling way left a skimming layer glazed over the top of the water that sat the pen's round trough. In time it would settle and add another thin layer, like the age rings on a cut tree, that, if wanted, one day could be counted and interpreted as to what kind of annual seasons the ranch had endured, and just how many years of cow work were built upon each layer. The sweet scent of manure hung along with the dust. Pungent maybe to some, but for those in the life refreshing and satisfying in its meaning. Rance could already feel it. It was at least five lifetimes felt in each layer in the trough for him. He could feel it to his core. He also felt something else, as his thoughts rose with the still building warmth of the sun resting on him. The air felt even heavier on his thoughts. He was torn in what he was having to deal with in that time of his ranch. Like the false joy he would need to portray outwardly when, and if, he actually would turn up this time at the Hall.

13

THE NIGHT WAS YOUNG

The Hall was situated on a hill, beside the St. Mary's Catholic Church, the sacred symbol of faith, and the epicenter of the German settler community built there by the refugees who found the hill while searching for a better way. They had come to that spot of the Texas ground late in the 1890s, and selected that expansive range to set up their settler community because of that mound. It rose a little over a thousand feet above sea level in height. It was part of such a slow sloping rise that one would have to know it was there before actually finding it to see it. The mound didn't look much higher in elevation than the community's seemingly flat, surrounding farmed prairie that encompassed it. But they saw it differently. To them it was the closest thing that represented a mountain that they could find of that bald top, red bed clay and chalk plain they chose for new life. To them, even though a small prairie dog mound to most, that small rise in the sea of prairie grass that surrounded it would be the closest relatable spot that would remind them of their homeland left behind. The closest thing to their "Zugspritze Mountain," forever gone to them and from where they came. That new spot, with that hill, would be the only thing in that region that might compare, even though its land was dotted with wild prickly pear and scattered mesquite. There were a few smatterings of creek grown elm and post oak trees that made the contrast that much easier – trees that shaded the creek and bottom lands, that the new settlers drew straws for its taking. But on that hill there was nothing and it shown out mightily to them in their first morning spent there. On the rising of their first morning's sun, a fog lifted under the morning heat and rose like a cloud in its cover of the land. At the distance, the knob of that hill protruded above the silent layer giving it the appearance of it floating there. It was decided that on that hill would be built a magnificent church – the strong point and anchor of the tight group that settled there. Beside it would be built the hall – the center of the community, where business meetings would be held, wedding receptions and reunions were expected and birthday celebrations and baby showers would be the norm. But its real value was in its gatherings, where the young would come to mingle and give release from the long week's work then solidly behind them. A place where outsiders were welcomed for the chance of out of community needs to meet new blood, discovered for young relationships to be had. The hall was the place where the band played loudly and the bringing of your own drink was expected and approved. A place where the toil of the week would be forgotten and the reasons for it were enjoyed.

Hank was definitely correct in his thinking, as the hall welcomed a few older, just as much as it welcomed the majority of young. He was also right in his knowing that in that German-bred community were some of the most beautiful girls ever to be seen, just about anywhere. Women bred for strength and outward pronounced beauty, but inwardly unaware as to how beautiful they truly were. Beauty that just about any man, including Hank or Rance, could ever want to see. Many a male came for miles just to get at the chance for their gainful attention – or the hopes of it anyway. Just entering that hall would leave a man to wonder just why so many of them were there, available, but not yet taken. It wouldn't be long in their reflecting on it, that it might have a simple answer; that most coming found reluctance in their pursuit, because of the absolute assurance that eventually they would have to meet up with their overprotective big Dutch fathers, and just as equally, their big Dutch brothers that might come along with the deal.

Rance had thought about it over the years and avoided the trap of it. He figured that it was surely the reason of the overabundance of untaken girls and their lack of takers. That reason alone left the average mixed-blood pup, as he was, uneasy about being bold enough to venture into that old hall. And for some the feeling, once there, of their inadequacy for the challenge. It had never interfered with Hank's marching right on in anyway. He was handily accepted as a regular fixture, never giving up on the hunt. They saw him as harmless and expected him there every dance night. Truth be told, he even felt the intimidation upon entry and found it fitting to prime himself a bit earlier. It would take him several cold beers to relax just enough to settle in. He was welcomed by the girls there. They were receptive to the visitors that respected them, and Hank had been just that. Outlanders like Hank and Rance had always referred to the tight-knit German descendants as Dutchmen, never really knowing the derogatory nature in its deciphering. They weren't Dutch at all. Who knows where the term originated? For Rance it just always had been. Ignorant to its meaning, he used the term loosely and at all times, with vigor, not quite ever knowing it most likely had been ill received, if not by him. He and Hank had been given a pass, so to speak, as the Germans knew in their ignorance they had meant no disrespect. They had been raised so near to the little town, and had so many dealings with the dairymen and ranchers in and around it, that the thought of ever correcting the two had really never been in the forefront of any of the Dutchmen's minds. No harm, no foul. However, those outside of the circle might not have been so well received. It had just been a part of their evolution, but it did leave one to wonder just what the German descendants that lived there called the outlanders in exchange. He only used it with common greeting, like "How all'yew dutchman doin taday? Or, "Who is that Dutchman over yonner? Don't believe I know'im." Casual routine speak that rolled smooth and innocent enough to show no disrespect intended by the old cowboy and his friend Hank. They knew just about everybody that lived in that community, and just like everyone there, he'd heard it used just as many times as well by the good citizens there. But he would have to admit, if he'd seen it, that it was usually in spiteful agitation between one and another.

The beer was flowing from every can and bottle brought into the little dance hall and the band was playing. Just like Hank had said, he danced with just about every free girl that night in the hall on the hill, and some that weren't. He was harmless and was known that way, even the boyfriends and husbands couldn't say no to the happy Hank, with his slicked back hair and belly that seemed to keep perfect rhythm with whatever tune would be playing at the time. Rance was getting glances from the ladies, some young enough to be his daughters, some older, but he sat quietly and drank his beer, relaxed in the moment and happy just listening to the band and watching all of the fun and festivities taking place around him. He was content. Reserved in manner. Not a loner, but just one to enjoy the quiet of an evening, the silent night sky above him, and the clear brilliant stars that adorned it. He had always been that way. He preferred it over the rowdy mix of a night ballroom, even if it was a hall on top of a hill underneath those very stars. He enjoyed the occasional visit to one, but felt a nervous uneasiness most of the time when he did. He didn't feel the need to mingle as most do, but was not beyond enjoying it, once there.

His eyes panned the room of lined tables with the band playing from the makeshift stage that sat at the end of the hall, completely opposite the end with the entry door. "Cotton Eyed Joe" was the song requested and he watched the lined partners, mostly in pairs, others in threes, sometimes fours, as they circled along with the tune around the salted dance floor. There, in caught notice, was a gap in the lined dancers that suddenly opened up, providing a view to Rance between each passing spoke of the circling dancers' wheel, as they moved around the dance floor. There sitting just opposite of Rance sat a very pretty girl. He would catch glimpses from time to time of her with each opening presented. She hadn't quite seen Rance through the parting rows of the patrons, as he had, or if she had she didn't allow him to notice. She just sat relaxed and proper in the moment of looseness that surrounded her. A whirlwind of motion flowed around her, yet she was the poised silent eye of the storm.

She was the most beautiful girl there. Her blond braided hair was simply pulled back and hung in the middle of her upright back. Though he could not see its length or where it truly laid, Rance could tell by its braiding that it must have been long and beautiful as she, and there was simply no pretense in her or her appearance. What Rance was taking in, was the absolute truth and purity in and of her. She wore boots, not the dressed up version of Rhinestone and sequin sewn, that most of the girls in that night were wearing, but worn down rough outs, plain and scuffed with delicate, but hard worn spurs that capped off each heel. Her jeans showed signs of true work wear and a rip had formed in them, just above her left knee – not born of fashion but of well use. She wore a shirt with boyish-worn style, and Rance was certain it was a man's shirt; not cut for female form, but worn well by her and worn in a comfortable fashion. Rance looked onto her. He could see that her dress couldn't hide the femininity that she unawareingly exuded. No other girls there, no matter their girlish ways, could come close to matching her natural God-given beauty, as far as Rance could gauge in her. Her hands were that of a lady; well kept, nails clean, short, yet still polished with a natural color, that Rance would guess that in her she still had her instinctive way of need of it. The want to feel pretty even though she had no need to force it out on anyone. Her ears were pierced and held dangling bits of turquoise, a color reminiscent of the old Tex Mex tradition, adapted from the Navajo silversmiths of old. She caught all of Rance's complete attention. There wasn't anything fake about her, and the look of her sitting with the closed-lip smile on her face only enforced it to Rance that she was very much like him and he wanted to meet her.

He stood up just as "Cotton Eyed Joe" ended, then caught himself outside the music, when the band quieted and the shuffle of the restless crowd faded. He caught himself and sat back down. He took notice of her once more. "What am I thinking?" He asked himself in his sitting. His mind's eye once again placing him in a picture of someone he was not. She must have been twenty years his junior, and it was her quiet youth and beauty that had been calling out to him, that he even noticed her in that moment. It was her youth and beauty unmatching. Everything he saw opposite of himself in realtime appearance. He did notice that she had been just as out of place there as he felt he was, but he much more, as she would come closer to acceptance than he. He felt it, and she must have felt it, also, being that the majority of the girls there were maybe at least ten years her junior as well. When another song had ended, the open gap of dancers split both ends of the outward edges of the floor as they made their hurried ways back to their chosen spots at the tables that surrounded the dance floor, leaving only a few in waiting for the next song to play. It was in that clear view of her still clapping to the songs finish, when the band struck up the first note of the old German song, "Fraulein," which was routine in its playing at that point of the set expected of the night. In its start, stare-bound Rance was caught looking right into the big blue eyes of the most beautiful girl he had ever seen, and she smiled back at him.

A multitude of thoughts raced through him, but one thought in particular stood out, as he stood up, turned to his friend Hank, who was leaning back in his foldout chair, cooling down from his battled round from the dance last played. "It just can't happen," Rance thought to himself. "Where'ya goin?" Hank asked as he settled all four of the chair legs back on the floor. "Goin home. Gotta big day tomorrow," answered Rance. "Why dontcha stick around Rance, the parties just gittin started." "Gotta go," said Rance, turning toward the door. Without one look back in the direction of the pretty fraulein at the table, he made his way out of the little hall on the hill of Windthorst, Texas, on his way to greet the night sky stars held above it.

He left her sitting, without a single attempt at introduction. He pushed his way through and past the crowd on his way out of the little hall that sat across from the church on the hill, clearing his mind of her and the smoky atmosphere, into the clean night air. His thoughts changing in wonder if Hank, after his late night, would be there still long enough to be an added small part of the next morning service of Hail Marys, from the Saturday night before. He left with no regrets. Back to his commitments and the ranch. He felt his mind and body would be where it was prepared and always meant to be – still the only thing on his mind fulfilling his inherent promise to hold the whole thing together.

14

UNCOMFORTABLE AS IT IS; COMFORTING AS IT
MAY BE

Rance sat the old worn out truck seat and managed the back and forth action of the steering wheel while struggling to maintain, from subconscious habit, without any notice of the old Ford's way in the lane it traveled. He struggled to see the road, as there was just as much dirt to the inside of glass windshield as there was on the outside. The only difference being his attempts to clear the inside of it with the occasional back hand swipe of its collected dust, mixed with morning dew, causing sometimes blurring streaks he would need to chase his way through, in his effort to see the trucks way in its travel. The outside of it rapidly collected the end of the day's ritual of headlight caught bugs, that he would never feel the need to take the time to clean off until there were no spaces left between them anymore to see. Most of the time he would hardly take notice of them, because of his lifetime of practice seeing around them. He herded the old truck down the road, and added a few more early morning grasshoppers to the night mix already cemented in place. They would need to stay there for a while as Rance was too busy on his way in routine trips throughout Clay, Archer, Hardeman and Foard counties. He would just wish for an early morning or late evening rain shower to aid in his cleaning them off, which would very likely not happen in that time and in that place of North Texas.

The doors rattled and the wind coming in both windows almost drowned out the rare opportunity of the dash radio being turned on. And the even rarer opportunity of hearing the Hollies singing along with the old cowboy, loudly and in contrasting tune to the song "Long Cool Woman (in a Black Dress)" that the local station, Quanah, Texas, 1150 AM radio was having a misstep in their daily programming for its playing. Rance turned it up until the vibrating speakers chattered in its playing, and the old cowboy's singing along with it almost drowned out the clatter and roar of the engine and the rattle of the loose right shock that was held in place only by one support bolt, as the left shock had been lost a long gravel road drive back. The radio had been usually turned off, but on this rare occasion of signal gained, Rance had the other speaker thrown up in high gear and listened to every reminding word of youth gone by. For most of the time it had remained off, its use mainly while sitting parked, both doors open, just to catch the news while working penned cattle and catching a few of the country songs set between local business advertisements. For the most part, Rance's travel was without it and the rattles and clatter kept him enough company.

Rance seemed to travel mostly alone. He just seemed to handle it better that way. He wasn't much in idle talk and with the occasional ride-along partner going with him on short pasture-hopping runs to catch work when warranted, he seemed to run out of things to say in closed cab conversation. Silence would usually overtake the majority of time spent in the ride, as even the other party would feel the restraint for interaction in the lack of return from Rance. Rance enjoyed conversation, it was just he never felt the comfort as most, in contribution to it. As long as it was enjoyed by others, he could sit and listen with ease and felt that was his place in it. Conversation listened to mostly over coffee during morning gatherings at the cafes or local gas or feed stores. His comfort was in the listening, with the occasional answer of a question that might be directed his way. He wasn't one to press his points or ideals. He would leave that to the braggers and politicians. In his own way, he felt he was joining in and contributing, even though in reality he couldn't. It was enough for most, him just being there. Beyond the talk of the weather or market prices of beef, he would stumble at best, as he never felt the great need to talk about his neighbors as if it was needed to be done. He had enough business of his own to keep him busy. Their life was their life, their problems their problems. He had enough of his own. He would stumble, at best, and fumble his way in finding a topic, which usually didn't fit most, well-rehearsed in casual speak. He was more driven and focused for the day at hand and saw anything out of his schedule, as wasted time. As for idle conversation, when the coffee was taken in, the visitation would end. He would simply rather converse with his horse and old dog than most any man acquainted. They seemed to get more understanding of what he truly was, and what he had for them to hear, than the coffee house words soon forgotten when each morning patron left their table chairs.

He understood that he was missing out. It was just that he was uncomfortable in it. He understood the importance of him showing up and the human need for interaction. It wasn't so much that he chose not to partake, or his want to, It was his way to himself – his uncontrolled design to not. He realized his lack of participation was a restrained trait he could not control, and had come to realize the value in learning so much more in his listening. A trait that would keep him from the simple questions asked. He accepted it. It would be something in his makeup that removed his ability to allow it. The long drives without company were always better for him. It was less time interrupted and his time to think over the day past or the one that he was coming into. For Rance, that was the one thing he could count and depend on, that each day there would be a lot to be thought about and a lot to be done. The world around him never seemed to know him or his inhibition. It knew him, and it knew his family name as he did, but he was like a distant ghost, always wondered about but never quite fully appearing for one on the outside looking in to get a handle on. It seemed false fronts were put up by him for the ability needed to navigate his way through. His portrayal, perceived and held by others, had not much truth in reality.

...

His family had come a long way from the small shack living, but with that long way came aging and less time for them all. More disdain than ever between all who had been branded by the ranch. The time of the false pleasant fakery was now gone, only created for the benefit of their mother's happiness by some and clear gain by its presentation by others. While Thanksgiving and Christmas time gatherings fell out of favor, attendance was tolerated to cover and hide the wishes expected by who was in the room at the time. Those gatherings of the family now in the past. Rance remembered the lackluster ceremonial-like expectation of each time spent. There was no real joy in it for anybody in attendance or the desire to be in each other's company. It was work just to be in the same room together – sad but true – and only to make a showing to insure a place for inheritance. For different reasons, attendance was always prompt but pretending, with no difference even for Rance and Hadd who were just as guilty of outwardly portraying false feelings in time spent in each gathering. Wasted time, never changing with hidden feelings and false meanings, left over the years uncomfortably upon the feast table. To Rance, those holidays only represented his assurance that business as usual was left in check. He couldn't remember a time after his childhood, and after his father's passing, of his want to ever be involved in any family gathering. It would be just the opposite; a structured, forced, way.

He often thought about it. He saw it in his mother over time. She was the reason – maybe the center – that bound the whole mess together, but he also saw in her the reason for the mess. Each of her kids different as night and day. Never knowing the need to just enjoy the moment. Each had felt their time unending, until the clock showed their waste of want, of what they might lose. Their programs set by their mother. Each cut from a different cloth with no set combined effort for goal. No joint assistance rendered, as greed ruled and entitlement expected, except by the two who had kept up their end of the bargain dealt. Two siblings obsessed with their own lives and two who saw the need in strength of sharing for the group as a whole, but all there, for whatever the reason, with nothing in common other than the prepared food for the party that would set the adorned feast table of each holiday spent. The difference always the same. Five ate the meals, while two were left to clean up the mess. It didn't stop with just the mess of the feast dishes. Two continually cleaned up every mess made by the other three. It would be Rance and Hadd always there to handle any mess made, and any cleanup needed on the ranch. Just as in those holiday feast meals, two would lay down all of the work needed and five would eat the meal. Rance's nephews following right along with their mother's values and patterned much after their Uncle Plover. Each never lifted a hand in the necessary work around the ranch. Rance would never remember a time of their investing back into the life the ranch had given them. Much like their Uncle Plover and mother Lindy they had quit more in life than anyone should. They would be the new generation trained in entitlement with hands out for inheritance with no thought of their earning or reasons why they should or shouldn't receive, in false belief of their right to anything by just being born. Birthright had not been a deciding factor of ranch practice up until Rance's mother made it that way. Because of that stance, there would no longer be the money built to buy any loafer out of their legal hold. Lindy's boys had learned a lot from their mother and their Uncle Plover.

...

Plover had been along for the ride, as they, before he was asked to leave the ranch by his mother's second husband. In his desperation to find the replacement to his own, he found another to fill that gap. Rance recalled her being the second female Plover had ever dated. He recalled her to be the only one to ever give in to a second date. After two weeks of her knowing, he married the girl of his dreams, twenty years his senior. He was comfortable enough in his decision to move into her home. She was all business and ruled over Plover, which rubbed his old mother wrong and she and new mother-wife built a hatred for each other. It made for some interesting holiday gatherings. As lazy as Plover was, Rance was certain his brother's worn-out new bride was even lazier. She never lifted a hand, either, with the meals, but enjoyed the food he brought to her, while she sat perched to lap it all up similar to the pigs once penned on the homestead ranch. She had a way about getting Plover to do what most had not. She needed a living and he needed a place to stay, and her solid convincing ensured the best way for him to meet his need was his success in gainful employment. Rance saw it; her eyes on the prize for herself and her homely stepsister-like daughters.

They were all looking very much for their glass slipper, which was their one-quarter of the operating ranch when the matriarch passed it down. She wanted what she believed Plover would be receiving. Mineral rights and oil royalty that would come along with the title of shared ownership. She had worked that thought out the minute she met her husband/son, and didn't quite think hard enough in her thoughts of the time necessary in wait, for his true mother to live out her long life. In their aging wait, Rance and Hadd, as morbid the thought, had placed bets on which mother would go first – the one so lucky as to give birth to him or the one that could have. In their aging want of it all they had been oblivious to the relation of time's toll on just how she would enjoy her new found wealth – if it would come to that – with the fact of her obvious overtaking of mortality to that of Plover. Rance often enjoyed the chance encounters made with old acquaintances of Plover's, when the "Oh, and this must be your mother," comment rolled innocently enough from the ignorance of the chance asker.

In times when Rance had been close enough to witness it, he could see the old wrinkles deepened under false smile and course correction on the face of the old hide.

Both he and Hadd seemingly wouldn't need to wait for a very long time in collecting on any bets placed, as Plover's ancient old nag was wasting away in her own right while lying in wait for their mother to die. Even though she wouldn't have much time to enjoy her spoils, unbeknownst to Rance, it would all come back eventually to bite him, and possibly the entirety of the ranch. According to his mother's will, Plover's own quarter would eventually come back in its entirety to the ranch, if there were no living blood heirs to pass it to from him. It must have been her way to protect the ranch, as well as Plover, from possible bad deals he had made post putting it all in her protection. But in her doing so, she almost ensured Plover's portion sold off in the event of her passing in order to enjoy anything from inheritance made. The leather-skinned bitch he was married to was none the wiser to the will as written, and spent her dried up time in wait for nothing. He watched Lindy fail in her wait as well, living out an old maid lifestyle – the only difference being she did have blood offspring to acquire what was left since her portion wasn't being sheltered by her mother. Rance and Hadd's work ensured it would be ready for whatever plan she had for it on her mother's death. Either way, Rance would not know that Plover's or Lindy's portion wouldn't stay combined in the estate, as it had done for over one hundred and seventy-eight years. They both knew the deal would be that, once acquired to enjoy it, they must get rid of it while still alive to ever gain anything from it. Rance had no way to know that all bets were off in ever holding the ranch together. It would be dissolved in his time to hold it and in his generation. What Rance worried about the most could happen, and he was without the knowledge needed to plan any type of fight to keep it from transpiring. He had worried about the vast sell off and the rush of it all to get it done. The worry would continue.

Lindy lived, but that was all she had done; between the date of her birth and the date of her future tombstone-etched date of death, she would never live the dash mark between. A waste of time, just enduring. No written story existed of anything between a disappointment of humanity and a waste of oxygen and food supply better afforded to one who might have been something, done something, or meant something. She would never accomplish anything other than bear entitled offspring.

Early on, she had married a boy from another state, a boy she hadn't known but part of one summer. She was looking for her escape, too, and he had the religion that was flaunted. He preached at Rance in short time given to him, and she had the religion also pretended. He talked to her in a flowing, soothing seller's tone in appearance given and all time portrayed. Rance never trusted him, but he tolerated him, given no reason otherwise to not. He had met her new husband's father just once, but that was all it would take for Rance's impression that he was in the presence of perversion. He remembered their meeting as Brick's father sat alongside his own poor wife, who Rance felt was none the wiser of the pervert she was married to. Lindy's new husband's brother was a preacher, therefore the preacher for the big wedding she needed. Rance was there and watched the oddity of it all. One brother to marry off the other and their father the pervert sat right out in the front row unblocked by the tall lilies that sat their bases on either side of him. He sat there, mouth open, taking in the young bridesmaids with awkward stare directly at their breasts as each made their way by him, not leaving out his chance for a sporadic glance at Lindy's, as she made her way down the aisle. It didn't stop there, he made his way through the young maidens at the reception with one-arm hugs and copped feels that the young maids winced at, but with no combined knowledge of what he was doing until after the partygoers had long left.

In the years after, Lindy popped one kid out right after the other. Three sons. True to the faith he sermoned, her new husband Brick, was being fruitful in his multiplication. Their wedded bliss, however, was short lived. Just after the third was born, Brick had other things on his mind. As church volunteer coach for the boys' basketball league, the saintly advisor spent most of his time with his best friend's wife. When their liaisons were finally discovered, Brick ran and hid for a while to a mountain cabin near Cloud Croft, New Mexico; his method for hiding from his former friend, in hopes of escaping the beating that was warranted. True to his character, he allowed his future new wife to end her marriage alone and didn't come back down from Mount Sierra Blanca until everything calmed down below.

Lindy moved back into the same little shack out by the new ranch house on the hill, with the three boys. She felt safe that she had taken them far enough away to hurt the preacher's brother still out there in the land of enchantment. She wound up with the home they shared, half of his business, and the total of the bank savings, in the divorce settlement. It all had come and gone in the four years following, in partying and spending spree. All that she gained – enough to start over that had been handed to her – gone. By then, she was living off the mother who had asked her back. No one ever knew just who the new found man of the moment would be, or just how many there had been. Rance rebuilt the little shack for her and had provided all of the monies, materials and labor to ready it for a new start that would never be. She was never there. The boys slept in chairs and on their grandmother's couch, instead of the bed alone next door. Rance gave her a gas cook stove and refrigerator that was never used and never stocked. It was his own stove that he had missed and needed to boil his morning coffee to ready himself for the day.

She left the care of the boys to her mother, with lies told she had taken a job at the local truck stop – the Hen House Cafe in the nearby town of Henrietta. The truth was she was having an affair with a frozen goods delivery driver in the parking lot out behind it, after their chance meeting at the station that sat beside it. Lindy hadn't a job. She had found a way to find the freedom she had never had before Brick came into her picture. He made it easy for her to run from one lover to another justifying it in her mind that if he could do it, then she would just show him up in the numbers. Rance had passed by that truck stop every day on his way to feed his heifers in the northwest pasture sitting just to the east of the town of Petrolia. Sometimes in passing on his way back, he would see her pickup and the chicken driver's rig parked out behind it. Other times, he would see it there with other trucks, even the UPS van that seemed to be a regular more than most. She wasn't a hooker – that was the truth of the matter – just "easier than most" would be the proper description. And the CB radio traffic off highway 287 kept her introductions easier than most also. Her catching up and acting out had not been unseen. Her boys had always seen the truth of it even if her mother had not, and wouldn't believe it anyway, even if the trysts had been taking place out front of the house sitting high on the hill surrounded by the single lone oak and the ponderosa pines.

Rance's mother married a good man, but he would never be his father and was as out of place, in a different way, dissimilar to the know-it-all "farmer wannabe" Stan Stepp who lived just across the country road named after him, opposite the Backed ЯB's north fence and a good man's place. His place resembled more of that of a salvage yard, or a trash dump, than that of a home. Trash in white bags lay strewn about the yard, waiting to be brought down to an open pit dug just south of his home. There, the wild hogs that roamed the night countryside, along with the coons and skunks, would raid it between its semi-annual ritual burning, whether it needed it or not. It was always burned on a north wind, so the stench of burning plastic could be carried toward the ranch and away from Stan's need to smell his own waste. Most of the time, Rance was busily removing the blown paper and torn up plastic bags that managed to be drug over by the wild coons that occasionally raided the pit, as well as worrying about the pits burning and possible grass fires started from it. The plastic bags gave him notice as they hung, caught like flags, in the north fence wire. Stan was the typical upstanding citizen who kept his nose in everyone else's business, but slyly. He would talk about everybody, without most of his followers realizing they were talked about. He had a way, an ability, to keep himself from being the subject unless it was his own portrayal, and only heroic in nature. He made sure he had a comment or involvement of most he had caused problems for. He judged the rest of the community, and made sure he was one to be seen and one that needed to be routinely brown-nosed by his choice few. By the look of his homestead, Stan could have used a little assistance and involvement cleaning up from some that he had judged to do better. He lived to be noticed, and for those fooled, upstanding and one to rally around at volunteer fire-fighter fund raisers and hootenannies, where his portrayal of a singer was as good as his portrayal of a good citizen, math teacher, or hero. He was a retired math teacher, but in reality that was questionable. His vocation should have been more of an "eluder" as he did a fine job of that in his avoidance of the Vietnam War, managing his way through the total span of his "historic" career, to be situated on a Navy base in North Dakota, going to class instead of battle, and earning him credits enough for his after-wartime retirement job. Rance was always amazed of just how many area folks kept their noses shoved up the crack of Stan's ass.

Rance's mother's new husband, though, was the complete opposite of Stan. He really was a good man. It was just that, in truth, he just didn't belong there. His cattle shouldn't have been taking the grazing that the family had rights to. The Backed ЯB ran stagnant, during the years he lived there. Rance did recognize him as being there for his mother and for never questioning her way. And he did well to finish the home his father had started, but then again it hadn't been for nothing, as he used it and the land around it just as long as any had for the remainder of his life. And there was more start than finish to the home on the hill with the single oak, surrounded by the ponderosa pine. Lindy attached herself to the old rancher and his genuine kind nature, and kindness, and used it as his crutch against him. After a few years, she had managed to help him spend his earnings down in loans left unpaid, and he near broke in the process. This was unknown to Rance and Hadd, as neither of them would have approved and would have stopped it. Neither of them ever took a cent from the old man that had married their mother. There would be no knowledge or proof if Plover had, but each was certain of it anyway. It was up to Rance and Hadd to pull up the anchors and keep everything afloat. There would be no other outside help, financially or otherwise, for their mother, her new husband, or their sister. Their labor and money kept everything running from that point on at the ranch house with the single lone oak tree surrounded by the ponderosa pines sitting on the hill in Clay County.

Hadd was a single man, reserved, but different in mind than Rance. He had suppressed a lifetime which Rance knew better than ever asking him about. He had experienced war, the only of their generation that had. He was affected and Rance knew it. He remained quiet most of the time and there were days he was not to be bothered. He was not to take on the responsibilities of a wife, and with the eldest brother, Plover, married to an old woman that had her womb removed several years before he reached puberty, there wouldn't be any sons fathered by him, which was a good thing, as Rance saw it. Rance wanted the chance, but the promise had taken him all but out of the opportunity. The way he saw it, then, there would be no namesake to carry on the line. His thoughts on that came more and more, as time and age came along with it. It was every day at this point in his life. Not only could he see the death of the ranch, but the death of past generations' work – and his blood line being ended in his lifetime. Hadd could not take on the responsibility of a wife, when the war was still taut in his mind, like that of a drawn rope dallied off to a wild steer that wouldn't settle in its pull. He was supplementing so much time and equity – along with Rance's contributions in equal parts – that his mind wasn't able to even think about latching a wife onto his gatepost. Unlike Rance, he never thought about it one way or another. Their mother was ending up late in life with nothing. For Rance, it was his way to keep everything protected along with his mother's pride, something Rance had recalled hearing that one shouldn't have too much of. It was written down somewhere in the Bible he never felt yet the need to read, but he recollected its meaning. He would ignore it anyway.

He would help his mother save face and keep her secret – a secret that had already been guessed by Stan. And already spread through the after-Sunday-morning worshipers during his idle gossip with church goers on his adamant journey to every Wednesday and Sunday service and gossip meetings. The only one keeping the secret would be Rance, not allowing his mother to know that her true worth was already on display. He would allow her to believe in her secret held. He watched the old man's money spent down by the debts made by his sister and mother. He watched them further the spending, that both might portray what in the past had been there but now without the means to live it. He had watched it first with the sister, then with his mother. It had come full circle. Hadd made sure there was always money in her checking account and that her bills were paid. Rance fought to keep his eldest brother and spoiled sister from getting their hands on anything. He made sure the ranch's expenses were kept up, and the operation was successful. That was enough in itself, mostly handled personally under ranch-earned pay, with the rest of what little time he had to spare doing as much outside daywork as possible. Under his and Hadd's partnership things ran smoothly and their mother's lifestyle upheld, but it had only run as smooth as could be afforded under the circumstances. It was another job added in keeping the other's hands out of it to prevent draining what profits made. Every penny pinched tightly, even when their mother believed secretly in the gifting of it out. That would be the secret known that bothered Rance the most. It wasn't the ranch money being given to his brother Plover and Lindy under the table; it was his own, most of the time. It had come too late in his knowing that his and Hadd's allowance to their mother often times found its way into the most worthless of hands. If too late found, it would already had been spent and gone, but if caught early enough it could sometimes be retrieved under threat of exposure and misdealing. It was a neverending circle of secrets held, of lying deceit, and self-entitlement to its core. And it was getting worse. His mother had mainly spent the rest of her husband's monies down, even before the addition of Rance and Hadd's contributions being funneled out with new loans to Lindy and Plover. The time before her new husband fell ill, Rances mother also spent in a rage, as in her own biased paranoia she worried that somehow her new husbands ex-wife would get her hands on some of it – that he might ship some her way. They had both shared grown children and Rance's mother knew well what a mother would do for at least some of her own children's needs. His mother being his mother, he realized the reason she spent the wealth down. The apple didn't fall far from the tree, as the same happened with Lindy wasting her divorce settlement – her fortune – for the same reasons of jealous spite and she had controlled it all. It had already been given to his mother with no possibility of the new wife reaching it. There had been no reasoning to her method, but it happened, anyway, just the same; spent to keep a ghost from getting it. For his mother, it would be an all-out race for her to outrun her husband's supposedly giving it away to them.

What had taken years in its building would take little time in the clutches of two separate women to take away. He, an old man, respected but never accepted by Rance, had been much like Rance. He had spent the completeness of his life time working or thinking about it. Deep down, Rance liked the old man, even though he would never admit it. It was just that he was out of place there and his time spent, too far away from the true heirs that were set in place to run everything. His cattle sometimes rotated on the grass that Rance felt should be his own to use. That was all, no spite toward him, as he really didn't know for sure the old rancher thought he was stepping on others' toes. Truth be known, Brick and Lindy's house had been built on her mother's race to give it all away. Rance had noticed their visits stopping when the money in that first phase of his mother's marriage had ran out. In that time after the old rancher's death, Rance's mother, in order to keep up the facade of prominence she once had, created substantial debt that Rance only discovered while making his rounds of his daily chores. He stumbled across a stranger that was busily counting standing cattle grazing, well inside the posted private gates in south Clay County. A banker Rance had not seen before was taking in the head count in front of him. It was Rance's own. His private bunched herd, unbeknownst to him, was the bankers secured collateral for his own mother's loan. Collateral to a note that was being called. A loan not of his making, and too late to stop the effects of it. Had it been anyone other than his mother, he would have fought it, but he would not see her prosecuted; it would not even be an option. His cattle took care of the debt. It would happen no more. He believed Plover and Lindy had a hand in that debt, as his mother had nothing to prove in purchase of a loan secured in that amount. From that point forward an allowance would be set and monitored, and Rance was forced to pull from profits shared, over time, to replace his herd.

He had no choice in doing it that way, and it furthered his ball and chain attachment to the crooked pair. In his protection to keep their hands from the till, his name would be placed on every note, credit card, and bank account that would be involved in ranch business, and secondary on his mother's personal account to prevent any money from being siphoned from it. He continued in constant watch over the two – a full-time job in itself – never knowing what trouble would be coming for the ranch by them. He believed the last monies slipped away had been to Lindy in her own facade to buy her sons' attention. She bought and gifted and spent her way to fit in with the parents and the groups that believed themselves to be "in" at the time, only to have them abandon her like her boys when word spread of the liaisons with the UPS driver from Vernon, Texas. Her buying didn't stop a thing.

She watched her boys, one by one, leave Clay County for a life in New Mexico, as each reached the court ordered age of deciding at fourteen. Brick's new wife would become "Mom." Lindy was back where she had started, with nothing, in the little remodeled shack on the hill by her mother's new ranch home surrounded with the ponderosa pines. The world spun by her and she was stuck in a time she would never move from – 1998, the year Brick had run off with Irene. She would never forget, and would never let anyone else forget, either. She chased off everyone around her by not letting them move on or forget the memory of it either. It was just her way. Still, everyone else eventually did move on. While they continued to try to insert themselves back into her life, her blame never seemed to cease, and eventually short visits became Facebook views, as she tried to follow her own sons' way through their new lives.

A hermit within herself is what she became. She simply was unable to move on. She would keep Brick's last name, saying that it was her only way to be relevant in her sons' lives, but they had long gone from her and didn't share anything with her. Their last names were the same, but their name was bound by their father's blood, where hers was just a signpost reminder of the bad time they all endured. The truth was that her reasoning was never for the boys and they had always known it. She kept it for pure spite toward his new wife. A gift she had been given, in the reminding that she was first, and hoping all along it would be a thorn in the side of the new wife and to Brick as well. In reality, the message was just another anchor she strapped to herself to complete the permanent process of holding down her motionless ship. Her sons recognized it even though she hadn't and it would leave them embarrassed and removed of any speck of respect toward her. They would have appreciated her more if she had reverted back to her maiden name and made most of what she had been prior to her never-forgotten divorce. She had the name of her ex-husband and by God she was determined to be that until death did she part. Rance, deep inside, was glad she didn't go back to the family name, just for the few out there who weren't familiar of her relationship to him – it would be easier for him and the ranch. For her, she would be unable to see it, and would spend the rest of her life truly ignored and never given a second thought.

Brick's new wife saw it differently and quickly took to his last name, erasing all ties to her ex-husband's last name, even though she watched her troubled children wear it proudly in defiance to the Sierra Blanca cabin boy who took their fathers place. She looked upon her new name like a badge of honor, something to be proud of as if her golden prize. She not only took Brick from Lindy, but she rubbed her new title in her face. She now owned the name, and took pleasure in the fact that Lindy was out there, branded like an old cow numbered, being extracted from the herd. Just as Rance had branded every cow on the ranch with the same brand, so it was with Lindy – along with the rest, marked but bred by the same herd bull. It was Irene's satisfaction in knowing that Lindy would never be his, and would be condemned to be the old bowed-back cow with his mark on her hip, turned out to pasture with the rest. Each child Lindy had given birth to purposely chose not to have her as mother. Time continued to move on for everybody, especially for the mother the children chose.

15

TETHERED BY FIGHT; MOLDED BY CIRCUMSTANCE

Rance would have given anything to have one more ride with his father. Maybe even roll the clock back to a better time to prevent the problems that he had no doubt his father would change before they could ever be. Things would have been different because, as father, he could decide where Rance, as sibling, could never be accepted. "Maybe things would be different," Rance thought. "Maybe not." If it were that easy then the world would just stay stopped. He knew his father, and had known his wishes; some told, some he just inherited from his way. His father had wished for the family (maybe an improbable wish) earned respect from outside, as well as inward, paid to each. But they were not their father. Maybe that had been the problem. Maybe they couldn't ever fill the boot print he laid. Rance wouldn't try, nor would he try to overstep it. He was his own man and he would leave tracks of his own. But, while in his father's realm, he often felt the comparison and the digs made when unable to live up to him. One thing for sure; in that realm he would tread as sure as any mule would tread, and not step out of the tracks made prior to him. Honest and hardworking children is what his father wanted, but that is not what was made. Everything he had wished in their portrayal, including Rance, was not as he envisioned.

Neither Rance nor Hadd filled their lives from greed. Moreover, either would have been happy peering out at the night stars from a lean-to shelter, listening to the bawling of a lone calf looking for its mama, or a coyote howling off in the distance, a well-built campfire with a strong pot of black coffee hanging from the fire irons and a plain pot of red beans sitting below it. Their entertainment simple enough; a well-told story or old memory brought back from a better time. It hadn't been their fault or their father's fault, the dysfunction that had been shaped the family as a whole that they were now living.

Thoughts shifting, Rance could remember his own well-carried smile, once. A long time ago. A smile that was projected outward, toothy and bold. A smile not just for everyone else to see, but for the feeling it gave him in its giving. A feeling deep within him. A smile that couldn't be contained. Tragically, it seemed long gone – far too long. His only recollection of his own earthy laugh, and possibly last time he heard it, might have been around the time of his hanging tree summer remembered, 1967. The world had seemed simpler to him, even though it was not. Life to him then seemed free and unsought. Now his time seemed embittered and angry at the ranch, with problems outside of it seemingly small. He had yearned for the old feeling and deeply regretted his inability in its finding. He hadn't for a long time seen it. Once, looking in his shaving mirror, he tried to force that long-ago smile past his leathered taught jaws. It almost wouldn't happen, but his forgotten stretching-for-it smile finally made was uncomfortable, and hadn't the look or feel of natural movement in its forming. That had been his only time in trying, eventually losing all desire to further the challenge. His grin was still there, and cheek bones showed even under mustache cover, so it would sometimes be seen by others, if he felt it at the time. But his outward laugh and toothy smile would not happen, and seemed to be gone for all time. Rance thought on it. Maybe that grin was not a grin at all. Maybe not even genuine in its showing, maybe just kept in forced practice from rehearsed expectation for the morning café coffee and the stale jokes that often accompanied it. His grin, a common answer to the regulars in their morning greeting toward him. A physical greeting maybe learned in need for expression to suppress his true feeling of disallowance of what was so natural to anyone else. He questioned often its true meaning and legitimacy. His laughter he couldn't remember, the only remaining of it was the sideways, close mouthed grin he managed in its place.

It wasn't that Rance was unhappy, far from it, but he wasn't content either. Just disappointment and shame is what he felt of how it was all turning out and how it had all come about. His loss of joy would be contained in the fear of the possible breakup of the ranch. It was all he knew and all that he had known. It was everything to him and two people in his life, attached by blood, were actively leading the charge with speed in its destruction. The ranch was his life, and Rance carried the full weight of it. Every day and in every way he felt it being pumped through his life's veins and that was the basis of his way – his purpose and life. Day to day, just like it had always been. Day by day, he knew that it most likely would bring most to their breaking point, but for Rance if it was a fight, then he was bred for it. He came by it honest – an inheritance bestowed in his makeup by his tougher ancestors, settlers who fought their way to hold their lands, a makeup passed down to some that had completely been missed by others. Just as in those earlier families before him who readily weeded out the useless. It was now his turn to do the same. It had always been there, in every family of every line. Every family had seen their weaker blood line. Rance believed it hadn't just been his, and he was sure he wasn't alone in the problem. A problem of the modern time of expectations, without the fight and laws that leaned for the unfavorable in so-called fairness. He had known of it, but had not seen it so easily as he had with his own. Did it just happen with all families? He wasn't sure, but one thing as plain as the Texas hot sun's rising: he was not cut of the weaker, and if a fight to keep it was in order, then he was just too far invested in it now to leave it alone. So a fight he would make.

16

REMOVED FROM SATAN'S BRIMSTONE

The old truck rattled as it made the one hundred and fifteen mile mark, ending its strain of past wear, up the slanted driveway of where his aging mother would now stay. She was no longer living in her ranch house home, high on the hill surrounded by the tall ponderosa pines and the single lone oak, in south Clay County. Lindy had taken the job of her care, but only by forced deception and trickery. His mother fully signed over power of attorney to her, both medical and personal. By the judge's order of the recording change initiated by Lindy, and with approval given by the mother being of sound mind, the legal go-ahead was given. Unbeknownst to her slowing mind, or the brothers Rance and Hadd, of it being done, Lindy managed the full control over her mother's being, as well as over her accounts and checkbook. This leaving both Lindy and her mother feeling very sly in its doing, especially for the fact it was accomplished under Rance's and Hadd's unknowing noses.

But only one would understand the truth behind the order, and it wasn't the ever-slowing mother or any of the brothers, including Plover. Lindy exercised her rights over her mother's accounts and shut everyone else out of its expenditure record, erasing her worry of the monitoring of where monies truly had gone. She controlled the money that would be deposited, but Rance controlled what would go into the accounts. He wasn't privileged to see her needs, and denied any chance to adjust her needs, but the ranch had to survive in order for anything to be deposited. The baseline for her allowance had been averaged and only Lindy would know of what means her mother was to be supported. His mother, who felt so good in her sly joining with Lindy, had denied herself, and her allowance now would be solely in her daughter's hands. Rance winced at the thought, and further guilted himself over his ignorance and not being able to stop it before it had happened. Every check cashed would carry his mother's signature, but Rance would not be allowed to balance the account. Lindy's decisions were covered, to a point, from the ranch's expense account, but she would find out soon enough that the trap she set for control also left her a limit – a cap – on the spending. With Rance no longer able to adjust the deposits to fend off the fees, Lindy would be on her own, which further reduced the allowance given. It would be all that Rance could do, and he rightly feared for his mother's upkeep. Everyone but Lindy was denied access to her mother's accounts, even the mother. However the funds removed were used, it was, sadly, all with her mother's blessings.

Lindy would soon set into place home health care assistance. Checks paid to her for her mother's upkeep, and free run of her mother's allowance, would let her give her mother what she would choose to allow her. She was now a risk owned by his sister. All spending was done by Lindy as she saw fit. She had even managed a life insurance policy with her being sole beneficiary in the event of her mother passing. A slip in conversation by his mother had confirmed it, somehow believing it a good thing – as if she would get the cash prize. Lindy had taken it out using her mother's own money to pay the premiums. Jackpot for Lindy!

His mother, under court order, would be forced to reside in Lindy's home. Bought by Rance and Hadd, with monthly payments made for that fact and subsidized by the government pay received for her mother's care, her mother's SSI checks and ranch money run through her monthly accounts. Her mother was nothing more to Lindy than her cash cow. Her used monies funded Lindy's trips to various vacation spots such as Cancun, the Bahamas, and various Indian Nation casinos that surrounded the areas just north of the Red River. All that play managed just as had been the divorce settlement and unpaid loans – her spending still unchecked and ill-used. She forbid her mother's small requests of a lottery ticket purchase at the local Allsups, along with the purchase of an occasional magazine she so enjoyed. There wasn't enough money from the ranch after its upkeep for Hadd and Rance to fight the order given. Both were caught between a rock and hard place. Any move made could be the ultimate fail of the ranch and that would be worse for the mother than she had it then. But keeping it safe, without a fight for their mother's freedom, was the ultimate chess game for Rance in his truth of leaving her there. Lindy, with the support of Plover, happily along for the ride, called out checkmate to Rance and Hadd. Because of her forced conditions and papers set in stone, his mother had been denied assisted living and lived her new time out in neglect and depression. And even further by suppression and oppression.

Lindy worked a home-based job, pocketing everything she made, yet over a six-year period, able to spend down everything her mother had to spend. Rance and Hadd had limited control. Their only way would be to open a. separate account for money transfer into their mother's account and deny Lindy and Plover full knowledge and access to ranch day-to-day budget. It would be a truth Lindy would have to except and agree to, once Rance closed down the initial ranch account. There would be nothing she could control in that as the trust had originally been set under Rance's authority by another legal recorded paper – his father's will. There would be sharing of the profits, but just how much would be decided by him until his mother's death. Lindy had brought more strife upon herself, and her mother was hurting because of her. Her only way forward was to accept Rance's deposits with only his original knowledge of his mother's needs as they were before Lindy. If that was not enough, then Lindy would have to bear the brunt of how she had treated the one that favored her the most. Plover was all for his mother's confinement there, just because of the fact that he had much to hide and needed time to protect it. He had saddled his mother with a section of property he also secretly placed in her name to hide and shelter it from being used to pay down debt owed from personal bankruptcy, and acquisition in collection of his debts. As in Lindy's case, his mother agreed to his use of her to do just that. In doing so, there would be no way to get assistance needed for their mother to be in a much better place of assisted living. The money was not there for it. Her false assets owned prevented her from qualifying for the care. It was okay by Plover, he had no worries. It was okay by Lindy, she would still draw a vacation check, but for Rance and Hadd their hands were tied, the outcome of their siblings' uncaring way. There would be no way to stop everything set in motion. They all would have to live with their own actions that had caused the way it would all be. Rance might carry the guilt of inability to change it, but was clear in conscience and heart that he had done his best with what he had to work with.

For his mother, she would live out the remainder of her days, unknowing, but making do in her surrounding attention given by the two who had reason to have that access to her. Her misguided impressions left in her a need to insure the ones that she loved the most were shown how much more she cared for them. All the while being used for their own self-appointed entitlement and personal gain. Neither of the ones she had interested herself in had any empathy or sympathy toward her, and Rance often thought they didn't even have the capacity of it for themselves. He saw them as actors, living a false life to show and impress others while hurting and hiding the fact from the ones who really mattered. His mother's new home was a tiny unkempt space in a small corner inside a newly fashioned makeshift bedroom, formerly a storage closet. In it was held a small twin bed, simple and plain, with a hard mattress expected to be more of the type for a younger body than that of a woman with ailments earned over time. The bed was centered between a row of Lindy's stored junk, stacked upward and to the ceiling in some spots. It was more of a hoarder's dream than a bedroom for her mother. Away from the door were stacks of old newspapers, for whatever reason only Lindy would know, piled comfortably one right on top of the other all the way and wedged for their bracing against the ceiling. One right after the other. Four stacked columns that resembled Trojans' Triumphal columns of Rome, more than of stacked Times and Record News, but that would be Lindys triumph in itself in useless hoard. The mother's room stacked with boxes and paper that seemed at any moment might collapse outwardly or into themselves under their own combined weight. Rance's mother would spend her time wedged among them with only a tight passageway leaving just enough space for her to enter and leave with sole purpose of leading to the entry door of the closet where the teetering towers of nothing leaned in for possible fall. She would be able to squeeze through, but only after leaving her walker outside of the room's entry door and using the brace of those very stacks to ease her way. She was only able to open and close the door after the repositioning of two boxes that would lay just inside. She placed them on her bed to leave, then repositioned them back, blocking the door to regain the bed for her sleep. It left no way to enter her room in case of emergency.

All of this had been unknown to Rance, as he was forbidden inside the home to see its condition first hand. Yet had he or Hadd known, all bets would be off and they would have entered regardless of the ranch and its future. They had no way of knowing just how bad it was. The room was dark, dusty and never cleaned. His mother had reached a stage of mild dementia and had not the faculties to recognize or address the need, even if her physical difficulties would have allowed it. A child-like mind was satisfied in her keeper and protector, that just was the way of things. The floor was littered with tissues used. With no way to discard them, they had formed a small stack that was rising with Lindy's columns beside the headboard of the little bed.

Lindy would give little attention to her mother and she liked it very much that way. The same judge that had issued power of attorney also handled the restraining order that would keep Rance and Hadd a hundred feet from their sister at all times. That was the way Lindy satisfied even more control over them both. It was her nature to control something and since her boys could no longer be used as control over their father, and Rance had eliminated her control of the ranch, there was nothing else but to set the design of how and when they would see their own mother. Open visits were acceptable, but only allowed if arranged first and only for pickup outside her yard perimeter at the sidewalk curb. Rance complied with the circumstances. His mother's only company would be an obnoxious untrained dog – also neglected – that ran rampant throughout the house with continuous overpowering and angry bark. All day, the dog would snarl and scowl. His mother was afraid of it, but there was no teaching or control of the stupid creature she was forced to share her loneliness with. She would never mention to Rance the prepared food he would rip from her meal plate with its voracious appetite and vicious approach. Lindy would plop a plate down beside her mother, and would leave to eat alone in the slightly bigger closet of her own. His mother continued to spiral downward, but Rance did not know the full extent of her neglect. If he had only known, he would have put a bullet right through the head of that stupid dog. He had no way of knowing her condition there, as he would never be able to set foot through that door, and his mother didn't understand it enough to tell him. He had no way of knowing that the dog defecated and urinated all over the house and it lay where it happened, never being ever cleaned up. It was not the way any of them had been raised and, as far as Rance knew, even Plover stayed clean. Something happened to Lindy that left her crazy in the way that it had.

"If only there was a way to git her outta there," Rance thought to himself, as he finished the drive that would end in his sister's driveway. Rance pulled his phone from his shirt pocket, looked around to see if there was any movement in his view of the clear glass door that led down the long entry hallway, showing the only clean room of the dwelling – another false front put on by the sister. It would end at the edge of a pit of what she would call a sunken living room that, if with no warning in it being there, one could break his neck in the fall to follow in stepping off into it. The only thing inside the glass, was the big black dog, doing what he was best at in showing that Rance had arrived on time. He texted the number from his list, titled "A-bitch," as in his listing it was alphabetically the first number. "I'm here." "Well?" Was the reply back. "Can I see Mom?" "I don't know. Kin yew?" "Ok, I'm here, yew said ta let yew know when I got here," Rance hammered out on the small keys imprinted under the screen. He was certain she could feel the anger build in his wording. Nothing came back. There was a lengthy pause. Rance sat in the truck just outside the yard. He caught glimpse of a sickly old squirrel, climbing its way through the branches of a century old half-dead and twisted oak tree that sat the center of her steep angled uphill yard. It was on its way to the home's eave where a long-time weathered-out hole had been chewed for its entry into the corner soffit.

A young mother walked past his sitting there, pushing a stroller on her way down the sidewalk path. In her passing she looked up at Rance and asked, "How are yew doing sir?" "Good Miss and yew?" "Yes sir. It sure is a beautiful day;" she answered back never missing a stride in her journey. "Yes Miss it shore is." The wheels of the stroller broke the silence of the afternoon, with every wheel tap, from every sidewalk crack they encountered, fading off as she was. Rance watched her in his rearview mirror. He could not help himself. After all, he was very much a man, single, and some things just came natural to him. He watched the sidewalk turn along with the curved street. His arm already lay curled up on the door frame window ledge, and he adjusted his side mirror in following the curve of the street. He followed the young mother with attention, but of no disrespect to her as common admiration of her shapely figure, had warranted his innocent look. Her hips young, but not. Her shapely butt moved to him like two trapped shoats in a burlap sack with every step she took. It wasn't of perverse want to him, more that he appreciated the female form as how it should be appreciated for what it was. She was pretty, and Rance approved. He watched her every step taken until she had completely left his mirrored view. He relaxed back into the moment as the thought of her was as fleeting as she had been. Immediately his thought went back to whether or not he had shut the water off at the heifer pasture before his leaving. His concentration in the moment only broken with another game-playing text back from Lindy. "Well?" Rance, hesitant, answered, "Well what? Gotdamn it! Am I goin ta git ta see Mom er not?" "Well it depends oan how yew act whether er not yew git ta see 'er now doesn't it?"

Rance hit the starter and the broken exhaust pipe hanging just below the old trucks manifold sounded off with each and every stroke of the diesel's fired-off pistons on that side. He had ensured everyone that lived within that confining city block would know that the old ranch truck had "kicked off." He put the old truck in gear, threw his arm over the back of the seat to relieve his turning head to see what was behind him as he ripped his way out of the driveway, pivoting out and onto the street. In his pivot and just before throwing the old truck into first gear in his transition to leave, he looked back up at the house and saw his old mother facing him, just behind her walker. Her weak shrinking frame was struggling to get out past the strong spring of the witch's glass door entry, without any assistance given by Lindy in her trying. Rance could see her desperation in not being left there, even though she was reduced in speed by age, she was in a race in her leaving down from the first entry step, avoiding the sidewalk stoop purposely in her way toward the grassy knoll. That knoll as steep an angle needed to damage her badly if she were to fall. She was racing without thought in the most direct route gained for the direction of Rances truck. He slammed the truck into neutral, set his brake, and leapt from the seat to make his way to her in hopes she wouldn't fall. "Don'tchew leave without me," she said as loud as she could utter it, followed with a grin that shown the absence of a front tooth, because of her forgotten misplaced partial that normally filled in the gap. Rance hadn't heard her over the trucks engine, but had known his mother well enough to know what was said, as he shut the motor off and before his departing the cab. He hollered out to her, "Wait there. Ah woan't leave'ya mom," and he raced to meet her in the yard.

"Well, where'er we goin?" She asked in her excitement, but knowing exactly where Rance had planned to take her. She still hadn't realized the forgotten tooth, even with the hiss of her breath escaping through the gap with each word spent in his reaching her. In that moment he noticed, she changed from her toothy smile, quickly retreating back to a tight-lipped grin in remembering her missing tooth. She was frail and pale in appearance. Although the weather was hot, she was chilled to her core and wore her favorite grey hound's-tooth pattern sweater. Worn with one button off in its fastening, clinging to her in crooked fashion. She smelled of neglect and her hair was matted and unwashed. It appeared to Rance it had been that way for a very long time. There was flattened area in the back where Rance then knowing by its look that she was spending most of her days in the bed. Much different from the woman he knew in her younger years. There had been a time when she would have never left the house unless everything was just right and she was made up to perfection. He remembered when, just going out for groceries, she would have the latest style of tight sprayed hair, her eyes covered with white framed cat-eyed dark sunglasses, snug fit stirrup pants with high heels, lips painted bright red, and her ears adorned with white pearl clip earrings joining the much larger ones hanging around her neck – and a pearl bracelet to match, tying her whole look together. Women were just that way then, and up until her advanced age and the changes it brought for her, she was still that way. Rance knew that if she had a little help from Lindy, she would still want to be at her best.

He continued in his helping of his old mother while carefully assisting her across the yard to the old pickup. Stopping with every other step to allow her rest and gather more strength and to catch her bearings on the matter, along with her bearings in the meaning of just where she was and where she was going. Her lips were still dressed in red, but in her application of lipstick, she had just missed her mark and the red wavered down to her cheek. Rance hadn't the heart to tell her, so he just began to talk about the squirrel standing watch from one of the old twisted oaks long dead limbs, on its way back into the cover of the few that still held leaves and shade. Rance removed his handkerchief from his back pocket and wiped his mother cheek, while her attention was being held by the now chattering rodent high above her. It had reminded him of the same nose clinching technique that she had used on him when he was a child. The roles now seemingly reversed and she was relying on his help now as he was then. He dabbed at her mishap quickly without her realizing her mistake. "What're you doin?" She asked, wiping her face in slight protest and quickly wiping her cheek with her left hand. "If yer goin ta kill me, don't try suffocat'in me. Do it with sumpthin that'd be quicker!" It was a rare moment of clarity and quick wit Rance was happy to hear in the moment. "Just gitten a bug offaya Mom." A little white lie to save her from her embarrassment of the truth. She again swiped her face with the hand in a more brisk fashion and said "It ain't still there is it?" Followed with a blow of air from her pinched tight lips. "No Mom I gott'im," he answered.

Rance caught the light sound of an opening door of the bitch's house and turned just in time to see the fat arm of his sister open the entry glass door and toss her mother's purse on the ground below the front porch stoop. Rance's anger he held in check at the disrespect she held for him in being there, and especially for her mother and the items she held dear. "She might need this, have 'er here by sevin," his greed-filled sister, full of hate, blubbered out, while turning and slamming the door. "Wait here Mom. You'll be okay. I'll be right back," he said. He made his way to the laying purse, with spilled contents sitting scattered about the lawn. When he picked up all of her things to put them back, he realized the small wallet she normally carried was not in the usual spot inside her bag. He could only guess it was Lindy's way of controlling her mother, or to keep anyone else from getting access to her bank book usually carried. His mind began to mull over the situation in that moment. Two siblings together; one in court-ordered charge of his mother's care, and both with only selfish intentions in her holding, and both without empathy or the least bit of sympathy for her in the waning years of life. Rance looked back toward his frail mother, standing and waiting, looking in the opposite direction – not really understanding why, but trusting in his telling her to wait there. For Rance it was a different story. He had understanding of his mother's feelings, and sympathy for the woman that he knew deep down never really wanted him in the first place and had forced love toward him. He wondered if her stillborn loss before him, had been the reason that contributed toward her feelings felt by Hadd and Rance. Hadd was the reminding survivor just before his departed brother's birth and Rance sometimes felt that must have been the reason for love lost for him. It had only been a theory, but without ever knowing the reason for sure, it would only be a guess – Rance's best, and in the moment – his only guess.

He looked back up at the glass door and behind it with crossed arms and smirking smile stood his sister gloating in what she had done. He knew she got pleasure of watching him down on his knees, with nothing he could do about it. She was backed by enforced rules when she tossed her mother's purse. Rance really looked at her standing there. No genetic propensity for obesity, nor was it from disease. Her whale-like weight was due only to her lackadaisical life, second only to her ravenous, gluttonous urge to make it to the trough, similar to the ways of their penned slaughter hogs, before the rest had a chance to get there. She was a glutton, and had remnants of a powdered donut still on her grinning lips, but there would be no rescue wipe from Rance's handkerchief in that moment. He glanced back down, but not before noticing her clammy, pale, complexion, and looking back at his mother and seeing it the same. He was just understanding it. They both were holed up in that pit, never seeing the light of the sun. In Lindy's need to control her mother, and the lifestyle money that came with her, she confined them both to a personal prison without either's chance of parole. Rance saw his mother's plight and was disheartened by the situation. He was guilt-ridden in his not knowing what, or even if, he might do anything about it. The money just wasn't there for the fight and there were two against two in the mix – and his mother still showing her favoritism and full love to the ones who were hurting her the most.

She in her old age, and unclear thinking, wanted to be there. Rance had always known it, too.

One last time the door opened. "Now yew have her back here by sevin. She has medicine ta take and don'tchew be late. Ya hear?" His sister 'bellered' out, resembling an old boss cow that butted every other cow in the herd just because it made her feel right by doing it. Rance pictured her in that role, knowing that, just like when the old bully boss cow would finally go down, the others she pushed around usually reciprocated in their downward head butt driving blows in payback until she would take no more. Then, with triumphant bellows, turn and walk off leaving her to die alone. "Why don'tchew give me her medicine and I'll make sure she gits it? An why don'tchew let her decide when she would like ta come back?" Rance answered. "Because I decide! Haven't'chew figgered that outchet? Do I need to git a crayon an draw yew a picture so you kin figger it out?" "Why don'tchew git yer oan crayon an draw yersef a picture an then take that picture and ....." Rance stopped short in his finishing. She had him over a barrel and he knew it. She had proven it in times past. She was good about calling the law on him any time she felt the need. Only the need was never taken serious and the local sheriff had a good time at her expense, because, like Rance, he understood her spoiled insanity. But this time was different. He couldn't see his mother's outing with him being stopped, as he knew she was living inside just for the chance to get out of that house for a while, and the Wichita Falls police might not yet know his sister as well as the sheriff of Clay County had. "Fine," Rance answered. "Ah'll have 'er here by seven." "Yew'd better! And yew better not be late!" She said this time, with muffin crumbs flying from her mouth as she slammed the front glass door. Rance watched her slouch her way back down the hall. He blisteried to himself of his cowering down to her, but understood completely why he had, and if it were to happen again he would do the very same thing. Besides, he knew, with patience, her day was coming.

He brought his mother to her favorite eating spot, she felt fancy in her going there, because once there, she was. The waiter always offered her a sample glass of house wine. She never took it but felt fancy in its offering, not really knowing it was just a sampling in hopes she'd buy the glass or bottle. She seemed tired to Rance this time, worn and quiet, and although she ordered she would not eat in its arriving. It was a beautiful day and she enjoyed her time spent there. It was just short of her eighty-fourth birthday. Rance made it seem like it was her actual birthday though, and even in shared enjoyed embarrassment of the wait staff singing "Happy Birthday" to her it was a nice way for her to feel special. And, on top of that, receive the free dessert that came with the celebration. He had faked her birthday many times in their going. He would have gladly paid for it, but his mother believed him to be mischievousat times, and expected him to perform the ritual of being that way at some point when she was around him. Rance knew she expected it so played along with the facade, and the unexpected surprise of the waitresses singing to her, before her real birthday had arrived, was something he knew deep down she'd find enjoyment in. She found guilty pleasure in Rances oft-times bending of the rules. They sat there way past the dinner. Rance watched as her food sat untouched. She did enjoy a small portion of the tiramisu, but Rance knew it was probably only habit that she did, because of her feeling of something special gifted to her. He asked the waiter for a box to go, which he promptly went to get. She sat there happily with the paper hat still strapped upon her head. Normally she wouldn't have and Rance didn't know whether it was just forgotten, or she was happier it being there as to hide her messed up hair.

"Well Mom ya ready?" "Ready for what?" "Ready ta go back." "Why, lands no, I'm enjoying this here. Are ya already tireda me?" "Well no," Rance answered. "It's just I have ta git yew back before seven so yew kin take yer medicine," he finished. "Just a little longer?" It was more of a question, than in her stating it. "Sure Mom, there ain't no rush. Yew just tell me when yer ready." It was getting hot, but it was a beautiful day. The bright light of the sun enhanced the green leaves of the Bradford pear trees that adorned the parking lot. Rance caught his mother's stare as if she was watching a play being acted out before her. Expressions changing, her forehead lifting and setting, grins forming, then serious look. She had expressions of joy in watching the now resting black birds in those packed rows, but in smooth line as they would fill the trees. Seemingly like choreographed dancers they would launch themselves out in a giant wave, then in unison curl and float their ways back into their treetop perches. "They look like fish," his mother broke the silence. "What? Asked Rance. "They look like fish. Ya know, like the ones in tha ocean. All movin tagether – what one does, they all do. I wonder how they do that…it's hard ta even git one'er two people all oan tha same page," she said quietly. In all of his time Rance had never noticed those birds in the way that his mother was seeing them. Maybe she hadn't either. Maybe they both had, but only in the learning minds of a child long forgotten. It was the simple noticing of a child that his mother's mind was pointing to him. Maybe this was life's fading way to bring it full circle and ease its end to her now. He watched. Sure enough, from their restaurant window the black birds did give the appearance of fish swimming in unison before them, and the window frame represented the aquarium view they both had.

One more hour passed and he told her again that they must go. He saw a sadness in her, he had never seen before. "What's wrong?" He asked. "Ya thank I kin buy a lottery ticket?" His mother asked quietly. "A lottery ticket?" "Before we go back. Ya thank we kin buy a lottery ticket?" She said to him, while she gathered up the extra table napkins from the holder and stuffed them into her purse. "Why?" Asked Rance. "Well, Lindy don't let me git'em, says it's a waste a money. She says ta me, why would an old woman like me have need of anything, much less a lottery ticket. She says I'm too long gone to spend it anyway if I won. She don't let me buy'em." "Is that what she said?" Rance asked, trying not to show his anger outward that was boiling from inside. "Is there anything else she don't let yew buy?" "Well I'd like ta git my magazines, but she says that's a waste a money too. I guess she's probably rite," she finished. Rance helped her to stand and placed her walker out in front of her. The waiter brought back the bagged up dinner, with an added few complimentary breadsticks for the road. Rance took it and stepped behind his mother. "Well Mom its yer birthday ain't it?" "Well land sakes no!" "Yes it is! Taday, especially. Whatchya say we go git yew sum birthday lottery tickets and sum magazines." Rance said on their way out to the truck.

He and his mom showed up two hours late, and he began his help to get his mother out and up the hill to the door. His sister had parked her car in the street crossways to the drive, to keep Rance from pulling up into it. It was dark, but the street light made it seem like daytime, only with reflections of flying bugs around them, at times hiding their glow. He stuffed a month's worth of scratchoff tickets and her two choice magazines into her bag, and they began their way up. Halfway across the night yard, the front door slapped back and the fat bitch stood before them. "I told'jew ta have'er back her by sevin an it's past tin. One more step an I'll have yew arrested for trespassin'," she blubbered out at Rance, who was steadfast in assisting his mother up the steep path forced and to the front door. He kept his way there, no matter the ignorant order received by the controlling imbecile ranting away before him. He bit his tongue the whole way, allowing his mother to stop at times to catch her breath. "Now Lindy I'm the cause a us gittin here late," his mother said, hoping to calm her out-of-control daughter. "I don't keer what the reason. Yew were told ta be back here by sevin," she said to her mother, all the while directing it at Rance in a slow, low demanding tone, through clinched teeth. Her face was red and the lack of physicality in her life had her winded in just the giving of her belligerent speech. The walk up the hill to the door took twenty minutes to accomplish. More than the five or so it normally would have, if Lindy hadn't blocked the drive with her car, in her unconcerned, offhand rage-driven tantrum. Rance listened to the berating, but was relaxed in giving his mother as much time as needed to reach the entry stoop.

Just about the time they both reached the door, two police cars arrived along with two of the City's Finest. For Rance, it would mean a quick handcuffed escort back to the sidewalk curb, followed up with his believed explanation of his and his mother's late return, backed by his mother's statement that she requested a little more time at dinner. A quick background check revealed past repeated calls unwarranted by Lindy from past Clay County Sheriff's department calls. The Wichita Falls police now knew what the Clay County sheriff already knew. It would be their turn in the job of dealing with a crazy lady that now resided in the house that sat on the hump with the half dead twisted oak at the end of the street in their city.

Rance would never be allowed on the property again. He could see the torment and toll that confrontation, in the late evening of that day, had on his aging mother as she made her way past her out-of-control daughter into the dungeon-like home. The only finite thread his sister had left in her sad existence would be her decisive action of being in control. She lived for it, as it was in her mind the only way to feel important; control of anything – or something. At this time it was control of someone; her failing mother. Rance made his way back into the seat of his old truck after the cuffs were removed and slowly pulled away.

Guilt at leaving her there, locked away in that hell hole, was whittling him down as much as the one with the proverbial knife of time was slowly whittling away at his mother. In his leaving, he just couldn't wrap his head around the problem dealt and the link he must endure with the siblings he'd rather not ever see again. His binding to them for the last thirty-odd years had nothing to do with family want or need – or the ranch for that matter. Instead it only revolved around each being trapped in a round pen lot tied with long rope knotted to a centered breaking point-post – their mother being that post. As long as the post stood there, each would be tied to it and tied together for its fact. In this case, she was not rallied around as being the strong matriarch that enforced the rules and was respected. It wasn't like that at all. She was only the center of control, as created by Plover and Lindy, from their on-running manipulation and unending greed. By then, she was used in securing crooked dealings and sheltering possible losses and it would be their only hope that she survived long enough to get them past the long-standing statute of limitations and be the protection needed to get them both out of trouble. To them, she was a bank that the pair could use as collateral to cover their ill-gotten gains.

Rance and Hadd would see she was collateral damage, to be discarded by them once their deeds were done.

Rance and Hadd were in the dark about it all, but once the secrets slipped out, they were dragged into it like a calf to the branding fire. It was forever two opposing forces in the constant protection of their mother's wellbeing and in loss prevention for the ranch and its holdings. The greedy pair, out of ignorance, were burning the whole thing that was built and worked by everyone but them to the ground. What was worse it would be without their mother's understanding, and with her own blessing. Their inability to secure means on their own, and separate her from their corrupt ways, would ultimately be the reason that everyone mixed up in it was force bound together by it. It was a bad way. Rance and Hadd hadn't chosen it and didn't want it, but the actions of the other two dragged them both into the middle of it. Both felt the guilt of their cover up, even though it was the only way to ensure the ranch's survival. What was done, was done, and the way it would forever be. Rance couldn't bear thinking about it, but was caught up in the fact that he and Hadd needed peace and separation that only time itself would enact. Harsh as it was to think about, Nature had the only way to handle it, and would eventually – along with time – catch up with their mother. He didn't wish it or want it, nor did Hadd, but that was exactly what the others seemed to plan for. Like two perched turkey vultures anticipating the rotted meal before them, in just the correct way and length of time necessary, to provide them with the biggest, best prepared free meal they could get. Rance hated himself for thinking it, but was tired of the worry and paranoia that came along with it – the never-ending secrets that could bring whole generations of life's struggles and labor to a crumbling end. He could see the secrets Plover and Lindy kept bringing the whole life down.

17

SELDOM, BUT HOME...

Rance drove into the city limits of Archer City, on his way up the lonesome street that held separate vacant houses not lived in since the last big oil boom for many fell. Unkempt yards. Tall grass and weeds, some with old scrap piles of trash where their weathered containment bags had long since rotted away, and contents once held lay strewn around. There were abandoned vehicles, still sitting upon flat tires, left to dry out and rot in their abandonment. The abandoned structures sat side by side, while an occasional black sheep being lived in shown out with kept-up hedge and mowed yard. The ones appearing alive standing in contrast to the others that were leaving the lonely occupied houses awkwardly out of place – completing the picture by their existence throwing the whole look of the block in disarray.

Rance rolled up into the drive that ran beside a little green one-bedroom house on West Walnut Street. This was the house of his childhood. It still had the covering of its original factory green asbestos siding that was common in homes built of its period. Out at the left of it stood the single stunted elm tree that sheltered one corner of its roof, protecting that lone particular corner from high wind, rain, and the occasional hailstorm that frequented that part of the region. The rest of the roof reflected that one corner's lost protection. The front entry had a crooked screen door with angled latching hasp that had been pulled loose many years prior to Rance, and poked its way through the door's rusted lower screen. It was all held in place by a strained hook latch still doing its job. Rance bought it in disrepair, and in disrepair it would stay, as he was not a carpenter and his lack of ability – unless by use of a rope, a brand, or a vaccination needle – was the reason it would remain that way. The little house shared the look of the unloved majority of others on that street. The only difference being that the yard was wrapped in a single electric fence wire strand, that when its gap was closed, was left to Rance's old horse to graze freely. His gelding, Yank, made his traveling, grazing, around the yard in even fashion. He kept the grass neatly trimmed for his portion of rent paid.

Rance had a half circle in the back where he would bring his old truck and trailer around and park for its rest. Earlier that day, he had done just that, before rushing to his mother's house for their routine dinner date. He unhooked the gooseneck trailer in his rush to get there, and had left his faithful steed inside, as he planned on getting back much earlier to relieve his confinement then. Rance's running late meant his horse would carry the brunt of his failure to schedule that earlier day, but it would have to be his horse that felt it. It certainly wouldn't be his mother, even though Rance carried the guilt of it as much, either way. The sun had long since set and his headlights startled the trailer bound gelding. Rance caught his excited eyes widen at their shine. The horse jumped a hop forward and calmed as Rance opened his door. "Woah boy, easy son it's just me." The horse replied back with a whimpering knicker. "Sorry son, didn' aim ta leave ya that long," he said, while stepping up and unlatching the idle trailers gate. The horse turned to meet him and instead of his usual backing out, paused just long enough for Rance to pull the looped neck reins from his neck, then without pause the big roan leapt from it in a buck, and spun back at Rance's tight hold and the touch of the bit to the corners of his mouth. He stamped his foot to the hard ground, agitated, but anxious. Rance answered his tension and unbuckled the well-worn saddle. As it was removed, the roan performed a full body shake, similar to that of a wet dog running out of caught rain back into the dry of a shelter, in ridding its coat of the water. Afterward, he exhaled with a lip fluttering snort, letting Rance know it was way past time for his drink. He led him to the half-barrel trough beside the back door faucet and paused, relaxed the reins and watched the horse drink. When Yank pulled up in pause, he removed the bridle, and the roan worked his jaw in a stretching fashion in relief of it being pulled. Relaxing, he looked at Rance and went back at the water. Rance tossed his saddle over onto the back of his truck, shut its door and leaned back a lengthy stretch and looked directly up in the Texas sky.

The stars were bright, he thought to himself, and a nip was forming in the air all around him. After the stretch, he patted his old friend there, called for his old dog Bingo to unload, and they both walked out to the front drive gap and pulled tight the hot wire gate to keep the horse from winding up in downtown Archer. Rance made his way into the door, just as the horse pulled back from the water and began ripping at the grass that grew under the backyard peach tree. The outside lights shown a dull light, sporadically lit up where the houses sat that were lived in. One flickering in its dying attempt to burn out. It made the night look eerie and silent in its twilight haze and the night's bats flew into them, catching pale insects fluttering found in their echolocation. He walked up the wooden back steps, hoping to miss the rotted out area of boards that topped it. It was an area in the shade, where the pole light couldn't quite reach and it was chancy, at best, of him not stepping onto through them. He opened the rear screen door, which was in much better shape than the front, as the spring made its familiar stretching song. With blind unease, he pushed his way in the solid entry door which wasn't quite as easy and drug its way to its three quarter open stop on the uneven kitchen floor. Once in, he released the screen door for its expected slap in its closing. He worked his way over in the dark room, right arm outstretched and waving in horizontal side sweeping action, searching to find the single string connected to the simple hanging bulb that would light up the room. Finding it, he pulled the cord, let it go, and the room lit up. Rance closed his eyes a few times for them to have time to adjust to it. The hanging light swung back and forth in loose link swinging, allowing the luminescence to dance, sweeping the room. In its movement, it presented the illusion of ghost-like apparitions moving about the small kitchen.

He made his way over to the old refrigerator that had come to him with the purchase of the house, opened its aging warped door and pulled out a slightly less than lukewarm jug of milk. Pulled its pressed top from it and heartily drank several chugs.

He looked around at the bare dull walls and stared in thought at slightly lighter square spots on the walls that stood out to him, halting him in their seeing, but not really.

Shades around lighter squares, where past pictures had hung by the past tenants who lived there. Their smoke removed when those tenants carried them away to protect new spots on cigarette walls where they were going. The light hung in the living room, where a single chair sat in the corner facing the television set opposite of it. There was an old wooden crate that had been perfect height and width, that dwelled as a makeshift table to set his food and drink, and also the occasional chair for the off-chance visitor that made their way to his house, namely Hank. He made his way over to his chair, sat his milk on the crate and opened the pack of devils food cookies that fueled his personal addiction. He grabbed the remote and turned on the television set in hopes of catching the weather, which was really the only thing that interested him and prepared him for the routine planning of his next day's work schedule. With simple bonus, he quite enjoyed watching the pretty weather girl in her delivering of it. His eyes peered around, seemingly searching the bare walls, after realizing he had missed the news. He looked at the nailed up sheet curtains that had shielded him inside from the nothingness of the abandoned house that sat across the street from him. He chose to live here even though he didn't, and wouldn't have, any other time or anywhere else.

Strongly, he had embedded in himself willed self-restraint to not move into the vacant ranch house on the hill, either. It was the ranch's house, it was his mother's house. It was his father that planned its being there. He hadn't earned it, and wasn't sure he would have with his mother's leaving, let alone the fact she was very much alive. Even in the knowing she would never return to it, it was not his to live – and would never be. But it was the headquarters, and for that fact alone, his being there was needed and his need to be there, was there. Rance was living and struggling in two worlds. The house sat there full of furniture, but was very empty in its need for her. Inside it was her lifetime of collected trinkets and it would have been very wrong for anyone to tamper with her past life there. In his present moment, Rance direly needed the money spent over that run down shack in Archer to make improvements on the ranch. His daily eighty-plus-mile round trip was breaking him. In reality, it could be much easier, just walking out of the door of the ranch house on the hill and working its ranch from there.

The house lay vacant, but kept up and centered on the very land that had been willed outright to him, aside from the rest divided out by five way split. Forty-one miles from his house with the stained walls and hanging curtain sheets. There was a green pasture there much better than the backyard grazing and a perfect set of welded-pipe lots he and his brother Hadd had built for the livestock penning. A round water tank sat the lots there with a stopping float valve that kept the stock tank full for needed drink but shut off the well when its feeding flow was not necessary. Thirsty pastured cattle walked their rutted path routine on their daily visit to it, where one could get a good check and head count, without so much as an untrailered horse or a let down rope in the process. Rance always saw it as her home and not ranch property. It was the only home she ever knew, yet now she would be housed another forty miles away to the north – away from her planted spring garden, her summer roses and the crepe myrtle bushes she so dearly loved. This would be the second year that she wouldn't be there to pick the early summer peaches from the small tree that grew out in the corner of the fence, just outside her backdoor. Her life was clean there, and even in her lonesome times she was happy. Rance was crippled emotionally. He was sure at this point she would have loved lonesome.

The house in Archer City was easy. It had been acquired for the sum of sixteen hundred dollars and change from a tax sale, but Rance's clearing his monthly bills of electricity and gas would peak his upkeep on both places. His fuel between them was the farm fuel money needed for the operation's equipment. It wasn't what he wanted, but actually the money was the same spent as if it was with the weekly rate at the Lonestar Motel, and he didn't have to put up with the Friday and Saturday night drunk patrons that kept him in many a sleepless night. He didn't miss the buzz of the passing traffic from Highway 25 just outside his window, either. What he missed was that ranch house on that little North Texas hill, and his mother being in it. There was nothing, absolutely nothing, he could do for her and he lived with that daily. His choice other than the Lonestar was a little rundown motel in the oil-rich town of Electra. It was far enough away, but close enough to come back if need be. On some sub-conscious level, maybe in some unrecognized reality supposed, he would sometimes feel a desperate need to just run – to get away from everything. That Electra Derrick Motor Hotel was always on his mind. Archer was the center of his daywork jobs, though, and with his winning closing bid, Rance now owned a piece of it. A place to keep the dust out was all the little house was, but it didn't keep much out. And on the days it rained, trash cans, pots and buckets were good enough to stave off the wet. The ceiling showed just where to sit the leaking water catchers. Unlike the motel, he had a kitchen, with a sink beside a stove that he used to prepare mainly his eggs and bacon, and a refrigerator big enough for him to retire his cooler. The water was supplied by the city water tower that centered the town, and at times smelled as fishy as what resided in the muddy lake it was derived from. He had spent a lifetime drinking from fresh water wells deep and cold – the water of his grandfather's finding and his father's drilling. It was hard to get used to coffee with a hint of carp and catfish. Still, Rance's Archer City home was so much better than the Lonestar, with its constant traffic just outside its cinder block walls, as it only had the occasional lost car or truck traveling the dirt street past it there. It happened more than it would have at the ranch house on the hill, but it was still left for his notice when one would pass and conjure up an uneasy feeling of "why would they be coming down his street at that time of night?" It was just his paranoia of confinement of the city, even if it was only Archer City.

He had thought on the possibility of moving a trailer house or camper out on the ranch, but he would have the need to tie into electric, gas, and septic system to do so, and with the problems with the ranch so touchy, and family dynamics in turmoil, he changed his thoughts on the matter – it would stir much more than he needed. The feasibility to do it would no doubt bring reprisal, even though the ranch house on the hill was centered on the property he owned. The ranch house surrounded by the ponderosa pines on the hill was on an undivided part of the estate, so Archer would be his home.

The land had been quartered many years ago, all but the ranch house and the acreage under it which was to be bought out, by ordered will, by the ranch operator after their mother passed away. Whoever would take on the duties of the ranch from others would buy it out. It would be just the house and the two acres it sat upon, ideally going to Rance, as his father left him the section it sat in the middle of. It was a good idea of his father, but Rance knew it wouldn't go as planned. His brother and sister with help of their mother would see to it that way. Rance would be left to deal with the others, even if they were out of favor as they were forced to deal with him. He and Hadd always shared in the operations and the other two were thrown into it, as their mother felt it was the fair thing to have them own their own share. Rance had never seen any fairness in it, as he had spent a lifetime working it and securing its place, while the other two were absent in the finances, expenses and especially the labor. Rance believed, as the working line before him had felt, that just because you were born into the blood, didn't give you the right to inherit equally in it. Something maybe, but not equally. As Rance saw it, inheritance should be earned and it was Rance and Hadd that had paid their dues many times over. The other two simply rode the coattails of the ones controlling the ride, but they were in it as if they had. Rance and Hadd were stuck in it against their wanting, as they were tied to the other siblings' greedy hold until the time of their mother's release of it all. Her death would be the teller of how it all would transpire. Likewise, the other two's need of Rance and Hadd, and the cover-up provided – the insurance needed – to keep their own holdings safe, as all was in their mother's name. For the time being, a running ranch was needed to protect them, and they had Rance and Hadd hogtied to it.

Rance had always seen it, but was hard put between a rock and a hard place. Rance had too much invested in the ranch, and so did Hadd. He could not see it going to waste, as if it had never happened in the first place. He was caught between his father's words of "take care of them" and his ever-tiring fight, giving way to his want to let it all die. In time, the hard decision was made by him to let the crooked deals of his brother stay covered up and hid, and not let the ranch suffer from those deals made. Rance would pay the price for the cover up. He felt the guilt it would bring – for the saving of it or in the loss of it, either way. He chose to put off the total liquidation of generations of worked and sacrificed for land and holdings. He knew that if a breakup would occur what he and Hadd, and their predecessors, had invested a lifetime in, would be in for a possible fall. They needed the other two quarter shares to pay down their loans for their future stake. Without covering the other two in their misdealings, the ranch as they had known it would absolutely end. He also had to live the guilt of leaving his mother in their selfish greed, but he saw no alternative to it, as she needed the ranch as much as they did to survive. Rance was wearing down and he knew it. He didn't know whether he was saving it all as he had promised his Father, or if he was only delaying its finish. He never knew what secrets were passing back and forth by Plover and Lindy, and what problems in his future would have to be dealt with. It was Vegas there in South Clay County, and Rance was forced to roll the dice.

He woke to the early morning sermon being given by a TV preacher that he'd seen at various times over the years. The preacher's time was sandwiched between the early morning infomercials and the local day-start news. His preaching irritated Rance to the point that he quickly moved from the corner chair, where he was awakened, and manually unplugged the television at its source at the wall. His irritation was that in the end, as most sermons, there was more talk of the passing of the plate than that of the message. He remembered sermons heard given by the old man with the black dyed and slicked back hair. His gold watch and large gold rings on both hands catching the light of the camera as he prayed for Rance, for his love offering given, and for the schedule for his tithing. A prayer for him, if he would "just take the time right now and call in his offering and talk to the first awaiting operator, on standby and waiting to pray just for him".

He remembered the preacher from long ago, appearing much younger than he would that morning. Now the old preacher's wanting, with fresh plucked eyebrows and jet black dyed hair, included tithing gifts which helped him with his new bought chin lift and botox stretching that still didn't hide his true age. His slurred slow sermons had only changed by the fact that credit cards were an accepted form for the tithe. Rance thought back on his older brother and his younger sister just in the moment of pulling the plug, and how they were both happy to outwardly portray, every chance given, their denomination and membership in the church whenever such performance was needed – and both without truth of it in their professing. Rance had been raised with them. He knew them. They, like the TV preacher, had no practice in what they would preach. Rance judged that old preacher, knowing full well by the good book's teachings he shouldn't. But he had made the choice just by being the recipient of the Rance way; that he'd just have to take his chance in hell, rather than burden Jesus for his forgiveness. He would have his hands full just trying to keep up with the rest of the sinners. Right or wrong, he always felt he was better off handling things himself. His decision was early in his life. Looking back on it, too early to truly handle it, but for him at the time he felt worthy of the task. He forewent the ritual baptism that Plover, Lindy and even Hadd had gone through as he felt he might taint the water to the point it would be useless in its way to purify anyone else that might follow him in.

He quickly walked into the kitchen and turned on the tap, allowing the rust from his old pipe plumbing to clear its rattling way through the valve and splash into the sink. Eventually, it had cleared just enough to fill the blue glazed coffee pot that he was long accustomed to using in the making of his morning start. He had prepared his morning brew in that old pot the majority of his life and the glaze-busted smooth rust dent and the lower separation of its handle added its use and value. In earlier times, an early morning wake would have him struggling – usually after a late night honky-tonk hangover forced him into it. Now, the struggle was still there, but it was primarily of age and wear of his own doing, and more time allotted for his waking.

The bags under his eyes slowly drew into their wakeup, as the morning coffee brewed. He watched the hinged-cap top pop up under the bubbling foam pushing at its rim. Long ago, its inner percolator stem was lost, and Rance was well-rehearsed in the change to the single scoop of coffee being dropped right into it, along with one leftover breakfast egg shell said to help settle the grounds. He performed the same ritual each time as if fact, but got the grounds in his teeth anyway with each morning cup and felt it just wasn't a true cup without them. Even though Rance would share in a morning cup of coffee at the cafe with friends, it just wasn't as good to him, as it just wasn't the same without the needed texture he was accustomed to from the brewing of his old graniteware pot. He poured a cup and remembered how many times he saw the old pot set over the morning open fire coals, where finished day of the branding and doctoring of the young calves raised the moon – where, at times, the fire told stories throughout the rest of the night. He also thought about how many times that leftover pot had doused the same mesquite pit fire with its boiled-down leftover just with the rising sun. Then to be tossed back in the tool box that sat his truck bed, just as ready to start all over again. He missed the smoky taste of the open camp fire to the coffee, but it was still his choice over the weak stuff fixed elsewhere, and the designer coffees that seemed to be in every convenience gas stop and restaurant dotting the highways he traveled.

Rance had only one cup, skipped a cooked breakfast and put his plate of scrambled eggs in the refrigerator for later. He grabbed the last devil's food cookie on his way through to his bedroom and his bath. After a quick dry shave, he stepped into the old clawfoot bathtub that was painted in a dark royal blue to hide its outward rust by the previous owners. He grabbed his makeshift shower hose, engineered by unscrewing the spout from the half inch pipe it was attached to, and with the aid of a hose clamp, attached a piece of half inch garden hose that had the handgrip sprayer attachment still attached – borrowed from his mother's flower garden hose not in use. The tub didn't have a curtain to pull around it, but with practice, he was able to keep most of the spray from the walls and floor. The rest he just soaked up with a towel. Then a quick drying off, his comb barely grazing in its catch through his short hair, followed in finish with a splash of cologne.

18

FIVE STAR OUTCOME AT A SINGLE STAR DINER
IN ARCHER CITY

He was right in the middle of putting his last boot on, when
his cell phone rang out with the programmed ring tone of
"On the Road Again," announcing that Hank was on the
other end.

"Yow Hank," Rance answered. "Dontchew ever just say
'Hello,' or 'How ya doin?'" Hank answered. "Whataya
need?" Asked Rance. "Ah don't woant nuthin!" Why do
ya always gotta accuse me a woantin sumpthin?" Rance
didn't answer. "Well ya bout ready? Thought yew'd be
ready by now. Ah doan't woanta miss tha buffet," Hank
said while trying his best to rush up his old friend. "Come
oan Rance, they gotta good buffet goin this mornin. All tha
pancakes a feller kin eat 'n plenty a sausage ta go long with
it." Rance didn't want to admit it, but as good as his coffee

was to him, it sure was needing something to go along with it. After all, he was invited, and he already intended on going. Hence the shower, shave, and cologne that for some odd reason his little buddy Hank ever insisted in his wearing. Rance sniffed himself before applying it in his wonder why. It had been a slow week and he hadn't any outside work lined up, so he'd agreed. "Yea, sounds good. I'll seeya down there." "Good man. About time ya joined in oan summa tha finer thangs," Hank had said. Just before telling Hank he was heading that way, his phone's screen lit up, informing him that Hank had ended the call.

The old stop was busy and Rance made his way in through the door. "Howdy Rance!" "Whatya bin up to Rance?" "How's tha world binna treatin ya Rance?" Every old acquaintance he passed sounded out in greeting when he entered the diner. "Over here Rance!" Hank yelled from across the room, as if Rance hadn't known where to go. After all, the pair sat the same table for the past thirty plus years, but usually only at noontime dinner.

There was a sign placed in reserve for "The cow hauler that's full of shit," written on a ripped off soda straw boxtop and placed into the table top memo clip holder for everyone to see and wonder, except for those who knew Hank. The sign had sat there for at least fifteen years, put there by a waitress of an earlier time of Hank's aggravation. She was long gone, but it was left in her absence for every waitress that had to deal with the flirtatious truck driver after her departure.

Rance made his way over and had just sat down when the waitress came over to the table. "Know whut ya want Rance or ya need a minute?" "Well Agnes, seein as ah just got here, I don't reckon ah know what I woant. Mind if ah see one a them menus ya got there stuck up under yore arm?" He pulled out and sat his chair, rested both elbows on the table, and looked right in the eyes of Agnes and waited. She looked him back with a scowl in complete defiance to his ornery ways, and handed him the paper that had a few items scribbled that they did have and lines through the ones they didn't. Without even looking at it, he pointed over at the buffet just as quickly. "I thank I'll just have that!" Rance unclutched the menu as Agnes grabbed it, turned and tilted her butt cheek at him. Rance and Hank laughed out loud knowing all of the implication of it. "Brang me summa that coffee Agnes while yer at it," he finished while getting up and making his way over to it. Agnes, in her pleasant way, shrugged and frowned at the extra time she had to spend doing her job and was busy ignoring her victims over at the next table. Rance was always amazed at the tips she seemed to get at the end of each patron's dining pleasure – including his. He often wondered if it was out of guilt at how each had treated her, or fear of what might happen if they didn't leave her one.

Rance rounded the partition wall to the buffet. The wall separated the front room of the cafe for the morning breakfast brunch, and the closed-off section slated for the evening crowd for supper. On this day, there was a larger crowd there than usual due to a book auction and a store's shutdown that would be taking place later that morning. The local reared author that had owned it was revered by some, ignored by most, and for a few just plain detested, for his painting of their little town in a rougher light than most felt it should be. Rance had seen it differently. He saw it as the writer had been dead on in its portrayal. Anyway, the store and his welcome try at revitalization brought in strangers unexpected, and change that the town had not wanted. Paranoia to those not written about and some that had been, with hints of realism to those who still resided there in truth and paranoia alike. The crowd at the diner was double stacked and there were tables set with an eccentric bunch in their waiting. The curbs were lined with

Mercedes and Lexuses, along with a vintage VW with flowers painted to its sides. The VW was more reminiscent of the time the celebrated author had written his first novel. It was even dragging a small trailer behind it and took up three spaces of the only parking area at the end, leaving Rance to park across the street at the Courthouse and walk over for his breakfast. Rance had his mind on the buffet bar but couldn't help notice the graying man with the long hair pulled back in a bun, wearing an oversized Hawaiian shirt opened in the front. His large clunky monkeywood necklace that hung to his midsection took most of the attention away from his tight white stretch pants and lady-like white thin strapped sandles that adorned his pedicured feet. Rance, in his looking at him, didn't notice the woman with the orange hair, bright red lips and flower covered sack dress standing in wait beside him. Rance looked over the extremely large and growing crowd, then focused back to the bar and filled his plate. Upon leaving, he made his way to the right of the partition into the evening dining portion that usually in that time of the day was closed off, but was now open to handle the oversized crowd.

There she was. Eyes meeting his. Sitting in a chair beside the single glass pane, with the light of the morning sun settling through it and around her – a blazing luminescence lit her pulled-back hair from behind, reflecting an aura she absolutely warranted. A plate of pancakes sat out before her on the red and white checkered plastic topper that draped the sides of the table. She was not there for the books, as Rance could still see her morning's work in her complexion. A pair of well-used leather gloves lay beside her plate, affirming his guess about her start. She sat there, fork in hand with napkin spread and placed on her lap – a somewhat unexpected bit of sophistication that Rance hadn't seen in routine outings to anywhere or anyplace that might serve food in his world, but seemed just right in its placement. Her jeans tightly held what seemed to Rance the most beautiful legs he would hope to ever see. They bunched to the tops of her boots that were enhanced at the toe and heels with slight traces of cow manure gathered there before breakfast. Her heels were also adorned by a pair of McChesney short shank spurs, with etchings of feminine touches in silver, portraying her style. A style preferred by Rance over than that of the ankle bracelets of that time some woman preferred, including the one worn by the woman with the orange hair who was still standing in wait with the greying long-haired man with the bun. There she was.

This time new; without the true-beauty-hiding makeup Rance reminisced her wearing. He saw more beauty in her then than he had at the night first seen at the hall on the hill. She smiled. Rance, with lost essence of time, was very much unaware of just how long he had taken in her appearance there. Catching himself in doing it, he stumbled out with "How ya doin Ma'm?" "Just fine, and yew?" she said quietly and with an integrity and honest pureness Rance had never heard. She said it never taking her eyes' hold from him and returning her look with a soft smile. Rance was beside himself in his struggling with just what to say next or his deciding, as before, just to leave her there and him looking foolish. He had an intense redness that was felt welling up inside and he worried to himself it would outwardly show. The feeling was soon followed by cold sweat, shortly after. Here he was: a man built for trouble, who feared nothing or anyone; stout and bullish; one to be dealt with and respected on that front by all men; afraid of nothing and forged into anything he wanted, attaining it with zest and vigor. But in this moment, he felt inept. She shook him to the core. His nervousness must have been showing through, as her grin seemed to widen and she politely pointed at the empty chair across from her at the checker board covered table.

Rance turned back toward the breakfast bar as clumsily as he had greeted her and caught glance of his buddy Hank around the corner grinning at him. Even though she was out of Hank's view, and because she was sitting around the partition wall, Rance suddenly had the feeling his little stubby, no-count friend might have had something to do with their meeting. Anger and gladness wrestled with each other inside Rance's mind. Now a choice of where to sit was at hand. Either back in the corner with his gloating friend or in the overflow room alone, with the cowgirl who had his full attention, separated only by a small round table. Rance stood there, then turned plate in hand, and caught sight again of the girl still looking at him with a pleasant grin. She pointed at the chair again. Rance made his awkward way over and asked, "Mind if I sit here ma'm?" Followed by her response, "Well now, if I did then I wouldn't have pointed out that chair now would I?" "Guess not," as he sat down. "My names Rance what's yours?" He quietly said to her in introduction.

Agnes rounded the partition wall with his coffee he had left at his other table. "If ya gonna switch tables midstream, might let a lady know!" She slapped the mug down and coffee sloshed over its rim. She turned and walked out, but not before pitching her hip at him, where again it was obvious now, not only to Rance but the girl at the table, its meaning. Rance looked up at her and watched her head tilt, with wide-eyed grin at what the bold waitress had done and Rance joined her in her grin. "Well yew musta done it!" said the girl. "Must have," replied Rance. Old Agnes without intention of it, and Rance without expecting it, managed to break the ice.

"Well?" Rance asked. "Well what?" What's yer name?" Rance asked her. She gave in with slight pause and answered. "Luddia," she said quietly. "Luddia, why that's beautiful," Rance answered outward, again catching himself off guard and beginning to feel the redness creep back in. "Thank you. I didn't think so much growing up. "Why?" Asked Rance, regaining his composure. "Well I am a girl," she answered. Rance looked puzzled at her answer and reached for the shaker and salted his eggs. "It was rough growing up with it, let me tell you." She continued with a roll of her eyes, followed with a nice smile. Rance was now finding it easy hearing her sound. "Well, what's wrong with Luddia? I think it's beautiful," said Rance. "Well I guess Luddia's not so bad, but I came by that rendition of it late, and come by it hard." Rance, not understanding, sat quiet and chose her pause to smear a little butter to his pancakes and cover them with syrup. "It's not that pretty when your given name is Ludwig and you're the only girl in Windthorst with it, and the only girl, period, with a name like it to boot!" she finished. "Ludwig! Why that's a man's name," Rance spoke out abruptly and without thinking. It was too late, but with correcting attempt he continued on. "I didn't mean it like that," he said apologetically. She laughed at his stumble. Her dimples showed and there was a look in her eyes, as it seemed that was not the first time she heard it, in the many times over the years and in the various ways she had heard it. "Why yes it is! Glad you let me in oan it," she answered. Breaking the ice for the second time around.

After a short pause and a bite or two of the now-cool breakfast, she spoke out unexpectedly from the silence of the moment. "My father wanted a son. I guess he had to settle for the next best thing. I guess, I was it. The one and only. I never knew my mother. She died having me," she said, taking another bite as Rance did also. It was a little more than Rance had wanted to hear in the first place, and in the first few sentences of their meeting. He felt it was something she had to explain routinely over the years, more just of habit or individual circumstance. "My father only had one name picked and they wouldn't let him leave the hospital unless a name was stamped to the birth certificate. The only one he could come up with was Ludwig Ann Schroeder. Ann was my mother's first name. People know me now as Luddia. For a while when I was little, it was Ann. Then Ludy Ann. But I felt that if my given name was to be Ludwig – well, I should own it – and in the seventh grade went by it. My friends called me Luddia in order to feminize it that much more. So it stuck. Ta-da!" She said it as if just performing a magic trick, and she said it with outstretched arms and slight head nod as a bow. "So Luddia it is," she finished. "It's great. It's a real great name. Luddia. Very pretty, and it suits yew." Rance said, and he meant it. "Thank you." The smiling cowgirl said. "What's yers?"

"More coffee?" Agnes hollared out rounding the partition, and topping off both cups without giving either a chance for refill requested. Rance, midstream in his answer, said, "Rance. My name is Rance." "What?" blasted Agnes, not realizing he was answering Luddia's question. "What's wrong with yew today" She finished and just as quickly spun back around the same partition and disappeared. The beautiful lady before him laughed outwardly at the unplanned interruption, but picked up where his introduction had ended. "I know yer name is Rance. Not just from the fact yew introduced yourself to me earlier, and for the fact that everybody in the building shouted 'Hey Rance! Howya doin Rance?' And yer buddy Hank repeating it a hundred times over just so I wouldn't forget it. How could I not know yer name is Rance? I'm talkin about yer full name." She questioned Rance outloud. Agnes entered the room again just to add, "Well I know yer name is Rance! What am I supposed to say? 'More coffee Sir Rance?' or 'Would you like another bit of coffee, Mr. Abernathy?' each time I fill yer cup now?" She moaned out in her leaving.

They both looked at each other again at her routine tilt of butt cheek pitch upon leaving. "Well, Rance is a good strong name." It was the way she said it that confirmed his belief in it, as he had spent his whole life being it. "Rance Abernathy," she said, hearing Agnes' grunt. "Well?" "Well what?" "What's the rest of it?" Rance looked puzzled. "Your name? The rest of yer name." She said, only without adding the word stupid at the end. He had only been called Rance most of his life, and never felt the importance of any other name to back it. Everyone he rode with just knew it, and that was the way it suited him, with the exception of the few roughnecks he worked on the occasional oil rigs with, or the old high school gang, that sometimes called each other by their last names. Rance suited him. His family name was Abernathy. "Rance Edward Abernathy," he said back, and she just stared in an off-guard moment of silence. No comment from her, just a delayed grin over her pretty face. Inside her mind, she was sounding out a quiet melody, "Luddia Abernathy; Ludy Ann Abernathy," without so much as Rance being the wiser. They sat and got to know one another.

Hank had long gone, along with most all of the book auction patrons. The breakfast bar had been closed and was in the midst of the changeout to the salad bar for the dinner crowd Rance was usually a partaker in. The supper crowd started their entry back in, bragging about their first editions and other books bought. He and Luddia just sat. For once, he just sat and talked about things Rance had never thought much about before – and with ease. Subjects he had never taken time to talk about. He found out she ranched her own place. It was left to her by her dad, who had long since passed. He died while penning a herd bull, but the bull penned him instead, crushing her father to his death inside a loading chute. Her story had been passed around the coffee shops, but he was a rancher one county over from the counties Rance routinely day-worked, and they never crossed paths. Rance just wasn't personal with the brand. He discovered that she had been married early on and divorced, as her husband only wanted her for her money. Quite the difference in most gold digging circumstances, when mostly the roles were reversed. She produced two daughters out of that marriage. The oldest was fourteen, and she was the reason Luddia was at that dance that night on the hill. Her daughter begged her to let her go. The condition, meant the mindful presence of her mother being there. Luddia was strong, tough and feminine and she was absolutely stunning and she didn't even know it. Rance saw a tenderness about her as she seen the strong in him. Rance's anger at his old friend Hank for arranging their chance meeting left him with every word she spoke.

The pretty German girl told him of how she met Hank, as she knew Rance was with him earlier at the hall, and asked him if he could arrange their meeting. "He told me to be at this diner and he would be sure to have you here. He promised me," she said. "Why didn't he just tell me yew were going ta be here?" "Because he knew you wouldn't show up! He was right wasn't he?" "Yeah probly so," answered Rance. "Well, I guess he's a better friend than you give him credit!" She said. Rance didn't answer, but he had always known Hank was the better friend that he never gave due credit. But then Rance was the better friend to Hank that never got credit. So the way he saw it was they were split in it. They just were. That's all. No matter what.

Over time, Rance met up with Luddia many times, but innocently in their rendezvous. They enjoyed being together and were establishing deep feelings on both sides.

They were careful in their dating. For Rance, the difference in their ages, the protection he felt for her girls, and it being the right time, all weighed heavily on his mind. Both were feeling the need to be together, but trying to be sure it was the proper thing to do. Rance was an old bachelor and realized the setting of his ways. Luddia was solid in her own independence and felt secure in herself, but couldn't afford to let her guard down for somebody she had just met. Even though it was unspoken, they both decided that way without each thinking it was a thought of the other. They continued to meet each other for drives around the open countryside just talking or dinner dates at the Wildcatter, the Derrick, the P2 for "red draw beer," or the Livestock Barn Restaurant on sale days.

...

Time moved on and they were along for the ride. Summer was easing off its powerful hold on their five-county-wide sweep. The rotating fluctuation between the suppressing heat closing and the cool of the fall season coming was underway. Eventually it would put out the fire that had dried the ground and opened its surface cracks under the sun's chase. Rance was left with pushing more and more cattle to the local sales. There would be no need for the routine plowing and planting for the winter wheat grazing in the huge fields, usually prepped by that time. Not afforded, as there wouldn't be enough left over from the sales to chance plowing and sowing them. Maybe just enough to buy hay, if found, and cow cake to get the rest of the herds through. North Texas was in a hundred-year drought. That being said, it didn't mean a drought lasting one hundred years, but a drought like no other that came around in like kind every one hundred or so years. For Rance, it seemed like he had experienced it for the whole hundred years. This drought consumed the Tri-County area he ranched in, and considerably more outside of his counties worked. It had encompassed the whole state. Market prices had considerably dropped along with the quality of the cattle flooded into the market. Feed yards were packed from the surge of more sellers than of buyers.

It was a hard time, hearkening back in comparison only to that of the Great Depression. Rance didn't know whether he would survive it, nor if the ranch as a whole would survive it. Compounded on top of that, his eldest brother and only sister's corruption added to the abnormalcy of dealing with the dry, along with every other rancher enduring the same. He wouldn't know if the addition of the two of them would be deciders of its surviving either. His leases coming due, his forced selling off of cattle, a payment needed for his lease of his sister's quarter and the same with his brother – via the hidden holdings in his mother's name and the direct syphoning of her check each time it came – left Rance in a bind. In essence, paying three leases, two on the same property, because Lindy's lack of keeping her false portion had Rance making up her difference anyway. This go-around, Rance was burning through his lease monies with feed costs and higher fuel prices, water hauling, and triple the amount of hay normally fed in each fiscal year. He had force sold all he could spare, and kept the best of his herd. It would be his best choice, and best chance of hanging on and making it through the already-longest drought in written North Texas history.

19

NEEDED WANT

Rance stood there high on the sandy bluff overlooking the dried up Pease River, at the set of pens, watching the wind ripple the water coming across the metal stock tank drying what precious water was left there. Water needed for the cattle grazing down below. He stood there watching, with indecision. What, or how much, of the herd – maybe even all of them – must be drawn off his pasture. With each small wave blown across the tank's open top, the float valve dropped, allowing the cutoff hiss as the water escaped from it. He had purchased the land joining the Pease River just south of the Hardeman County line. Foard County is where he stood, on the same land that the great Comanche War chief Quanah Parker and his tribe had sheltered in search of the wild turkey for food and for feathers to adorn his war club and shield. The river split the land, flowing from underground aquifers and coming to the surface, making water usually readily available in most years, but not this one or the past ten preceding it. The windmill well had been converted. A new solar pump was added in place of the sucker rods pulled. The old mill was locked down and its turning days for the moment were at rest, but it was ready to be put back to work if the time and place warranted it.

Rance needed that pasture, and he needed the cows that were on it. The place hadn't had any grazing for the last five months running. All had been burnt off in its finality, yet even under this strain of the drought, the weeds still seemed to thrive and were taking over. The wind was cool and he looked back to the north and watched the clouds banking and building up. Blue clouds turning black in their building and growing rise of their height. Rance concentrated on the dark build. It looked to him like a huge ocean wave coming right at him – a wave very much in contrast to the burnt dead sky that it was forcing out of its way on its move southward. Up overhead he heard the flock of circling sandhill cranes rushing to stay out front of what was coming. Their rolling warbling calls were there, even before in his view for their seeing. He could not discern whether the flock high above was rising in flight or circling in order to land for their hunkering down in the impending winds coming. Their leading lookout, high in the distance, was seemingly the same in want of decision and seemed to be playing it by ear as Rance was. The world was alive around him, contrasting to the dead of the drought that had invaded the last hard life known as Texas. The leaves of the black jack oak were already curled and brown, as was the hackberry that was prominent there that hadn't the moisture needed to produce its berries. The chinaberries had already watched their leaves blown away and their scattered stands looked empty, as if the change from winter frostkill had already performed its duty. Those who lived it knew different. It was a long time coming before frost. It was the dry hard wind carrying the extreme summer heat that had already taken that pleasure away from the fall.

Rance watched the north. There was something in the cool breeze that brought out the life of the living around him, as if knowing, needing, and anticipating a change coming down. Rance's eyes shifted at caught movement to his left, and he watched a growing flock of Rio Grande turkeys in serious fast walk from the short brush thicket that was their hiding. In long line they walked out toward the sandy bluff with no walk path down below it to where the river Pease lay. Rance watched as they launched and lifted into the cool air, one by one upon reaching its edge, gliding their way down in synchronized flight to the sandy river and its one still-standing waterhole. He closed his eyes and was sure he felt the waft of each broad wing in their fanning rise, while each bird left the high cliff edge. They continued to talk to each other on their full way down, taking care in their way that all would be grouped and accounted for in their landings. The breeze had become cooler, and the wave of blue coming closer, as the old windmill above him rattled in its struggle to break free from its latched down stop. The wind then hurled its way in. A cottontail rabbit made its way behind him to the adequate hole that lay beneath the water tank and quickly disappeared into it.

A wall of wind erupted and swept up debris blown into the cloud of picked up range dirt that came with it. Rance covered his eyes and nose in its passing, then the blue collided with what little humidity there was to catch and it happened. A rarity in that time and in those years. A large drop fell at his feet. It hit the hot dry sandy loam soil. Rance believed he saw the steam of its impact. It formed a pocket when it hit and the dirt curled its cratered sides as if it had formed wanting arms forcing upward, praising the sky for more. It created the bowl shape similar to the small mud pies made in the cool sand that lay under the old sycamore tree of his childhood. Then another hit, and another, no lightning or thunder yet, but the pounding drops planted themselves in the dry soil with impact thunder. They grouped together and rumbled in their tightening sheets of rapid moving lines of waterfall-like passes. The heavy rain splattered on the parched earth, which drank it in as fast as it fell. His disbelief of it happening and his forgotten feelings of how it felt coming down, had caught Rance off-guard and his wonder of it being a reality held him there as if in a dream. The purge funneled its way off and over his soaked felt hat brim. This was not a passing phase. It was building and Rance was sensing its normalcy in its returning. The feeling of its power was welcomed and he never wanted it to end. The cottontail peered out from under the water tank, where now the hole was rapidly filling up with the flowing runoff. This would have been the first time in its short life that it had seen rain. It stood there outside, wet and shivering as each drop soaked its being.

Rance stood arms outstretched and looking up, caught up in exuberance and in subconscious primal praise for its providing, as each wave pelted his soul. This was the drought buster coming. He didn't know it for sure, but felt the Good Lord had made his point to the heathens below. The end of the hundred-year drought. Rance saw the goodness in it, and knew it must go on. So he thanked God that day on the muddy top of the flat overlooking the land he owned and stood; the land overlooking the mighty Pease River Valley; the land that sat the North Texas county of Foard. For precious deliverance, though, how much would be enough?

...

The system stalled in its race, directly over a twelve-county-wide area allowing the rain for weeks. The ground soaked up several years of depletion and was coming alive for it. Creeks swelled and their runoff flowed the dry creek beds supplying the rivers up and out of their widening banks. The deluge washed out whole bridges and roadways. It filled and washed out dams and muddy waterhole tanks over hundreds of square miles. Eleven days of heavy rain, then with breaks followed by weeks of spaced but continuous rain – each day a third of a year's worth, making up the eleven years lost. Whole stretches of long fence lines had been layed flat, or taken completely out, by flowing debris caught on the water's race toward the gulf. Cattle that had been turned loose, and not drowned, were rounded up and later separated by the brands showing their last place before escaping the bottom lands of rushing water. Not one rancher complained about it, as they had gotten what they prayed for and that much more. There would be no way, after that wait that a prayer would be sent up for its ending. God would let them all know when his replenishing was done. Rance, on the other hand, had no qualms about asking. "Lord it'd bin asked for an yew brung it, but quit a beatin us around down here. Anuffs anuff. Amen." The work began. Rance must have had a better understanding with the Lord than most might think he had; the never-ending rain did, as suddenly as it had arrived. Followed by a temperate fall and even milder winter to follow. Now, when the new rain came, it was in perfect timing with the sun and made great for wheat fields planted. It would be the first time in a long time that Rance wouldn't refer to his cow herd left as "boneys." They were steadily head down and Rance would swear that he could hear the fat growing on each grazing head.

Calves were bringing top dollar as created shortage was had and those who hung on were naming their own prices. Rance passed over the sale barn lots, as he could get more on the hoof for each head readied and buyers came to him for a change, racing their way there for the choosing. His choicest were bringing a dollar or more over what the auction ring would bring and he could do it without sales commission given on each head sold. It was a good time for the ranchers in his tri-county range.

...

But, even in all of its good time, time itself marched on from that drought-ridding spring. Time was racing off. To Rance, the rest of his siblings and their mother were showing the signs of it the most.

Rance watched his mother failing fast. He hadn't lived it before, so what to him seemed just common aging was not that way at all. It was unknown to him at the time just how his mother would age at the hands of his sister. Rance could not distinguish her abuse from life's normalcy in one's growing older. He kept his outings with his lonely mother, in contrast to his sister who wanted rid of her badly but couldn't without losing her control over something – control she still exercised as much as possible. She would choose who was allowed to visit and set all rules pertaining to it. Visitation of mother with other family would only be for a few days at most, as she would dictate her mother's time out and control of her money. Rance would be allowed to keep her a few days at a time at his home, but only allowed when his mother, tired of Lindy, made multiple requests to the point of irritation to his sister. He would be demanded at that point to pick her up. Rance did the best that he was able, but she had needs he wasn't always comfortable in his providing. Without the comfort level she needed, and the proper caretaking he couldn't provide, at times he was forced to bring her back early. She was feeble and slow in response and sometimes would fade off from obvious things going on around her. She would often resort to one word answers to repeated questions, but, at other times, have complete conversations as if sharper in quick wit than ever. Rance needed help in those times, so he asked Luddia if she would help him in those awkward times while his mother visited. She never minded in the help of his mother. She never knew her as Rance had, and only knew the woman just met. She was kind to her and his mother responded to it. Dementia worked its way into her, closed the door, and seemingly locked her up inside it. Luddia was the one who held the key. Every time the two were together his mother seemed to respond and come back to a place that Rance believed she needed to be. Hadd would keep her at times in the home place house on the hill, where she moved freely and seemed to come awake in just being there, but it proved to be hard for both Rance and Hadd.

For Rance, when he watched her, he sensed his own time waning – his own time as measured. It seemed just a short while ago she had been the same age, even younger than he. She hung on in the ritual, though. For Rance, the longer she had the better, but in the same time her hanging on carried the clock even further, with his own sense of time's eventual mortality.

Plover was showing his depletion even more than his aging mother, and Lindy was even more the worse for wear than the both of them. Her wear, in deceit and wrong living, seemed to be shortening an already sad existence. There they were with the clock ticking and life wasting away, both waiting like buzzards, ready to gain what was left of their mother's remains while seemingly doing everything possible to speed the end. There was no obvious care given from their standpoint. Rance eventually saw it, but too little too late. He believed that Lindy was actually trying her best to shorten their mother's life, just for financial gain.

Unbeknownst to him, when the final funds were depleted from his mother's personal account that would be the press of the stopwatch button that would regulate just what kind of existence and how much time for her was left in store. Plover went along with every decision Lindy made, good or bad, for his thoughts were in his worry of what he might lose if her dying happened to soon. He was in silent agreement with Lindy; it would be easier for them both if she did. His only thought would be in the timing of it. He needed at least one more year, so he could be in the clear. If she died, after that time, his secret would die with her – or so he thought. But his thinking would be all in vain, as he wouldn't know that Rance and Hadd already knew all that he had to hide. Just like he needed their mother's time for one more year, Rance and Hadd would decide if they would give him one more year or go right straight to the authorities.

20

SAD, HAPPY, AND SOLEMN WAS THE MOOD

Thanksgiving was skipped by everyone. Christmas had rolled around one more time. Rance bought his mother a small gift, because she didn't seem to want or have the ability to use anything. He gave her, out of want, a glass heart. He acknowledged it wasn't much, but asked her if she was able to hang it inside the small window of the dismal hole of a room she resided. There, alongside the obnoxious barking dog and the clutter of junk that confined her that much more, he had hopes that it might brighten her day when its reflective rainbow beams of color made its way into her. He was hoping it would add life to the bland box walls that lined her bed. Rance wouldn't be allowed inside the home to hang it for her, and wasn't exactly sure if his mother would be able to do it. He couldn't know of the conditions there, and it may have been for the best that he didn't know; after all, he couldn't do anything to change it. He wouldn't be allowed in to hang it for her, and wasn't even given the permission by Lindy needed to deliver his gift, but he would do that regardless. He called his mother to let her know he was bringing it by. She met him there at the glass door of the witch's castle, where she was happy in his coming. That evening he called her again and asked her if she liked it and asked her if she had any trouble hanging it up. She loved it and she thought it was beautiful and it meant so much to her. She let him know that she was unable to figure out just how to hang it, but whenever she wanted to see its rainbows, she would just hold it up to the light. Many times afterwards she would retell the story, not recalling that she already had. It seemed to remind her of watching a rainbow from when she was a little girl and she had recalled a memory of her being inside of it. She said, "Isn't that silly Rance? Thankin yew kin be inside a rainbow?" "Not at all, Mom. Sounds mighty pretty." He was proud each time she told him the story. It sounded better to him with each telling. "A glass heart. Who'da figgered," looking back on it he thought to himself. Rance was just proud that something so simple would bring her so much joy and he was proud he had given it to her and proud he was able to bring that good memory back to her. It was a good one, too, for her as well as Rance; something good between them to share over and over again. Rance felt good about that Christmas; he saw spirit in her that gave him hope that all was better for her. If it wasn't to be for her there, then he sensed something had changed in her relationship toward him. His certainly changed toward her.

The sparse little house in Archer was gradually becoming a home. Luddia came over many times and seemed to leave something for it each time she would visit. It was a good time for them both as they had become relaxed enough with each other and were spending more time in the evenings together. Both enjoyed sitting on the small porch at the kitchen entry leading into the back yard. It was very cold out, but they both held onto their cups of hot chocolate Luddia brought in from Allsup's Corner Store to keep them warm. Rance would rather be outside no matter the cold as he'd spent most of his life there, but it was even more satisfying being there with Luddia. She hadn't said the same out loud, and for that moment she would keep that thought to herself, but if she were able to tell Rance, she would tell him that she was just where she would rather be; spending her evening with him and feeling totally at ease with the idea of spending many more. Yank was standing out by the trailer happily enjoying a couple of flakes of alfalfa hay Rance had earlier placed there for him. The horse could be heard grabbing bits of it with his head nod shake for each bit. It was calm and cold and the stars shown out brightly, as there were no yard lights taking away from their shine. They were immersed in conversation so much that they didn't notice a stray cat make its way over to drink from Yank's water barrel trough, continually kept in a thawed state by the floating heater that sat on its surface. It must have been the only spot around that wasn't frozen over as he chanced getting that close to them for his much needed drink. He lapped the water quietly beside their sitting, taking in a silent drink and glanced around before stealthy moving along his way.

Luddia leaned into Rance and pulled her lap blanket over the both of them. In that moment, both guards went down. From that time forward, Rance didn't feel old, and she felt truly wanted. Her girls didn't remember their father, as it was early in their lives in his leaving. Never would he return. They hated him for it and loved him all the same, but had never trusted any man outside of their grandfather and that had been a very long time ago. They had taken to Rance in a way that he had not expected, had never wanted, and never experienced before his knowing them. He did, however, take to them just as much, if not more. He felt a genuine love for them and for once believed himself worthy of someone's affection in that particular way. There was a time or two that Luddia asked him to her ranch house, but with the still unsettled future of the ranch and not wanting to place his needs over that of them, he could never see himself moving into her place. When, or if, the time were right, he would do it proper. It would be *their* home, just out of respect for all of them. He couldn't expect them to live in the little green house on West Walnut; it wasn't good enough for them or large enough. When the time was right, he would do it proper and they would all move into a home of their own, outside of it. It would be built together, or so he would hope. For the time, he would stay in his little green house in Archer until his future, in all areas, would be settled. He would stay the course there. Out of respect for the girls, he never asked her once to stay over; he knew that out of her own respect for the girls she would not have if he did.

Rance loved her more just because she put them first. He knew that well as he would base the existence of his herd cows in the same way; he would cull a cow that didn't place her complete attention and effort in her calf. Luddia was a keeper and he had no plans to let her go. They made time for each other, but always discretely and with sound judgement that was respected by anyone who, at any point, shared feelings in the manner in which they did. It was natural in its progression and Rance would ensure not to do anything that would elicit shame upon her or embarrassment to her family. Yes, they were human, and with shared feelings there was intimacy, but it was out of true love shared and Rance had never taken advantage of the situation. They were learning each other and dealing slowly with the direction they valued. For the time it worked for the both of them and that would just be how it would be.

...

Time passed, but not much, before Rance noticed small changes taking place in his little home on West Walnut. Just little changes he would see when coming home, changes that were not his. Kitchen walls that had been washed clean. No more were the showing lines of where old pictures once hung. On one occasion, Luddia had brought him two framed photos, one of him and Bingo together captured out beside the round water trough at the working pens. He remembered the day; after gathered stock worked and waiting for the water to fill. There was another of her and the girls while everyone was out enjoying a picnic at the lake. Rance, never a one for photography, was proud of that one as he had taken the memory himself and was happy that Luddia thought the same of it as well. Both printed and hanging, making good use of the once bare walls. A calendar filled the space between the living room windows that had new sheet-replacing drapes that were just as surprising. Rance had given her a key to use anytime she wanted to come and visit, although she, as well as Hank, never had the need to use it because of the fact he never locked the little house's door, anyway.

Over time he walked in to find a sofa, two comfortable chairs and something that caught him completely off guard; a soft and larger queen bed to replace the hard and well-used twin that he'd grown accustomed to so much that, it not being quite the same, he chose most nights to just sleep on the new sofa. For him, it would be a better replacement for the twin, but he was sure not to let her know that truth. Changes were spaced and subtle. But on one night's late return, on his searching mission for the bathroom's pull-chord light, he wound up completely tangled in a new shower curtain that Luddia had nailed into the ceiling that was draped in a circle inside of the rim of Rance's claw foot bathtub. It was certainly a nice gesture by Luddia, but a little too surprising to him. The shock of it being there had him fighting his way around the dark room trying to find the culprit who was trying to put the tow sack over his head. He found fresh stocking to the pantry; mostly with items simple in their making but really giving Rance a sense of home. There were actually things in the refrigerator that could be prepared and eaten. She was beautiful, and he missed his not catching her in the days she was there, but accepted that she had planned it that way all along.

Christmas time was nearing. Rance arrived one night and was surprised to see a fully-decorated, live-cut Christmas tree, it looked similar to the ones that had set out front for sale at the Allsup's – the ones that hadn't quite the wanted look and were waiting for the final countdown to Christmas Eve. Decorated with a single string of lights, all of beautiful colors in the spirit, reflected against the glimmering tinsel icicles draped along every limb. There were no other decorations but three cards had been left upon staggered branches. Left for him to clearly see. Once opened, he read the separate wishes for him, as well as some of their own expressed. He silently wished "Merry Christmas" back to the three who left their cards there. Two strands of smaller blinking lights were draped around the window frame and their faint colors shown through the curtains. It really felt like Christmas for the first time in a long time. He actually noticed its coming. He recognized the feeling and was drawn back to the Christmases once remembered, when a young boy, before the times of deceit, jealously and greed, when everyone enjoyed being there together.

His thinking back prompted a call to Luddia in his wish to break their own self-applied rule. He invited them all over to the little home on Walnut Street that very Christmas Eve, and he felt comfort in the asking. He asked her if she and the girls would stay the night, in wait for a nice evening spent and for "Ole Santy Claus." He was excited, that she had felt the same and agreed to stay. So excited, that he raced down to Allsup's and bought out the complete toy section, even though the girls were beyond the age of most items he retrieved from the store's peg board display. He bought candy for each, and twenty dollars' worth of scratch-off lottery tickets to place in each of their pulled-off cowboy boots that would sit the doorway entering the little house. When the timing was right and both had drifted off to sleep, he would wrap their toys in newspaper and tie them up with hay twine, leaving them placed under the Christmas tree boughs. The stock string would tie in its natural white with blue twist overtone, and he would place them with love for each under the tree.

It was late, around three in the morning when all arrived, but seemingly wide awake in the spirit of the night. Rance helped Luddia carry a pickup-bed load of presents into his home she had brought over from her home with promise that this would be the new start needed for their own Christmas traditions. That was Luddia's wish for Rance, written out for him to know, and left in the pine bow branches of his tree. The little green house on West Walnut had never felt so happy.

They all sat around singing Christmas carols and drinking hot chocolate that Rance had got each straight out of the all night hot drink machine at the Allsup's. With the cheer of singing, they hardly noticed it had been brought back to life by Rance's microwave. The little tree was full and so was the little house. The early morning hours peaked, and sleep needed finally appeared for the girls. Rance fixed them a place, helped by Luddia, and placed each sleeping girl onto the couch. One head at one end and one on the other. Both completely out from the late night time – still in age transition to not believing, but still in hopes of seeing "Ole Santy Clause," mainly for what he "brung'em."

...

The time was right, and Rance led Luddia to the bed she had gifted him in his room. In complete quiet and intentional slow ease, Rance and Luddia gave each other the beginning needed for all spending Christmas in that little house in Archer City.

It was a beautiful morning. The girls were excited. Luddia had slipped back into her prepared spot beside the couch before their rise. She had no sleep, neither had Rance, but made it appear that she had, from the floor mat where she lay covered by a blanket, actually in quick slumber, when the girls awoke. It was not early, closer to Noon, though it seemed like first light to them. The gifts were divied out and the morning sounded with excited laughter while all there watched the handing out and opening of the gifts. Each girl grabbed their boots and dumped out the contents, as what was placed in them scattered about the floor. They might have been older, but maybe not so much, as the candy and toys Rance picked for each seemed to be a big hit. Especially the stick-on tattoos and the glow-in-the-dark fossilized dinosaurs hidden inside small round egg-shaped molded chalks, with hard plastic mallets, digging picks, and personal cleaning brushes perfect for their hammering and amateur archaeologist pleasure - but not recommended for anyone under 4 years of age. When the girls had chipped and brushed their dinosaur skeletons out, Rance shot them dead with the pink rubber band gun that he bought for Taylor, while Kaylee, the older of the two, laughingly did her best to block each shot. They had almost forgotten their other gifts brought by Luddia. They both quickly rebounded from the games played, and opened the boxes brought in from their own home tree, becoming even more excited at their new clothes and shoes. Luddia also surprised Rance with a new rope, a new lever action Winchester 30/30 saddle gun, and a brand new hand-tooled saddle boot to go with it. In return, she was given something she longed to have.

Rance held out a small box and opened its top. Luddia's expression fell to a more serious, but sincere, look as her cheeks turned a rose-blushing red. Rance leveled down on one knee and gently spoke to her. "Luddia, will yew marry me. Will yew an' the girls have me? I woan't havya less yawl agree to it. But Luddia, I'm askin. Kaylee, Taylor, I'm askin if yew would let me protect ya and love ya for my own. Thank about it bafore ya answer." Before he got it out he was met with an immediate hug and kiss by Luddia, and the girls, forgetting all about their presents were up and dancing about the small living room saying, "Yes! Yes! Yes! Say 'Yes' Mom, say 'Yes!'" Rance knew it though if even not spoken right away. He saw it in her eyes. She rushed in to hold his face with both firm but gentle hands. She looked him straight in the eye and said "I thought yew would never ask. Of course I will marry you, Rance. I would never have nobody else." Her answer would be Rance's Christmas present – the one he had been waiting on his entire lifetime.

They spent one more night in the little green house on West Walnut Street, celebrating the night after the girls had gone to sleep.

21

A NEW WIND BLOWING

The next morning, Rance pulled into Four Corners Station for fuel and feed. It was cold and the frozen sleet peppered the drive in its build. He was on his way out to the Bar L for a day of vaccinating calves. He was going to meet up with his day working partner, who was no doubt already out there. Seven a.m. and the blinds opened up at the old station, but there was already black smoke boiling out from the pipe stack of the oil fire heater that was heating the old gas station home of the owner. The closed sign that hung inside the frost-covered window was quickly flipped to open by the familiar hand seen. Leonard walked out of the rickety station door carrying an air hose in one hand and huge bucket with its water sloshing over the sides in the other. The spillings of it instantly froze on impact, when colliding with the subzero driveway. The north wind was brisk, and he quickly fought the hose into its chuck, mounted on the closest roof support post nearest the pumps. He hung the rope-like coil of the air hose on its hook just to the post's opposite side. Two antique station pumps sat in line atop a platform of concrete with rounded-off ends, giving the only artistic decoration in the architecture of the otherwise plain structure's design. At the end of the pumps sat the bug buckets with their squeegees plunged inside. The two pumps were simply labeled "gas" and "diesel." Both words had been doctored with white paint so much over the years that the letters spelling out which was which started to blend together, forming one single unreadable line in their distinguishing. The only real difference in the telling would be the oily, dirt-soaked, hose being diesel, and the other greasy one one from Leonard's unwashed hands was not.

Rance pulled the nozzle from its resting slot, then removed the gas cap from his truck and shoved the nozzle into the tank and left it there. He leaned over and spun the toggle on the old pump's side and zeroed out the slot machine-type numbers under the shield glass. He then tilted the pump switch to on and the pump began its hum simultaneously as Rance pulled the nozzle trigger and wedged his gas cap under it to hold it open. Diesel poured into the tank with each click of the rotating dials. Rance had an ear for filling the tank. If he timed it just right, he could pop the hood and check the oil. Sometimes the tank was empty enough to give him time to even wash the windshield before the tank topped out. The wind was blistering cold. The temperature plummeted already into the teens and still dropping. The March winds directed the chill on Rance and he was feeling the pain of it. He buttoned the top button of his canvas coat and rolled up the collar to cover his neck, but he still raised his shoulders and pulled his head down into new formed pocket similar to that of a turtle pulling his head back into its shell. "What's that bucket for Leonard?" Rance asked, slightly stiff-jawed from the cold, in his routine agitation toward Leonard. "Morning?" The old attendant said, either not hearing Rance or just plain ignoring him. He walked back into the station door and set out a rack beside it and began filling it with oil. He had shelves inside that would hold all that he would sell in a day, but that's not how they did it in the old days. Maybe Leonard just preferred his oil frozen. "There shore ain't no bugs out here taday!" Rance said. The pump clicked away; one big clunk for every gallon pumped. Rance was coming up on seventeen gallons on the rotating dial. "De-icer!" Leonard yelled out. "Might need a little de-icer oan a day like this," he finished. He was right. A little freezing drizzle was starting to form on his truck's back glass as he stood there waiting on the fuel to rise.

"Ya hear tha news?" "What news?" Rance answered. "Tha Slash 7's sellin out." "Whadidja say?" Asked Rance again, not quite hearing Leonard. "Tha Slash 7's sellin out! Sum big outfit outa Fort Worth," he said again, wiping Rance's windshield with a swipe or two of deicer along with a spit of tobacco just to give it texture. "Rumor has it they offered three thousand an acre for it. Thirty-five if tha minerals come with it," he added. "Says they're makin tha same offer to anybody that woants ta sell out in South Clay an North Jack." He finished. "What for?" a puzzled Rance answered back, hearing the truck's tank just about to top out, and quickly removing the wedging cap from its handle and hitting the shutoff switch, quickly quieting the whining pump. He placed the nozzle back to the pumps cradle. Leonard penciled down the gallons spent to his talley, while Rance cleared the dial out of courtesy for the next customer. "Doan't know. Just know they aim ta buy up everythang they can." With that Rance told him to put the diesel on his tab, and forgot about the few sacks of cow cake he usually got at each filling. It was just too cold to load it that morning, and he had the Slash 7 on his mind. He let Leonard know he'd get it the next go around. He signed the ticket and made his way back into the old truck where the motor struggled in its running but still kept it warm.

The old diesel clattered its way out onto the blacktop, black smoke boiled from it, in his way up the hill in the direction of the Bar Back L and his meeting there with Roy. The old truck hammered its way down the rough gravel road. He could see Roy already there hadn't waited on him with cattle caught, separated, and a working pen and chute already packed full with young calves. "Bout time ya showed up!" Roy quietly said, as he'd never seemed frustrated or angry at just about anything. "Wontcha kill that ole rattle trap affore ya get all these calm bovine ah caught here, withoutcha bein here ta hailp in it, stirred up," he said with a shudder from the bite of the cold air encircling him – knowing the whole time Rance's old truck was limited in its starting ability in warm, much less the colder, weather. "Why don'tchew just mind yer own bizness. If they git too riled up, yew kin just step aside and let a real cowhan hannle'em, now caintcha?" Rance blistered out his response. Roy laughed out inwardly, then answered, "Maybe ah will!" They both laughed, then committed with no more talk, to the work at hand. That was the way it was with them. Few words in introduction, then a few more words and a cold beer or two in completion. That's the way it had been for over thirty years, and it just worked.

Roy was a lean fellow, his appearance seemed more to emulate that of storied Legend Ichabod Crane than he realized. He was long framed. His skinny legs and large felt hat seemed to greet you before the rest of his body caught up. His neck tilted forward, as his arms seemed to dangle at his sides just a little farther behind him. He had a dipping bow to his long neck and the protrusion of his Adam's apple seemed to go along with the size of his parrot-beak-shaped large nose. He wore shirts with sleeves never quite cut from factory sizes to reach all the way to his wrists for him to button at the cuffs, and he wore button fly 501 jeans that were tucked in all the way into his eighteen inch tall custom-made Olsen Stelzer boots. His worn black hat reflected much of the region's style they lived and worked, and it was similar in creases to Rance's. The only difference being Roy's was seemingly always pulled down hard over his head while the only thing keeping it from shielding his eyes were his two large bent ears under its brim. He wore thick glasses that made his eyes double in size, to an almost bug-like appearance when looking at him. From one corner of his mouth, a bent pushed cigarette that had been snuffed out, shuffled its way back and forth; a habit in its saving to be lit up at needed break to be finished, or at cold beer time when the work was done. He looked lanky and awkward, but there was no finer cowboy around that could match him in skill, when it came to the rankest of the wild cattle to be understood and caught.

One right after another, the side gate opened, turning another worked calf out into the holding pen. They were separated only by their sexes with eartags and brands placed to them all. The bull calves of the Bar Back L would be banded in their castration. It was the choice of the day-working ranch hand what method would be used. Most still preferred the knife, but on this cold day, it would be the bands. Cows were turned out to feed, and the calves were quickly loaded to each gooseneck trailer to be hauled away and turned out on another section for their weaning.

"Time for beer," Roy said about as quickly as the last calf was loaded. "Yep," answered Rance just about as quick. "Been'a good day, even if ah had to do the most work," Rance said. "Yew must be blind as well as stupid. Ah don't thank ya have four arms now do ya?" Roy spit back. "Them cows didn't jump in that lot all by tharselves," Roy finished while making his way over to his pickup bed chest and retrieving a cold beer without offering his old friend one. "Ain't ya goanna give me one?" Rance asked. "Nope." "Why not? Aintcha glad ah showed up?" said Rance. "Nope," Roy said, while popping the top and guzzling down half before wiping his mouth and looking Rance right in the eye. "When are yew gonna buy tha beer?" He asked. "Ah brung it tha last time," Rance answered. "You've bin a saying that for thirty years now, but I'd rather be gullable than be blind and stupid like yew!" said the man with the coke-bottle-bottom eye glasses just before grabbing another cooler beer and swiftly tossing in to his antagonizer. They both settled, drank, and enjoyed the day that was finally beginning to warm, along with the money they both had earned in the process.

...

Old Fred Atterbury, owner of the Bar Back L, was the last of the dying breed of ranchers who had known nothing else but the life he was raised into. The same as Rance and Roy, them being day-work cowboys that were in it for the long haul and understanding the pay didn't always add up to the work. Atterbury was thirty years their senior, but Rance and Roy were feeling the gap closing in fast between his age and theirs. Just their time spent working his spread dated them, as well. At eighty-six, the old man was wiry and had already outlived most of his clan. The place was expected to be willed over to his only surviving relative, a nephew who had shown no interest in the place and its inner working, except an inherited portion of oil production that Fred had given his sister, who had left it to her son, his nephew, when she passed away. He had been pushing his old uncle to deed it all over early, on a promise of setting him up for a more peaceful place to spend out the remainder of his life. "It'll be better for you in the long run Uncle Fred. Those apartments are ni-ice. They'll haul you anywhere you need ta go. You git three meals a day an maid service. An people like you and your age all around'yew so yewell never git lonesome. We'll come visit'cha every week and yew won't have any bills ta pay or anythang," his nephew pressed at his uncle. "Well," was the reply, "ah've been ta jail bifore and that's what it sounds just like ta me. Thank I'll take my chainces oan tha outside, if ya don't mind. Could always start sellin drugs if ah need extry. Hear there's good money in it." That was his response to his nephew's ignorance, but as far as the ranch was concerned, he knew he could depend on Rance and Roy to keep him in the business, and that was good enough for him.

...

"Howdy boys, How yawla doin?" Fred hollered out the rolled down window of his old ranch truck. "Howdy" said Rance. "How boutchew Mr. Love?" the old man hollered out to Roy, who readily recognized his family name, as if he already didn't know it and the fun that Fred was poking at it in his love of saying it upon their meetings. "Howdy! Ya doin aurite taday?" Roy answered back. "Fine, ah guess yew boys woantcher pay now, doantcha?" "It'd be mighty nice a yew ta settle up with us, since we're tha only ones in this county who ain't goanna turn ya in for starvin them boney sons a bitches down, now ain't we?" "Guess ya gotta point there, young man. Ah'll git my checkbook out if ya toss me one a them beers over yhere," Fred said as he started rummaging through his glove box for his book. "Yer as bad as Rance. Ah ain't knowed yew ta brang any beer out here in tha last thirty years, neither." "Well, shore took ya a long time ta notice that now, didn't it Mr Love?" the old rancher said, still searching for the checkbook. Roy thought better of tossing the beer over to the old man, as if he didn't catch it, it might knock him over or break a rib or something.

They all drank and laughed and listened to the restless calves bawl for their mothers and rock the trucks as they sat idle on their spots. "Yew boys hearin about tha buyouts takin place?"The old rancher asked, quieting the time they were having. "Yep," said Rance. "Just taday. Why?" "Yew had an offer or sumpthin?" Roy quickly interjected before Atterbury had time to answer. "Yep. Shore did." "Mind if ah ask how much?" asked Rance. "Nope, don't mind atall. Three thousand an acre. Thirty-five if I'm willin to give up my minerals. Ain't gonna do it though. The royalties ah'ma drawin off just them two wells yonner already beat that offer in the last two months. Don't know what my nephew might do though if it were turned over ta him. "Don't be talkin like that yew old fart! Here have another cole beer," Roy said, handing him the last one the old cooler had to offer up. "Wull it's bin fun, but we gotta git these aunry thangs over ta yer north pasture bifore they walk a hole through tha bottom of that sorry trailer of Roy's," said Rance in his getting up from the slightly warmer ground he was sitting on. "My trailer! Wull them old rotted tires oan yers probly hadn't bin changed offa there since the day yew bought that pile a junk back in 1976," Roy followed up, while both meandered their way back to their trucks still mumbling out insults along their way.

After unloading at the pens and the older rancher long gone, Roy turned to Rance. "Yew know that's just what's goanna happen. Atterbury ain't got much time left and that's tha first thang that boys gonna do!" Roy said to Rance. "What's that?" asked Rance. "He's goanna sayle it. Nuthin' ever tha same anymore is it?" "Maybe. But yew referred ta his nephew as a boy. He's our age. Hell we went ta school with that no good son of a bitch," answered Rance. "That's my point exactly, we'll hafta deal with tha son of a bitch. Our whole days out here will be a son of a bitch. We'll hafta take orders from a son of a bitch. We'll hafta wonder how we'll get paid by a son of a bitch and our workin lives here will be a son of bitch. Ain't that a son of a bitch?" Roy blasted. "Yep," answered Rance, as he realized his friend put it how it would be when that took place. "Well, see ya later Roy." "Seeya later Rance," and they both headed back home. One to the three-house town of Antelope and the other back to Archer City.

22

HANK AND CHANGING TIMES

Rance made it home and found Hank curled up on the new couch Luddia had adorned his small living room with. But just not in the knowing that Hank was there at the time, Rance was startled as he made his way over to the pull string of the living room light, after making a rare entrance into the front door of the home. Hank suddenly sucked in a snoring snort that caused Rance to flop face first, in his escape, right over a new coffee table that Luddia had added, unbeknownst to him, to the room. Before his stumble, he had already grabbed at, found, and yanked the light cord, causing what was left of it to whip about the room, Rance landed, string still in hand from the broken weak link of the snap chain giving way in his fall. Hank jumped up swinging. Lucky for Rance he was still face down on the floor. Unlucky for Rance, Hank drove a boot heel into the back of his hand as he spun around in his fighting turns, chasing the swinging light shadows about the room. "Stop!" Rance yelled.

A half asleep Hank spun one more round before focusing in on Rance on the floor. "Whatareyew doin down there?" he asked. Rance struggled to untangle himself from the upturned coffee table resting on him. "The question is whatareyew doin here?" "Well hell boy ya gave me tha key, remember? But since ya don't never lock yer door anyhow I didn't need it ta git in," Hank said. "Well that explains tha key and how ya managed inside, but it still doan't answer tha question," Rance said. "What question?" "Never mind." Rance eased himself up on the couch and leaned back. "Howdja git here? Didn't see no truck when I pulled up," Rance said to his friend who was busy rubbing sleep from his eyes. "Walked. It's parked over behind Kings Grocery, in the alley. Jake said it'd be awwrite as long as I moved it outta tha alley bifore tha milk truck gits there." "When's that?" asked Rance. "Nine a.m. Got plenty a time." "Whatareyew doin here?" asked Rance. "Ain't got no money 'til payday. Lost it all in a poker game in Wichita. Cain't afford tha Spur Hotel. It's loaded with book tourists anyway. Thought you wood'n mind me comin here. Hey whendidja git all this furniture anyway?" he blurted out while panning around the room. "Just never yew mind. Yew better git sum sleep if ya woant ta git that truck moved outta Jakes way bifore nine."

"Maybe yer rite. But wheredidja git all this stuff?" "Luddia! If ya just gotta got damned know. Luddia fixed it up for me. Ah didn't ask her to – matter a fact told her not to, but she did it anyway." Rance firmly answered Hank with a rise of his angry brow." "OK. OK. So Ludy put it here. So what? Ludy's fixen 'er up. Yep!" Hank said with pause. "Yep what?" "Well, just yep." "Yew meanin sumpthin by it?" Rance asked, knowing all along Hank knew his meaning and answer and so did he. "First thang ya know Rance, she's a fixin yer house up, then fixin ya dinners, pourin up yer bath, then..." The silence broke with the slap of his two hands. "...she's got a ring in yer nose, just like them worn out ole bulls I haul around," he finished with a laugh. But with the expression on Rance's face, he realized it was something he knew might ought not to have been said. Rance gave no response to it. "Hey I was just joshenya. That ain't goanna happen to Ole Rance! Yew ain't tha one to fall inta a trap like that," he said, followed up by a hearty pat to his best friend's back. Rance just raised his head and looked at his old friend. He was biting his lower lip. Hank sensed something in him he'd not seen before.

"I've proposed to Luddia," Rance said quietly to a stunned Hank. "What?! Huh! Well I'll be! Yew and Ludy. I ain't bilievin it. Well, boy, yew shore throwed me for a loop with that one. Yew'n Ludy. Ah just cain't believe it! How in the world did yew git that pretty young thang ta agree ta marry yew? Ah mean, yew ain't bad and all. A bit old, but not bad. Yew and Ludy. Of all thangs, married! Ole Rance is getting hitched. Ah ain't bilievin it. Rance and Ludy. Well, congratulations ole boy!" he said, with another slap to his back, followed by a stout vigorous shake to Rance's hand. "Well, it just happened. I wasn't lookin, and yew aughta know how it started, since yew set tha whole thang up." "Well, maybe I did, or maybe ah didn't, but yew woan't find no finer a woman round here. Nope. No finer," he finished. "Well I've had enough a this. Ah need ta git up early and so da yew. I don't woan't Jake to be pissed at'cha too. There ain't many places yew can park that ole bull rig a yers close enough ta walk down here. We'll talk more about evrythang in tha mornin." "Yep yer probly right. Ah better use this here couch while ah still can," Hank said. "Mind gittin that light? I caint reach it, its missin its strang." Rance righted back up the coffee table, stepped on it, and pulled the stub that was left of the cord chain, obliging his old friend on the couch.

The next morning Rance beat the sun coming up and woke his old friend. He had a sleepless night, as Hank raised the roof in his snoring. Rance, no longer able to take it, shook him awake. "Let's go git some coffee down at the Dairy Queen." "Let's go," his old friend answered while rubbing his face, and stretching it out with both hands for the readying. Hank had enough left over Vitalis in his hair he was able to just drag his fingers through it once or twice to bring it back to life. Rance didn't have to wait for him to get dressed, because he was still in everything he'd been in from the day before, down to his boots and suspenders. Rance had time to shower and shave and even slapped a little Brute to his face. Fresh shirt and fresh starched pants, he looked like he was dressed for "Sunday go ta meeting." He had only one thing on his mind. This was his day to pick up his mother and take her out for her favorite time, at her favorite restaurant.

23

REGULAR RANDOM COFFEE WITH THE IRREGULARS

Rance and Hank made their way into the Dairy Queen, where the regulars were already talking about the events of the day. "Yep I hear tha Flat Bottom U is a thankin about takin their offer," Dobber Maes said, while coming back with hot, as well as hard, black coffee and making his rounds warming up the cups of his friends. "Hello Dobber," Rance said, pulling out a chair, and Hank doing the same. Dobber was a retired driller and had punched many a hole in the counties surrounding Archer. His life on the drilling rigs showed, as he was missing a couple of fingers from each hand and his language proved at times to fit more on a drilling platform than it did anywhere else. But anywhere else he chose to use it the same. He had a flat-topped haircut that blended well with his high cheekbones and flat crooked nose, and carried the strong arms of a man forty years his junior. "How tha fuck are ya, and how's that gotdamned son of a bitch Hank doin over there?" "Good. Yew can ask me, though, I'm right here." "Fuck yew," Dobber answered, going back to his buddies Jim Hanson and Rankin Meeks, old hands that spent years working for Dobber, and now the rest left in Social Security retirement. "Gitcha a cup over yonner and I'll fill it up while I got tha pot handy," he said looking at Rance. "How about me?" Asked Hank. "Rance, git this little fucker a cup too while yer at it!" Rance leaned over and grabbed two cups from the counter right beside them and Dobber obliged. "What's that you were saying about the Flat Bottom U?" "They's thankin about sellin tha whole fuckin place to that mother fucker Yankee land grabber!" "What Yankee land grabber?" Asked Rance. "That Fort Worth fuckin Yankee that's a buyin all tha range up round here." Rance had forgotten that anyone or anything outside of a one hundred mile radius of Archer County was either a Yankee or owned by a Yankee, according to Dobber. And if they were about to buy inside it, then they were "sorry muther fuckin Yankees." Dobber was on a roll in his coffee filling. "Them gotdamn sorry muther fuckin, son of a bitchin Yankee land grabbers. What gives them tha gotdamned right to buy here anyway?" "Well, I guess money," Jim Hanson spoke, knowing the whole while it would strike a nerve in Dobber.

Jim was a little man. He wore tan khakis, shirt and pants, long sleeves rolled up mid-arm and pants rolled up at the bottoms so they would hang top high to his lace up steel toed work boots with the worn-through spots on both toes showing the steel. He wore a hard hat or a long billed geologist cap, which ever suited him that day – although he was performing neither of these jobs and hadn't been for about twenty-five years now. He smoked cigars. When sitting, he had his legs crossed playing rope the knot with a piece of sash chord that had a large steel nut attached to the end of it; he would dance that nut all day.

"Oh who asked yew, fuckin smart mouth," Dobber answered back at him. Jim shut up and the other Knight at the round table, Rankin Meeks, coughed out a laugh. Jim didn't shush out of fear, it was just he didn't want to give the old blow hard another reason to overtake any conversations wanted that morning with another different long winded story. "What tha fuck are you laughing about Rankin?" Rankin, even though he never punched a cow, always dressed the part of a cowboy. He roughnecked in cowboy boots and a Stetson, as if he were riding the range. So his attire, even though long since retired many years before, didn't look that much different than Rances. "Nuthin," he answered. "Who is tha guy and what's he buyin it all for?" Rance asked. "Son, ainchew bin afuckin listenin? Aintchew got no fuckin sense? He's a buyin it bicause them gotdamn Yankees up there are moving west. Ya fuckin hearin me? It's all them fuckin huntin shows. It's gottem in a fuckin frenzy makin this fuckin area worth sumpthin. The fuckin locals here ain't got tha fuckin money ta keep up with them sorry muther fuckers," he blasted as the door chime sounded out, signaling that a young mother and young son had just walked into the restaurant. She quickly turned upon hearing the old driller's rant, and walked right back out, with both hands cupped over her little boy's ears. "They say he's fixin it all tha fuck up. Puttin high fuckin fences around every fuckin thang. Building fuckin cabins every fuckin where, plannin oan breakin it all up, and flippin smaller fuckin parcels out to as many a them rich fuckin Yankee fuckin bastards as he kin find!" "What's his name?" Hank popped in. "His name is Cage. Ah call him Mr. Fuck Yew Cage. Some say he's got more fuckin money than God, and if he ain't got it he's got enough a them Yankee fuckin bankers down in Dallas oan a strang ta git it. He's done took advantage of a bunch a them poor bastards northeast a Four Corners an ta tha south a Buffalo Sprangs. They just opened up their doors an welcomed tha muther fucker in. With sweet smiles an sweet talk, he plum talked 'em outta that fuckin land, like a duck outta water." "What's that supposed ta mean? 'A duck outta water?'" Jim asked. "Yea that don't fit what yer sayin," said Rankin. "Why don'tchew two go fuck yer selves. Yew know what ah fuckin mean," Dobber said, slapping the coffee pot back on its resting hot plate. "How come I ain't heard nuthin about this?" Asked Rance. "Don't fuckin worry, yew will. That ole junk yew bin tryin ta graze oan is tha kinda stuff he's buyin."

Rance finished his coffee and slipped two single dollar bills on the table to cover the cost, leaving whatever change left for the tip to the young early shift manager nervously struggling to keep up with pickup window traffic coming through; covering with her own loud talking in an attempt to squash Dobber's expletives and awkward jokes cast out boisterously from the Knights of the Round Table. "See y'all later," Rance spoke out on deaf ears as the three old men were rapidly going over the meaning of the phrase, "a duck outta water," and how it should be correctly "fuckin used," while Hank, unaware of Rance's leaving, was left sitting there enjoying the show.

24

THE WAY IT ONCE WAS IS THE WAY THAT ONCE IS

The Archer highway was quiet that day as it led through town. One pickup was the only vehicle at the Allsup's and the driver of it was only there for fuel, and maybe to grab a cup of coffee to go along with it. Rance passed the court house where it seemed a bit busier as a trial was going to be held that day. For what reason, Rance wouldn't know. He recognized some of Archer's finest as they were showing up for jury duty. In his quick stop at the blinking red light, he recognized the widow Walthrop, who seemed to be called more than most. She was wearing her trademark flower-wrapped straw garden hat, half-glasses slid down her upturned nose, loose spring dress that was more reminiscent of a time forty-years prior than as of late, and red sneakers, hobbling along as fast as she could with her walking cane being carried more than it was allowed to rest in its bracing to the concrete sidewalk that lead into the courthouse. Rance honked and waved, but the old widow never seemed to notice as she was entranced in her journey to civic duty. Rance looked up in his stop. Above him a mockingbird had found the perfect place to build its nest in a lower lip of the hanging signal. The intersection really didn't need that blinking light anyway as there never was enough travel to warrant it. Most wouldn't have stopped even for it being there, but most did anyway – even Rance – because Chard Williams, Chief Deputy and local traffic cop, was sitting there every day right behind the courthouse and between the police station and the old Royal Theatre across the street. He was always ready to slap the wrist or the pocket book of any motorist who didn't heed the light, depending on how pretty or otherwise they were. Rance pulled off and tipped his hat to him as he returned the gesture.

He passed King's Foods, and saw Jake arguing out front with the milkman, who was certainly complaining to the fact Hank's big rig was blocking the service entrance in the back closest to the coolers. Rance laughed at himself. It would be another few minutes before his old friend would realize he'd been left, and another hour before the Knights of the Round Table broke up their meeting and would offer him a ride. He could just picture Hank trying to catch up to retrieve his truck. He passed the Walsh Brothers Corner Station, long closed down and the old pumps rusted in. He remembered the time more innocent, when kids played outside at the age of three or four. Rance recalled slipping out the window of their West Walnut Street home – his home now – and he'd walk to that old station and rest his bare feet on the cool concrete in the shade of the station cover. His mother hadn't known he'd gone, as she napped the same time every day. Rance couldn't read time at that age, but he could tell by the lunch crowd leaving the diner it was time to get back before she awoke. Rance could stand there for hours, if able, watching one of the brothers burn patches in on the old tires set up on the spreader. Climbing on the pile of tires that were waiting their turn, he watched the inflated tubes being placed under the water, with patch after patch, some overlapping others, in their efforts to cover the mesquite thorn holes that were readily punched by the never-ending supply of them that grew all over the area. He also remembered at least one of the brothers giving him peanuts and an occasional sody water; usually a six-ounce bottled orange soda taken from the Coke box sitting just outside their little station door. He'd watch as they would drop a dime into the slot and let Rance slide the bottle down its hanging rack to freedom outside the locking flipper gate. They would hold him up around his belly as he would lean over the top to accomplish it. Rance thought back on it; it somehow reminded him of stacked cattle in a loading chute being pushed up one at a time awaiting their turn through the head gate.

He remembered the the brothers' every Christmastime treat for their customers. Just inside the station's door was a two-gallon open top wash tub that sat on a little table, just as a customer would enter to see. It was made available for any patron who wanted to partake it in when entering the little corner station. There was a thick towel on the top of the table and atop that sat a big block of ice. Centered on that block was the wash tub, with dipper overhanging its edge into the milky yellow and cream colored nog that lay chilled inside it. Rance remembered his brother Hadd asking their father if he could have some. His father, with his famous grin said, "Shore son. Gitcha a drank!" Hadd got the dipper plum full and drew in a full mouth's worth, before the burn of it set in. It had been a well-known expected spirit of the holidays that the whole town looked forward to every Christmas season, but Hadd and Rance were just too young to know that this egg nog was one hundred proof. His brother's face shown in its discovery of what the meaning of true Christmas spirit was. He was caught between spitting it out on the floor, or going ahead and giving it the whole gagging honest try of swallowing it. He chose the latter as his dad, Frank Walsh, and an old man Hadd and Rance had never seen there before, who was happily sitting behind the nog trough, busted out in laughter at what the wet-nosed kid had accomplished. Rance watched tobacco spit fly from the laughing old man in the chair – right out into the open top nog tub. Hadd did too, which prompted a run outside of the little station around to the tire rack, where he relieved himself of his morning breakfast. Whatever flew out of that old man's mouth, Rance thought to himself, wouldn't have mattered anyway because what was in that tub of nog would have killed anything that happened into it. Rance laughed at the memory of it and continued down the highway past all of the closed down businesses along its way.

He spotted Crosses Laundry, where the family washed their clothes once a week whether they needed it or not. He passed the new roustabout yard and drilling company that replaced Big Star Drilling Company many years before. The look had changed, but Rance still recalled the feeling of it being the same. He remembered the jack knife rigs, stacked two at a time, being readied for their next locations. The racks loaded with drill stem and collars being tested to be sure. The roughnecks and the roustabouts working together to break down whatever was needing work at the time and overhauling them to perfection. Welders burning their flashing rods throughout the night as it was cooler than taking on the hot summer heat. The old autocars plowing their way through, poles raised to latch onto whatever need to be lifted and moved in their repair. It was a boom, and there was no expense too great. "Git the job done," was their motto; painted in big letters upon the gates. Across from it was the Big Star Hotel opened for the workers brought in for the work there. It was still open, but just not quite carrying the same look that it had in the early 60s when the high class ladies of the night drove down from Wichita, just to see how big the bankrolls were for the taking from oil tycoons found. Rance remembered the crap games held on tables, right out behind the hotel, where company men there at the time staked their fortunes not only on the oil that lay in large pools under the county, but in each roll of the dice thrown. It had been a time like no other, and nothing had been quite the same since. It was a feeling of, "Get it out of the ground no matter what." If there was regulation to it, it wasn't talked about nor practiced. Permits and a look the other way were handily bought. Now, it's no longer the guess, the speculation, of what might be. Now, just distant memories of what was. The oil flowed, the ranches grew. "It was a time," Rance thought, "Shore was."

The once barren lands that skirted the long highway into Wichita Falls, with salt flats of old locations and rusty pipe half jutting out where cut, left exposed from the ground and washes, the cleared out vegetation and exposed red dirt, with some finding its way into the East Fork of the Little Wichita River, wasn't the same driving by now. Instead, new brick homes with manicured lawns dotted three quarters of the drive into the city. Wichita Falls was closing in. The salt water washed basins where the Comanche roamed was nothing as it had been. He made his way into Wichita. There to his left was a new Walmart and its row of leased-ground small businesses that generally came with one. He passed the "Easy Loan," with its row of beat up old cars which had carried in the recipients of what, to them, was momentary financial salvation, but in reality to the sharks that welcomed them and held open the door, each sucker that walked in represented a hundred dollar bill gained.

Rance made his left turn at the stop, toward his mother's keeper in the house on the knob. He felt happiness he was getting to see her and frustration out of whom he would be dealing with in order to get that chance. He rounded the corner of the block and was indifferent to what he saw. The big oak was still standing, but still in its winter loss of leaves. The bare stringy twisted limbs showed an eerie cold look that roared with death; not inviting, as a poised welcome sign might be in the place. Maybe it didn't look that way to others, but to Rance that home represented death. He knew it was no place for her, but had no way to change it. The weather of the day was a bit warmer now as it had changed, but there was still a chill the south wind was bringing back to replace the late day's warmth.

His mother, who had now resorted to a seat walker, was sitting there upon it. She sat there under the oak tree's dead and dormant limbs, waiting. She had her well-worn favorite grey sweater and ear muffs to fight off the chill. She saw him round the corner and make the drive up to the curb to get out. She met him with a most pleasant smile on her face. "What are yew doin out here Mom?" Rance asked. "Aintchew cold?" "A little," she answered. Rance hurried and tossed his spare tire off of the bed and onto the ground. He rolled it over and placed it just below the passenger side door of his old truck. It had become a welcomed ritual in her struggles to enter his cab. He looked up at the glass doorway knowing the bitch behind it had placed her out there to be picked up in similar method of the trash being left beside the curb for its pickup. "Have yew bin out here long Mom?" Asked Rance, as he could see the chill in her and the redness to her cheeks and the cold in her thin hands. "Not long. I'm ready for my bean soup," she said as he fixed the seatbelt across her and latched the buckle. "Me too," Rance answered, knowing she was talking about the minestrone soup that she loved so much, and that even he had acquired the taste for. It was a ritual for each outing in taking her there. She loved that restaurant and felt excitement and contentment in her going – Rance liked going too. He noticed a weakness in her that he had not seen in their last outing; her short exhaled words and a shortness of breath. It seemed she was struggling to be there, but was entirely happy in it still, even with her difficulty. Rance felt she had struggled even more because of waiting out front for his arrived. The fact of seeing her that way was working on him as much as her labored breathing at the time.

They sat by the window in her favorite spot, overlooking the trees in the parking lot. It was as if she couldn't see the painted lines designating each parking space and the asphalt paving where they lie painted. She was always looking up into the trees, as if some long ago forgotten memory was again in mind. Again, the blackbirds came in unison, curling in flight. It looked like a wave of a flag that was rippling in the wind as they'd land, then launch just as quickly in some routine, over and over again. Rance watched his mother, in her watch of them. "Just like fish in a ocean," she said with an outward exhaled laugh. Rance enjoyed seeing her happiness and joy of being there, for he knew she had enjoyed him being there as well. Her company was appreciated so much that day. He wanted to stay longer, but the clock said their time together was coming to an end. He didn't want to leave, but neither did he want the conflict for her over not being brought back in the allotted time. He would bring her back to the bitch and her sadness – right after another welcomed portion of bean soup.

25

ALL THINGS START WITH A PLAN

"Well when ya doin it?" Hank asked as they drove along the green April roads of Foard County, on their way to the cattle that were grazing on the flat above the Pease River. "We're shooting for May," Rance answered. "Well that's good. It's about time, but ah doanno what ah'm goanna do. You'll be all hen-pecked an ah woan't have no place ta go. Yew bein fulla family 'n all." "Yer probly rite. Yew woant!" Rance answered, holding back the grin inside. "Well ya don't hafta be sa damn cold about it. After all, ah bin'yer friend longer than yew know'd her," he blistered out. "Maybe so, but she's got more ta offer than yew, and it's the rite kinds of offerins. Ya know whut I mean?" "Guess ya got a point there, but ah still cain't say as ah like it none." "Well you'll just hafta try yer best ta git used to it." "Wull she's got yer place fixed up real nice, but them daughters cain't sleep oan that couch and it wouldn't be right ta share in that one room. Are ya goin to build oan, er sumpthin? If ya are, ya might build an extry guest room in case ya git a visitor every now'n then," Hank hinted. "Well I was thankin bout that, but I might sell it and move us all down to tha motel. There's plenty a room in there an each could have their own bath and closet," Rance answered, still holding back his grin. "Wull that's just plain stupid. That woman's gotta house sittin down there in Young County yew could put five families in. Aintchew got no sense? It even has a swimming pool inside it!" "I cain't swim," Rance answered, looking at his buddy building up under pressure. "Wull, so whut if yew caint swim," Hank started. Just about the time it dawned on him. "Yew can too swim!" He blurted, followed by a mumbled "Stupid idiot!" Rance busted out a laugh at his little now steaming friend sitting over on the truck seat beside him. "Looks like yew beena doin a lot of thankin! How'djew know she has a pool?" Rance asked. "She told me that's how. When ah asked her where yaw'ld live if yew wus ta ask her ta marry ya." "Oh ya did, didja?" "Yup, ah shore did. And don'tchew worry about it. That's my bizness!" "Talkin about me and Luddia is yore bizness? How do ya figger?" "Well don'tchew no never mind about it!" That would be all that was said by both on the long ride back to the little green house on West Walnut in Archer City.

Rance had thought about it a lot and really hadn't made a decision. His little home wasn't good enough or big enough for his new family. But moving in to her ranch house would have him believing himself to look like a gold digger, plus most of her hands he'd day worked with, and it just wouldn't feel right to him. He'd have to think about it long and hard. It would put him between a rock and a hard place, them seeing him as a boss, instead of a hand who earned his time, moving up. He mulled it back and forth, but with his own ranch house not available, and the little house in Archer not enough to handle the need, it looked like that would be the only way it could be.

It was quiet when Rance pulled up his drive, and Hank got out and opened the electric wire for him to pull through. He did, then shut off the engine just inside the yard. "Whatareyew doin?" Asked Hank. "Well ah got ta thankin oan it. I guess ah'll have ta sell ole greeny there or just give it to somebody," he said, looking over at his grinning buddy. "No... No. Ah just caint take yer place. No... Yew ain't rite. Whataya mean? Give it ta me? Ah caint take sumpthin like that for nuthin," Hank, looking strangely serious, said. "Wull, ah didn't mean yew. Ah said, somebody... Somebody that needs it!" Rance answered back. A calm rolled around that old cab, sort of like the calm before the storm, then, "Just whut tha hell do yew mean? Ah ain't nuthin to ya? Ah ain't nobody that would be in need of it? Ah ain't good anuff for it? Ah ain't bin yer friend when nobody else was? Go ahaid. Yew just let some other yayhoo out there have it 'n see if ah keer." "I would," Rance said, "but chewd hafta give me tha key back first." "Ta heck with that key. Ah never had no use for it anyhow. Ah doan't woant that house nohow. Tha thieves probly already got it marked cauze ya don't never lock the dang thang up anyway and tha screen door oan the front is crooked." Hank blistered out. "Well, ya talked me out of it then. I was halfway decided ta give it to ya, but if that screen door's a botherin ya that bad, it wudn't be rite ta do a friend that way. It just wouldn't feel rite with a possible thief a breakin in, an it havin a crooked door'n all," said Rance. "Wull, suit yerself," a pouting Hank sullenly gruffed back.

26

WEDDING DAY

The church was of a Protestant denomination and Rance, unknowing of the difference, felt that he couldn't be that much different than most, although he'd never set foot in a Protestant door until he and Luddia made their pitch to the preacher. Rance didn't know how it would go, since he didn't frequent churches much in the last fifty or so years and he'd never being baptized and Luddia being Catholic and all. He couldn't know whether this preacher would perform it anyway, especially after the preacher asked them both if they'd be joining his church if he performed the ceremony in question. Rance's response when asked was "Probably not! But ya might woanta thank twice about not doin it, come workin time," he finished. After all, Rance had been the choice day work cowboy in working the preachers livestock for the past fifteen years, and the

Lord certainly wouldn't hold it against him helping a brother in need. So the minister agreed it would be the Christian thing to do, and wouldn't dally with the small details.

The wedding date would be set for the end of May with only close friends, Luddia, the girls and Rance in attendance. The minister would meet Luddia and go over everything. Rance was adamant there would be no speaking in tongues by either of them. It would be a simple affair, and it was. Once the date was decided on, it was duly noted in the Archer County news, circulated throughout the county, written down in the upcoming events section on the last page.

The time had come. It was a beautiful day, as a spring storm had hit the town the day before, and its collapsing high winds had managed to litter the streets with broken limbs and a smattering of roofing tin and shingles from who knows where. The air was crisp and the trees were clean-washed, shimmering brightly in the clear sun. A rainbow appeared over in the east and was a picture sent to help calm an old bachelor's nerves. "Yew ready?" Asked Hadd, who was standing in as best man for his brother and currently straightening the crooked bow tie at Rance's neck. "Guess I'd better be," said Rance. "Everybody here?" He asked. "Yep, all but tha bride. She got some sense and skidaddled outa here." "That ain't funny. Hank ain't still mad is he? Me pickin yew an all ta be best man?" Rance asked his brother, who was struggling at the tie, as he didn't know how to tie one either. He knew how to tie a half hitch knot, so that's how it would be. "Not likely. Well maybe. But he'll git over it," he answered after finishing the knot. "There," he said while giving Rance a firm two-handed pat to both shoulders. "Well. They're playing that song we're sposed ta come in oan." Hadd opened the door leading into the sanctuary and he and Rance walked up to the front and stood.

The preacher was waiting and most rows of the church were pretty empty, but the front few pews were filled. A few offshoot friends that inclined themselves, not unexpected, to show up anyway without the formal invitation, were scattered in spots toward the back. Rance saw his mother sitting in the front row with a grand smile from corner to corner as proud of Rance in that time as he was, and as proud as he was for his mothers happiness found. He had brought Luddia along with their last few outings and she had grown fond of her. She grew to love her as much as Rance had, and cried when Luddia told her he had asked her to marry him and showed her the engagement ring. On those outings, a time or so, she had met the girls and fell in love with them as well. Hadd brought her to the ceremony, and as expected, their two siblings didn't show up. Rance had already known that they wouldn't, as did Luddia, but for their mother's sake Luddia thought best both should be invited anyway and did. Hank sat beside their mother and kept her company with his corny jokes she seemed to always get a kick out of. There were cousins, friends, and neighbors. Even the widow Walthrup was there with her flower wrapped garden hat, and bright purple painted lips, already crying while dabbing her painted tears with her handkerchief. She believed it her duty to represent the ones who had been neglected in their chance at invitation and their wish to cry at weddings. Deputy Chard, still in uniform, wouldn't miss another opportunity to control the wedding traffic and his chance to direct it away from the area Rance and Luddia had parked their wedding truck for departure. Roy sat with Fred Atterbury in aisle seats in the middle area by themselves, caught up in conversation nearly the whole time about Fred's neighboring rancher's cattle breaking in on Fred's wheat after their bulls fought through the fences. Just the usual bunch, most who wouldn't miss their union, along with Luddia's ranch hands, too many to mention or had been expected. Rance was proud of the ones who came and was happy they were all there.

Preacher Josh stood in front of the pulpit as rehearsed, black suit and slicked-back hair. He was practicing inwardly for the nontraditional ceremony he would perform, worried about making it suit, but not crossing the grain too much from the Pentecostal way, the Baptist way, or the Catholic way. Anyway, he was ready. There was no one there that day that could play a piano or guitar, so Roy stood up to the right of the pews and with his Hohner harmonica played out the best rendition of the wedding march that he could muster. The more he played, the more it leaned into Willy Nelson's "On the Road Again," but for his rendition the troubling similarity was soon overlooked, as all heads turned to watch the most beautiful sight that day – possibly ever – there in Archer County.

Luddia's youngest daughter, Taylor, led the way down the aisle in her beautiful dress and white shoes. Rance had never seen either of the girls outside of boots and jeans. In his wait he could see very much her mother in her. She wore a flower crown and a huge smile that he was happy to see. His eyes perked up with Luddia's following just behind her. Luddia's hair was in a long braid and she had a look about her Rance wasn't privileged to see until that very moment. Her dress was long and hid her feet in dress high heels. She looked much different in her carrying, than when in her boots. Luddia's oldest daughter, Kaylee, managed the train. She was in matched dress with her sister, and it completed the whole picture beautifully. Luddia was glowing. The bouquet covered her hands as she stood proud in her walk, and she held the bouquet level, centered about her waist. She didn't wear makeup as a rule, as she had a natural beauty not many had, but for the ceremony she put on just a hint. Rance saw her differently when she moved down the aisle and came to him. In this moment, she wasn't the rancher, but the model of femininity, moving down her runway. She would carry herself proud, which made Rance proud. He had always recognized the beauty and strength in her, but she was showing her strength along with her feminine poise. She was all woman – a woman that could stand on her own; who could have anyone she wanted, but chose him not of need, but because of her want of him just as he had for her. In that moment he was affirming that with all his being he truly loved her and her beautiful girls. A real love felt more than he had for anyone before. "I pronounce you now man and wife. Go ahead Rance. You may kiss your bride." Rance did just that. "And now, to all the friends and family who have come to celebrate this marriage, it is my great privilege and honor to present for the first time anywhere, Mr. and Mrs. Rance Abernathy," Josh finished. Rance kissed Luddia again, and brought her down the steps of the raised stage. He brought her down with pride, forward to his mother sitting on the front row. She wasn't crying, she just sat with a pleasant smile and Rance could see the joy in her at his choice. Luddia knelt down and handed his mother the bouquet and gave her a huge hug. His mother blushed at her giving, as she had felt young love in the gift. The ceremony took all of thirty-five minutes.

There would be no reception to follow. Hadd shook his brother's hand and hugged his neck. "Don'tchew worry bout mom, we're going ta stay at the ranch house tanight." "Ya hungry?" asked Rance, "Yea," answered Hadd. "How boutchew Luddia," "Yep" she answered. "Hey yawl lets all go down to the Oil Derrick, my treat," Rance hollered out. "You too Josh," he finished. Fourteen dusty trucks, cars and one ole bull rig left the church following Chard's patrol car, with lights flashing through the town. They took up all of the spaces at the courthouse, just across the street from the Oil Derrick Diner. Wedding dress and all, they feasted on the daily special of chicken fried steak topped with white gravy, and their choice of baked potato or fries with ice tea, coffee or coke – whatever fit their fancy. It was the beginning of a happy life for Rance and Luddia, and he was the proud cowboy to have her as his wife and by his side for it; the whole of it.

Hadd took their mother back to the ranch, the girls went with one of the hands back to their Young County home, and Rance and Luddia spent their honeymoon in the little green house in Archer with the crooked front door on West Walnut street, while Hank slept in the bull rig out behind King's Grocery. Love was made as they both met the sunrise. Their honeymoon was short, but as need of their lifestyle warranted, was expected as such. Rance had day work on the Lazy J and Luddia would see about the girls and be home waiting for him to get there.

27

THE CLOUDS HANGED LOW IN ARCHER COUNTY

Rance drove up to the alley behind King's and woke up his old friend, just to be sure he and Jake wouldn't be on bad terms with him blocking the delivery trucks that were sure to be arriving that morning. He tossed him the key to his new house. "Here ya go," said Rance. "She's all yers." "Thankya Rance shore appreciate it. You just don't know how much." "Yea ah do, and you're welcome. I got ta come over and get all my thangs out, soon as I get caught up. I already boxed them a week ago. Just have a pickup load there. The rest is yers – a house with all the fixens," Rance added. "Well, looks like ah gotta permanent parkin place now. Ole Jake won't have nuthin ta complain about. Won't he feel lonesome," answered Hank. "How's it goanna feel livin way over in Young County now?" "Fine, just fine. See ya later Hank, I got calves to work." "Be careful now, I'll catchya later, Mr. Schroeder," Hank said with a grin. "An tell Mrs. Schroeder ah aim ta come over and use her couch sometime anyhow."

Rance ignored the last comments, given he rolled up his truck's window and was on his way to the Lazy J where Roy would be waiting on him for another day. Rance drove up onto the flat short grass drive at the turn in of the gate. It was the cool of the morning, but had an air about it, leading into Rance's way of thinking that it was going to get hot. The clamminess of the early morning dew was already giving him the feeling that his body heat was being held inside. He looked around, checking the dust of the road to see if anyone was traveling up it or for any hanging dust that somebody might have left. Only his own was still settling, and nothing from the red bed valley below in the direction of where Roy would be coming. The gate held its locks, still damp under the wet morning rising, and had the look they'd never been touched. "Hmm, that ain't right!" Rance said out loud to himself. Roy had always been there; usually before him. In the thirty plus years of them knowing each other and day working together he had never been late. He usually would have the cattle already penned and waiting for ole Rance to roll up just for something to complain about. Rance looked back into his trailer at the perk-eared roan that stood ready. "Good ole Yank," he said to him as the waiting horse stamped the hollow bottom of the old trailer with his left front hoof. "Guess we'll have to do all the work this time until Roy gits here." he finished making his way over and unlocked the pasture gate. Pushing it open erased the quietness of the morning with the squawk of its pipe-sleeved hinges.

The old cowboy and his old horse drove the trailer-rattling road a quarter section in, to where the portable pens had been set up in permanent fashion two years earlier by the new owners of the Lazy J. The ranch was owned by R.

J. Fitz, who had been much like the rest of the old time ranchers, spending the rest of his years in the old folks' home in Archer City. His daughter and her husband now ran the ranch; her being raised in the life, and him about as city dude as one could get. His being that way, it had forced out the ranch hands. Over time, they filtered their ways out to outlying ranches, leaving the couple in dire need of help. As cowboys, their loyalty had always been to R. J. They had always seen Melba as spoiled by her father. She had grown out of it over time though and because of their quitting, a different side of her shown. Rance saw it. Maybe because he wasn't there at all times to be jaded by the perception, but for her day with the bunkhouse empty, the past was forever over and it was left to the dayworkers to handle the cattle, farming, and fence-mending end of the Lazy J.

Rance shut the old truck down, set the gates to the trap pen, and closed off the chute. He unloaded Yank who dipped his head immediately just to test Rance and the new grass grazing he was afforded. "Come oan boy," Rance said to him, giving him time for a mouthful, then led him over and looped a rein over the top rail of the catch pen. He left him in his expected routine procedure, readying the working pens in their usual setup for the work to come. Rance fired up the old truck once more, pulled it around, backed it up to the chute, and shut the motor off. He sat the seat and quietly looked out at the distance for any sign of rolled up dust from Roy's truck traveling the gravel road. "Nothing," he thought to himself as he opened the pickup door and made his way out to the standing tied roan waiting at the portable pen rail. It would be a long day for him and Rance. It was the way, if only one had showed up for the job. He'd stay until all of the work was done, even if there was no help in arriving for the task.

Dark had fallen and Rance finished the work of the sacked up herd. He penned and doctored all that was there. The roan stood again tied to the rail, lathered in dried sweat from the day earlier spent. Rance and Yank had to do the work of three, and it was cowboy hat off and headlight strapped to Rance's forehead to finish cutting the old boneys out and loading them for the hauling up to the livestock sale in Wichita. Every once in a while he would glance up to see if anyone was traveling up the road. Out at a distance he saw headlights dipping in their travel as they made their way nearer in their course. He couldn't see any trailer lights behind it, but it wasn't unheard of for Roys worn out old rig to blow the fuse shutting them down. There had been many a time Rance acted as wingman behind him, just to keep him from getting a ticket on a late night ending drive, through the county's back roads on their way to where they were going. "Bout time," Rance said to himself. At least he's good for a beer if nuthin else." He finished, while happily seeing the lone lights, as they danced their way out in the darkness on their up and turning way into the pasture gate.

The lights bounced, making their way up to him. The blinding of them grew larger and brighter in their facing him through the runoff creek and the half mile it took to get to him, as they hauntingly closed in on him through the darkness. Even though he knew his old friend was coming, it was an eerie roar into the lateness of a very lonely place. The truck kept its course and the wheels bounced against its shocks, before having one final turn out away from Rance's parked truck in front of the chute. The headlights dipping with each bounce over the rough rock terraced ground still coming. With a sudden quick turn away, the brightening headlights slightly startled Yank enough that he pulled against his tying and wide eyes shown white in the bright glow reflection. Once the flicker was gone he had moved sideways, but relaxed to it and let out a loud knicker at the pickup turning away. Rance, still seeing Roy, walked over to the running truck and said "It's about time you showed up!" When just before reaching it, he was met with the opening door and the driver exiting it in the dark.

"I didn't know you were expecting me. I didn't even think you would be here today," a female's voice spoke from the darkness. "Melba?" "Yes, Rance it's me." "Whatareyew doin here?" There weren't no reason ta come out an pay us tonight. I was just plannin ta pull our commission outta tha cow checks, that tha bunch brung after tha sale," Rance said. "You don't know?" She asked. "Know what?" "I just thought somebody might have toldja," she said to him as she walked over and gently grasped his arm. "Told me what?" Asked Rance. "Well, Rance I don't know how to tell you. I wasn't expecting you to be here, or I would have come earlier. I just saw yer lights in here and thought we'd better check it out." "We?" "Yeh, me and Jonathon," she said, pointing out her husband sitting in the passenger side of the ranch truck. "Tell me what?" Rance asked again. "Rance, I don't know how to tell you this, but Roy and Fred Atterbury were found dead this morning." "Dead! Roy and Fred? Whah – what happened?" Rance said, suddenly weakened in the thought of it and making his way over to the trailer and sitting himself down on the nearest fender, completely not hearing the shuffling load of bawling cows moving about the trailer. "How?" Rance asked. "They found them upside down, still in the cab, straight down under the water at the Turkey Creek Bridge. Looks like they both drowned, so they say." She replied while moving over and leaning up beside him, as he sat with both hands resting his forehead in the rawness of the news. "How?" He asked again. "Don't know. They sent them both to Ft. Worth for autopsy. Everybody's guessing that since Fred was driving, he may have had a heart attack or somethin, 'cause there was no sign of braking. Looks like he just missed tha guard rail and drove rite straight off tha road into that ole creek. The bank seemed to roll them both inta tha old muddy hole just enough, they couldn't get free. A passing truck driver saw the truck wheels up and still spinning when he came by, but there weren't no way ta gittem free. He fought real hard tryin, so they say." She said.

Rance sat there, the dark hid his tears, but the suck in of life breath air, and the sniffles that followed it, sent the feelings out and no matter how black the darkness Rance's moment was given away. Melba moved in and hugged the old cowboy and stayed there with him throughout the night just to be sure he was okay. Rance lost all track of time. Yank still stood tied and saddle-bound just like his owner, untested for it.

The sun broke the horizon and found them all sitting there in silence, and Melba in genuine concern. That day Rance was drowning in his sorrow for losing the best day-working friend and cowboy he'd ever known, and a great friend and ole time rancher he'd had the great pleasure of working for The old time ways were dying out in Archer County and Rance was dying inside with them, but in the night turning into morning not only had he found peace in his worry, he discovered the fact that he had completely misread Melba as much as her quitting cowboys had. She was a fine woman and a proven rancher and Rance was proud to know her and would be determined to set the record straight about her going forward – determined in siding her as she had done with him. She was a rancher. All rancher. And a rancher who had taken the time to set with him and give him comfort for the whole night needed for it. He also misread and earned respect for her quiet husband. He stayed as well and without complaint in his allowance for her to stay.

Rance and Luddia, just one week after one of their happiest times, visited two funerals of two great friends – one in Archer City and the very next day one in Jermyn. Two friends buried thirty-six miles apart. Rance felt the two were needed together when called by their maker to manage his range – both working cattle; one making the decisions and one bossing the cowboys that made it there. Rance's hope was that they were holding the range together for an eternity and were readily awaiting for the rest of the boys to join along when their times came.

28

DOUBLE DAYS BEARING DOWN

It was again a hot, hot day in summer. Winter to spring had gone by quickly and the world had instantly grown into the climate made normal in that part of North Texas. The sweltering of it, with the early starts and the cooler ends of the evening led to double days as the old cowboys called it. They would take advantage of the mornings to keep the stress of the working down, and the horses fresh. A mid-day rest would ready them to finish the day's long turn in the remaining, slightly lowered, temperature change of the evening. For Rance, it was a harder time. For Luddia, it was of mixed emotions to her. She knew that it was harder on Rance, but she welcomed the daily routine of seeing him and caring for him in his return for break in the day to rest and welcomed getaway from the middle day heat.

She partnered with him now, as Roy was gone, and he had no finer partner than the cowgirl he had married. She could hold her own with any man out there – including Roy and even Rance. She was tough, feminine and poised in any task she needed to get. Although Rance would always miss his old day working friend with the tucked-in pant legs and the coke bottle bottom glasses, he wouldn't trade his time with Luddia for anything; unless it be a trade in his never losing Roy in the first place. He admired the way she sat her big grey and the swiftness and smoothness that she let down her rope and the drive and seriousness of the throwing of her loop. It was poetry in motion to Rance, and it sometimes caught him off guard in her method and put him in her watching, instead of participating in the catch at hand. The couple worked her spread and were a welcome crew, along with her two daughters Kaylee and Taylor. Although young, they also could keep up with the best. Especially Kaylee as she could handle just about any rough stock out there, while Taylor was slowly closing in. The four worked the day work scene as needed while pulling down their own work alongside the full-time hands on both Luddia's and Rance's ranches as priority, without faltering to their promise of the outside work. This was the way in it for Luddia to keep up with the routine as she knew it, and show Rance she was in his backing in the life he had led before their meeting. Combined, what Luddia had inherited and what Rance had worked in estate and lease, the work was around thirteen and a half sections of ranchland scattered throughout the counties of Archer, Clay, Foard, and Young of North Texas. Enough to keep them satisfied and busy for the moment in their lives. All scattered range, but ensuring at least one area would be thriving, while another rotated out in the offsetting weather pattern changes.

It was a hot time in Archer and it was coming up on the 70th Annual Archer County Rodeo – a time that Rance had looked forward to most every year. It was a get together of the ranches and the hands that worked them competing in old ranch traditions dating back to the first days of running rough shod over wild-caught Mexican cattle. A chance for them to fight back against changes of the new times or chase closer to the memory of what was. It was a time he had looked forward to in his youth, but now was the time (and had been for a while) to hand over the reins to the up and comers of the life. Now he enjoyed the parades, and stayed away from the ranch roping events he used to be driven to. He certainly missed the passed-around beer and old lies told, but most of the old passers and old liars of his time had long gone. He wasn't old, it was just the gathering of cowboys meant more for the younger than it did for him. The only time he wanted to be tied to a caught bovine was in his working; even that was learned to be avoided as much as possible, and only performed when in need of it. He participated these days in a four-county-wide daily rodeo that kept him sharp in his skills and self-satisfied in them – his personal day work rodeo. His days of proving himself were over. He and his kind had already done so. He had earned his right a long time ago to top hand and the title that came with it. It was a hot time and again he would skip the event, as he had seen too many of them. He was busy in his work and busy in his holding on and set odds out of his favor were against him in doing so.

Rance had not intentially neglected the weekly trips to Wichita and his outings with his mother, but it had been some time that he had joined her in doing so. She hadn't been forgotten by him, and that was the worse for it, as it would have been better on him if he had. He was feeling quite guilty in each visit missed out on, but Luddia had made time for them. She made the trip in to Wichita with her girls. In her trips in and to the house with the big oak she didn't see it as something to dread, as Rance had, but took pleasure in each visit as if his mother was her own. With pleasant affirming tone she forced her way in, even if not invited, freely past Lindy, as if her sanctuary was of no interest. Without trepidation, in her pursuit of an untimely and unannounced visit to an old lonely woman, she would brush right by the obese bitch that had been neglecting her mother as if she were a stranger. Luddia recognized the neglecting of her new mother and wouldn't have understood it even if it had been by a stranger's hands, but at the hands of the daughter spoiled in her raising was just unbelievable to her. If only she had have been blessed with a mother of her own – one she never had – she would have catered to her every want and need.

Luddia had a way with Rance's mother and loved her so much that she would call her grandma, as if she were her kids' own. His mother would light up every time a visit from her and the girls presented itself. Luddia and the girls would pamper her. Special moments to take and dote on her; things like getting her hair fixed and nails done. These were things Rance couldn't have known were needed for her – not by knowing and neglect, just in ignorance that this was something enjoyed and needed by her as he had never witnessed personally its need. Luddia even understood the importance of a pedicure, something else Rance had not known anything about and especially its need to be done for a woman. He never witnessed the importance of them from his mother, so he just couldn't know. It took Luddia to lead him in silent example of the feminine point of view. He was grateful for her knowing and was proud of her being there for his mother when he could not be.

Time passed so quickly and the rodeo parades had come and gone. It was time once again for celebration. It was just one week before the city's Fourth of July gathering on the courthouse lawn where vendors of homemade ice cream and fried turkey legs would raise their awnings and pitch their sales through their concession windows. Trailers would be set up and opened for business a couple of hours before the parade was to roll on by. It was a fine time for everyone around Archer, and even though the time would be hot, the humidity most times would be low – the heat of it wouldn't feel as bad to the body as much as the rainy times followed by the sun of the early spring.

29

HANK'S SURPRISE

Rance hadn't seen his old friend Hank for about two months. The last he heard, he was down around Del Rio moving cattle for the Hernandez brand. He had been wondering lately what had become of him, since it had been way longer than usual in hearing from him. He was normally in town during the Fourth of July ceremonies. Rance made his way into the Dairy Queen, and rounded the tables to the pot for his late, but much needed, morning cup of coffee which had been traded for the early morning catch of a rogue cow.

The cow had wandered its way off the Castleberry spread and made her way up several runoff creeks, finding her way into the deep ravine country leading down to the Little Wichita River basin. He was to catch her at all cost as she led many good cows astray and raised havoc on the fences that lay between the ranch and the river. On Luke Castleberry's orders, if that ole cow was caught he was to get her "old wild ass loaded," and as fast as he could right straight to the sale if she could be kept inside the trailer once put there. If she couldn't, he'd given Rance the okay to put a bullet in the ornery reject's head. Rance had managed the first order given, so no bullet required from his still booted saddle gun. With the help of his old dog, who seemed to come alive and live for the chase as Rance did, Bingo caught hold of the rank, bellowing, long horn's nose just outside a short brush thicket. That gave Rance enough time to get a loop over her horns. He was half the morning working that throwback cow – with taut rope, the help of his big roan and Bingo – back to the trailer, slowly wearing her down at the end of his horn-wrapped dally. The mile from where he placed his loop to where he had parked his rig was quite a jump, and without trusting to tie her off on one of the mesquite trunks, he and Bingo worked her on up into in the trailer. It meant a hundred and seventy-five cash dollars for his efforts – well earned.

Upon his entering and making his way to the coffee pot, and the upside down cup on the bar, he was received by a "Howdy Rance," in unison by all three Knights of the Round Table. "How yaw'l doin?" Rance answered back. "Better than yew by tha got damned looks of it!" Dobber said back, referring to the half-ripped tear that ran down the back of Rance's shirt. "Whatayew bin into?" Dobber asked, referring to his mesquite-thorn undressing received bringing that beast out from the river to the trailer. "Whadaya bin in Rance, a fuckin cat fight? Dobber threw in. "A cat fight?" What's that supposed to mean?" His buddy Jim asked out loud, not putting much thought on who and what he was asking. "Yea, that don't make no sense Dobber. A cat fight is a fight between two women. Rance ain't no woman!" Rankin added. "Oh what tha fuck yew know bout it. Yew spent yer whole fuckin life a never knowin what a woman was!" Dobber pelted Rankin with marvelous, quick and melodic insult. "Hey Rance, hear yer buddies back in town," Dobber just as quickly changed the subject. "My buddy?" Rance looked puzzled. "Yea, Hank's back. Saw his rig earlier heading up toward his place. "Is that right. Well that ole reject didn't even tell me he was coming. Guess I'll hafta go by an see 'im. See if he wants to make a trip to the sale with me," Rance said as he sucked the single cup of coffee down and tossed two bits to the table top in his leaving. "Yew be careful Rance," the Knights again said in unison – a common way to say "see ya later," in those parts, and from men of their day.

He left for a surprise visit to the little green house on West Walnut Street, and his buddy Hank. Rance pulled the pickup truck with the trailered longhorn cow, the worn out horse, and the one-eyed catch dog out in front of the little green house on West Walnut Street. Sure enough he could see the old bobtail bull hauler sitting behind it, circled out and readied for its next run in Rance's old spot. He shut the motor off, kicked open the badly sprung driver's door and patted Bingo on his head just before telling him to stay there on his way around the trailer and up the drive toward the backyard kitchen door.

He pulled the old screen open and shoved the main door back to its stopping halt on the uneven floor, walked his way in and made himself at home. His old coffee pot had been taken with him on his move to Luddia's and was replaced by a fancy coffee brewer brought in by Hank that he had no experience in the running of. Rance stumbled around the kitchen pantry for the filters and coffee that the new brewer needed in its start. He rattled the kitchen drawer for a tablespoon to measure the coffee with, filled the glass pot from the faucet, poured it into the holding reservoir, set the pot under its spout and pushed the button.

The door of the pantry was still wide open as Rance placed the coffee and filters back from whence they came, then commenced to shut the door.

"Woah now!" Rance yelled and half fell over the kitchen table chair in a stumbling retreat from the strange newly-startled and screaming half-dressed Mexican girl wearing a morning robe, fuzzy slippers and holding a butcher knife. Both stood there screaming, each not knowing why the other was in the room. Hank rounded the corner from the living room holding his britches up with one hand and his Colt .44 revolver in the other. "Whuh-huh-whut tha hell is goin oan?" he hollered, coming in behind the little woman with the great big knife holding a very confused Rance at bay. "Rance!" Hank hollered out, dropping the gun, still cocked and ready, down to his side. "How tha hell are ya?" He said, as he rounded behind the young Mexican as if she had been a ghost and wasn't there. Sure is good to see ya," he said as Rance and the girl relaxed into the knowing that each was okay to be there. Rance, still dazed in the moment, looked at his old friend, then back to the Mexican girl, who had now joined his old friend in a big smile. A welcoming one, as a matter of fact, while the coffee maker rattled and spewed out its last percolating burst for the mid-day round. "Why in tha hell didinja tell me yew were comin?" Asked Hank. "Well why in tha hell didinja tell me yew were back in town?" Asked Rance, still looking at the little brown eyed beauty standing there holding the butcher knife. "Fair anuff," answered Hank.

"Hey Rance, let me innnerduce ya. This here's Merna. Yew remember Merna doancha?" Hank asked. "No," Rance answered. "Sure ya do. Rodrigo Flores's daughter." Then it came to him. "Merna Flores?" Rance said out loud. Little Merna Flores of the Triple 7?" "Yep," Hank answered. "But she ain't Little Merna Flores anymore.

She's Mrs. Hank Thompson!" There was a pause in Rance's thought that shown outwardly. Merna was thirty years Hank's junior and was way too young and pretty for the stubby-legged, potbellied, britches-holding man that stood before him. Then Rance caught himself in the quickness of that thought and first impression of the situation. "What was the difference from that of him and Luddia?" A grin started forming over Rance's face. "Well I'll be. Yew old coot. Congratulations!" He said to his old friend, reaching out to shake his hand. Hank accidentally unleashed his held up pants in reciprocation of the gesture, catching them before their fall with his pressing left hand that was still holding the Colt revolver with the cocked back hammer – stopping the possible show that nobody needed to see. Even Merna, who was now privy to it didn't need to see that. Rance turned to the pretty Mexican girl with the big beautiful smile and the long flowing braids, and with a big hug welcomed her into the family.

After a great visit with coffee and excellent authentic Mexican breakfast to boot, Rance and Hank made their way up to the sale and unloaded the wild cow, as she was now the problem of her yard handler who was rapidly vaulting himself over the alley gate. The hammering jar of the impact and open mouth bellowing of the wild thing woke the yard hand up as she hammered the wall below him, bringing attention of the other stocked pens of sale cattle of their auction outcome waiting. Rance tagged her in, with his order to the barn to hold out his catch commission – the total of what little the wild crazy bitch would get from the sale. He was beginning to wonder if he should pay *them* as he watched her half clear the alley fence, front legs caught and hanging, back legs in hopping push, struggling to make it all the way over and out of her unappreciated confinement she so readily opposed.

Rance made his way past the office and down the ramp leading into the sale barn cafe, with Hank following right behind. Upon their entering, Rance looked around, his eyes spanning the full length of the table area, and was realizing his days were changing. Most of the old faces he had known were now just a distant memory. Their replacements were now folks he couldn't know. The young buyers and new-blood ranchers sat and watched the two old friends make their way to find a seat. "Not like it usta be is it?" Hank said first. "Nope. Don't recognize nobody, do yew?" "Nope," answered Hank. "Times are a changin," Hank said, as the crowd relaxed back from their coming in, and all but ignored the two cowboys that sat the corner. They waited for the waitress with the menus to come around. She didn't, and when Hank called out to her for them, she pointed out the little folded paper that lay the table. On it was just four items, not the way remembered in his many times there. He wanted something normal; something he used to order there. He turned over the paper to see if what was missing was written on its back. It wasn't. So he hollared out across the room at the waitress taking another order, "two burgers with chips, put a hard fried egg ta each and two cokes." The waitress wrinkled her brow at the outward request, yelled "OK!" and went back to taking orders from the table she was standing.

"Well have ya heard whut's goanna happen to the Bar Back L now that Fred's gone?" "Nope hadn't heard nuthin. Don't thank nobody knows. I know one thang; it's goin ta ruination when that sorry nephew a his gits his hands oan it." "Ya got that rite!" Hank answered, while happily eyeing the two Texas burgers with the added eggs making their way to the table. "Where a them cokes at?" Hank asked the young waitress with the turned up brow, who seemed to be still stewing over his hollering way of placing their earlier order. "Well why don't ya just give me time ta go over an git 'em," she sassed back. Rance laughed and they both worked on the burgers that sat in front of them, as he thought to himself that he was watching Agnes' very appropriate future replacement.

For Rance and Hank, it was a good ride back to Archer. They both made plans for the Fourth of July meeting on the court house lawn, a turkey leg and a round of horseshoes. Then finally a beer and fireworks finale out at the Archer City Lake would be in their plans.

30

GOOD DAY WITH FALSE HOPE FOUND FLEETING

Luddia and the girls made their way up to Wichita to the crippled, twisted, diseased dead looking lone oak tree yard at the closed dark house in Wichita. A meeting time had already been decided and thus their driving in, even though still early in the day. The heat was rising and the outward temperature was already reaching upper double digits, just before its timely rise into that of the triples, expected by noontime. The heat was sweltering and there his mother sat at a tapered angle upon her chair walker, oxygen in her nose, and same grey sweater cover to her frail body. Two bags sat on the ground beside her. A row of ants crawled in line over the smaller one, on their way up to the oak tree trunk that sat behind her. The smaller was for her medicine, and the larger for her change of clothes she readied for herself the night before for her three-night stay with Rance and Luddia. Luddia looked at her new mother and felt sorrow for her in having to be in such a destitute place. She wondered if she would be able to handle the outings planned for the Fourth of July celebration that she looked so forward to.

Rance had not known Luddia was on her way to get her, so he and Hank, after their sale barn burger ate, traveled up and rounded the corner in time to see her there on her way up the hill to greet his mother. He looked at his mother there in that moment, recognizing fully for the first time in a long time, her rapid decline. For the first time, her appearance hammered home the need for his guilt felt, in his not making time to visit her and leaving it all up to Luddia. He made his way over to where she sat waiting and witnessed the stress and toll the heat was putting on her sweatered small frame. She grinned her wide grin, showing the missing tooth in front. Had she realized that it had been left exposed, and not covered by her forgotten and left out partial, she probably would not have smiled so brightly. Rance was angered for the position she had been left in her waiting, but did not give the satisfaction to the fat bitch in the house in showing it.

"Hello Grandma," Luddia greeted her. "I'm fine and yew," she responded as if lost to the greeting. Rance retrieved her bags and placed them in the back of Luddia's Expeditiion. He began, with Luddia's help, the arduous process of leading his mother down the hill and to her place in the cool front seat sanctuary. Rance looked up the drive at Lindy's car parked sideways, purposely hindering them from entering into the drive and creating a longer distance and more difficult challenge in helping his elderly mother to her place. She struggled to walk down the steep grade, adding to an already tough time. His eyes swept sideways and his peripheral vision caught the separation of the front window blind snapping back together from the dark lonely inhabitant behind it, leaving her buried in the dark hoard-filled dungeon of an existence inside.

The animal inside had spent her lifetime in jealousy of Rance, and did her best to control the only thing she could control over him in that moment – their mother. Rance looked back at the shade in the window once more and only one thought came to his mind. That one thought for him in that moment was that his mother would absolutely not be going back in there, even if a fight in court would be warranted in his not bringing her back. It would have to be jail or judges order that she would. For Rance, at that time, would be certain he wouldn't be bringing her back to that hole without one. Rance traded his old truck for a ride back with his mom and Luddia. Hank agreed to drive it back to Archer and turnout Yank to the backyard grass he hadn't seen in a long while, then meet them later for the festivities awaiting.

All enjoyed the celebration in part, but his mother needed breaks from the heat, so Rance rented the only left room at the Lone Star motel. It was just right for the cooling naps and rest needed between activities through the day. He would make trips back and forth to check on her, and at one point brought her a bowl of much appreciated homemade ice cream from the Court House Square. With her help, he reset the TV to a channel she might enjoy at the moment, then let her know he'd return from time to time just to check on her. In his saying of it, she would just as quickly respond back with the same well-intentioned phrase: "Don'tchew go ta all that trouble, I can git by just fine. Yawl just enjoy yer selves. I think I'm just a bother and shouldn't have come." "No bother, Mom. We wouldn't have it no other way. Just git some rest and I'll come back and gitcha for the fireworks show tanight," Rance answered. "Ok, I'll be ready," she said to him as he made his way out the door.

Rance folded out the chair and helped his mother to the spot closest to the lake's shoreline road. She sat there with a blanket across her lap and Rance watched her expression change with each flash in the night sky. They all were entranced by the beauty of the display overhead as the plumes of colorful sparkles were seen in doubles, while the reflection from their skyward appearance erupted down below, laying itself out on the smooth, still lake. Rance watched Luddia and the girls interact with grandma, and they all shown of luminous grins, enjoying each reflecting light that brightened the dark of the night. In the hearing of each "ooh" and "ahh," Rance felt happy and becoming at peace with all the wasted time in life's joining with his mother. With new found relationship with her, all was forgiven by him toward his mother and hopefully of him by the now happy old woman watching the fiery night sky spectacle from her resting folding chair position situated at the shore of the Archer City Lake.

On that night, Rance had made the decision with Luddia, to extend, without Lindy's approval, her three days worth of packed gear into a forever more, even it if meant buying her new everything for her stay. Rance moved his mother into the shared ranch home in Young County. Luddia had insisted that they begin in the building of a small cottage-like bedroom to suit what his mother's ways and needs would dictate while there. Their plans were to incorporate a full bed area where she could have her own privacy built into it, with her own independent heat and cooling for the want she would enjoy on any particular day. They had installed a big screen TV and began the pouring of a slab to cut out the southeast window to install full glass patio doors that maybe she might like. This would give her access to either sit out in the quiet country air and come and go with ease. It would be life long, and it started that day.

She was truly happy and enjoying her stay there. Rance had noticed an attitude shift for the better. Even in her limitation, she was up and stirring. She seemed energized; offering daily help in what chores were needed around the house. The girls performed all of the inside work needed, but left her small things to do, because it made her feel needed. He could see she was happy, but she would never see the room finished, where they had all wished "grandma," to stay.

It didn't take a court battle, just a judge's solid threat of what it would cost Rance in fines imposed, plus jail time, promised him. He was forced to give in, and forced to live with the smirking grin on Lindy's face after the next order was handed down. He and Luddia would move her back to the despairing hole at the end of that lonely city street with the twisted dying oak. The dead house with the front dirty glass door, attached to the long dark hall. The hole with all of the nastiness of clutter and noise from the untrained and ignorant big black barking dog and all of the filth the big fat bitch afforded her.

Lindy couldn't be concerned about her mother. She couldn't care any less about her, but she had a way, with quiet talk and practical way, to convince anyone outside of her shield that she did, with false portrayal. She had the ability to show it in her rehearsed pretentious way, that she was upstanding and gracious to have her mother to care for. Rance and Luddia had spent many hours on the subject of just how the truth of her reality could be shown. No one really knew her, not even her closest friends – friends who were only there under the lies of false knowing what she was truly like. All fooled, and all fools for their believing in her. The only thing Lindy was worried about were the government handout and program checks mailed to her door for the supposed care and upkeep, as caregiver, and the access to her mother's bank accounts by power of attorney given, and the 24-7 access with just the push of the bank access PIN number 1919. Rance's intentions were not to take any of that away from her. He wouldn't block her from any of that, he and Luddia were going to care for his mother no matter what. They worked hard for their money and had enough not to worry about what Social Security fraud she would perform or how much money could be pulled from an old woman's bank account. Both felt confident that Lindy could still take what was there, and they would just turn and look the other way at what she was doing and what she and Plover had done.

Lindy thought she was being crafty, because she had Plover fooled. Rance and Hadd, had always known, but it wasn't about that for her; she couldn't care less if they knew. She just needed control over something, and to keep it away from Rance. The bitch knew they knew. She had always been believed, by them both, to be Plovers leader also. She thought she had him fooled, along with her friends, but maybe not. He always covered for any deed done and more than likely went along with her, feeling he couldn't be outed if all figured out his truth. So he just relaxed to Lindy's misleading along with his own. Rance and Hadd were just beginning to figure it that way. Maybe Plover had Lindy fooled. Then again, both were keeping such close tabs on each other and the joint scams between them, maybe they were now believing each other's lies as much as they were believing their own. The reality of it, ignored by both and caught up in all of it, was the old woman. In the moment of Rance's telling that she would be having to go back to that nasty pit with the obnoxious dog, she clearly whithered, as her heart visibly sank in his telling. She was going back to the dark bitch's castle on the knoll where the twisted oak tree looked like death – forever leaving her new plans and spirit gained. Rance sensed her end that day she was told.

31

MOMENT OF EASE EXTRACTED

Fall was here again. Rance stepped the long step down from the tractor in his final planting row of winter wheat into the plowed earth of Clay County. His drilling in of the new crop of grazing winter wheat was now ready for rain and the growing needed for his cattle. He had already counted the new spring bales with every seed sown, and those few bales left over from his last harvest, on his way down to his planting. He knew he had a hundred rounds to sell that would offset the cost of the planting. He had less cattle than ever, but what he had was enough to keep him in business. He looked at the sky and watched the floating wings of the southbound geese as they floated. Different groups, layered at different heights, in their open V's. Some caught in jet streams, traveling at altered speeds by it, and separate groups sounding various tunes in their honking high above him. He listened in their passing and the variations of their sound set by the difference of distance from each flock heard. It was melodic as well as medicinal to him, as he felt the coolness of the fresh planted sandy loam soil at his feet. The sky was clear and a fall brightness came with the change of the cool breeze sweeping just enough not even to rattle the slightest grain of fresh damp turned soil in its waft. Sky of pale blue, with swatches of powered dust-like white clouds sparsely in contrast; somehow it kept Rance's mind alive in its goodness. Another day of honest work, and he never felt better for it.

The solitude of the morning was broken when, at a distance a white Suburban, heavy chromed with a full ranch grill and manicured expensive wheels, pulled into the south gate and stopped. Its tinted windows shielded the driver. Rance wondered if it was someone lost, as he didn't run in the same circles as someone who would have driven something like that. In time, a man of medium stature and polished boots, fresh-starched shirt and white felt hat that had never seen the honest dust this life hangs on one who works, walked out to greet him. Behind the Suburban he saw the passenger side door open, and very large woman – too far to see who – had stepped out and stood peering the whole while at the man in his walk up to Rance. "Howdy," said the man. "Howdy," was the reply Rance gave followed up with "Can ah hep yew?" The man drew closer and reached out his hand in greeting. Rance pulled the working glove from his hand (that had not completely eliminated from it the overburden of gathered hydraulic oil that Rance's old tractor had spent throughout its working day), and grasped the strangers hand in a greeting hand shake. The stranger pulled back after the shake, looking down at his hand and briskly worked his fingers back and forth to each other, seemingly annoyed at the oil Rance left in his wake.

"How ya doin?" The stranger asked. "Good, how boutchew?" Rance answered. "Good. Good. Mighty fine day to be a planting, ain't it?" "Can I help you?" Rance asked again, annoyed at the feeling and the vibe given off by the stranger. "Just got this paper here I gotta give ya," he said, handing Rance a note that brought back old memories in the look of it. It was in the same shape and form of the eviction order handed by his aunt to his father. Rance looked at the man without opening it. "Who are yew? I don't recall yew introducin yerself bifore givin me this paper!" "Cage is the name, Pilfer Cage," he said. Again reaching out to shake hands with Rance, who declined in his learning "I'm not interested in sellin to ya Mr. Cage. Don't have no need for anythang you've got ta say oan this ole paper here," Rance said, wadding it up and tossing it on the ground. I don't woant no dealins withya. Heard too much about ya for that. Ya just need ta be oan yer way. I've got work ta do," said Rance. "Yew don't understand. I don't want to buy yer place, I just wantchew to git off mine. You got fifteen days to git all yer junk off my place. Sure am lookin forward ta the nice stand a wheat coming ya got planted for me. Ought to come in mighty handy," Cage said to Rance, in matter of fact tone. "Paid cash for it last week. Deed's already recorded, and those are my terms," he continued, as Rance just realized who the large woman standing out behind the suburban hood at a distance was. "Lindy sell you this?" Rance asked. "Yep, Plover said his was tied up at the moment, but said when the time was right he'd be selling me his too. It's lookin like yers is tha only piece, besides your brother Hadd's. That is his name right? Hadd Abernathy? Well when I buy his up, I guess since yew ain't sellin we'll be be building a horseshoe shaped high fence right around yew. That is, unless you sell to me first, then you won't have the annoyance of it and I won't have to spend as much in the building of it." "Why yew...," Rance started. "I wouldn't if I were you, the sheriff's sittin out yonder on tha road just ta make sure this all goes peaceful. If I were you, I'd pick them papers up. It's yer legal notice of eviction. Fifteen days. That's what you got."

That's the last thing Rance heard him say that day, as his big hydraulic oil covered hand met the slickers face with enough force to lay him and his starched shirt plum out. His obese bitch of a sister was out of view from seeing, although Sheriff Lymon, sitting the county road, had full view. Charges were dismissed in the whole matter as the Sheriff, who disliked Cage just as much as Rance, said he didn't know what had happened to him. "Looked like he just slipped and fell, looked like his face mighta planted itself oan tha drill's runnin board in tha fall. Those alligator-skinned boots can be mighty slippery to a feller tryin ta git traction in that sandy loam down there." No proof in the confirmation meant the matter dropped. From that point on Cage cut a wide swath in any chance he might run up on Rance, no matter where that might be.

Fifteen days later everything Rance had was moved from Plover and Lindy's places. In her way to get back at Rance and in Plover's rush to pull his property from the sheltering of his mother, they both had sold out, and were no longer land owners in south Clay County, Texas. That left Hadd who also refused along with Rance to sell. His land was mostly rocky and tree covered. Both needing pasture, and no workable fields. Rance watched the fields he had planted grow. His only way now, because of the late summer's drying of the stock tanks, was to get an old Aerator windmill back to pumping, and haul water daily to his remaining few Clay County head. Foard County ground still had all it could handle, but the wells were good and the cattle stayed fed on their own. There was one small fifty acre field sitting atop the flat that would keep plenty of winter wheat grazing if the moisture held out, plus there was one low-brine water well he could use to flow water into the rows, if needed. Too much salt to solidly water the cattle, but not too much to occasionally water the wheat. Luddia's ground, with moisture from the occasional rain, held out and he never had to use it. The ranch was carrying itself, but Rance felt that his way, along with his mother's life, was withering away.

32

HIS TURN IN THE CIRCLE

The fall had come and gone. Olive Garden outings were well looked forward to by him, Luddia and his mother. Old ranches were worked, with new ones reaching him in the giving of new work.

Rance stumbled across a new hand ready and able to do the jobs with him; young but eager. To Rance, more like his old partner Roy, this boy was a younger version of him; never late for the leaving, usually there first for the task at hand, and just barely 19 with a lot still to learn. A boy still wearing the size 26 waist, skinny as a rail with a clumsy gait, but true for a boy of his age. He always had a fast saddled horse and was raised in the life, as was Rance, so he knew how to keep it that way. He was settled and had a much older way about him than most his age, and Rance saw a lot of his younger self in him on that note. He wore a shovel-brimmed black felt hat that was the style of his time, creased in appearance that to Rance made it seem as if it was being worn backward, something he could hardly get used to. His boots had square toes and light tan tops that had the look more of what women would wear in Rance's time. But other than that, the boy was a worker and cowhand, and only his look deceived what Rance knew better of. He was a cowboy that didn't miss a loop he turned. He was good, and Rance was proud to have him.

His name was Solace; given to him by his father who lost his wife in childbirth of him. The only two things good from his loss was his newborn son and the boy's Christian name. It would be his father's comfort in the time of his great loss. The boy was his father's right hand up until he joined his late wife, leaving the boy running to catch up in a man's world. He was a good young man and he was solid in his work. His first name was Solace and his last name was Hand, befitting just what he was, and Rance was proud to know him.

33

WINTER COMING DOWN

Thanksgiving was coming. Hadd would be coming in to feast, and Luddia, with the help of their mother and the girls, was preparing the dinner. His mother was allowed a two week reprieve for the holidays to stay with him, as Lindy was lazy and used this time to take off from her at-home telemarketing job to go visit one of her three boys who didn't want her around in the first place, but tolerated her coming anyway. They had lost interest a long time back, when she had sold and spent their inheritance. Plover avoided any time spent – unless in secret – with his mother because of the fear that she might slip in her dementia and let out what Rance and Hadd had already known he was hiding. Rance and Hadd just liked it better, in their not having to see the leach because of that fear. They never let on that his lying and cheating had never been hidden from either of them. It would catch Rance off guard at times, as he thought his relationship with his mother had finally been proven, only to hear her say at times, "Poor Plover, poor Lindy, just nothing ever seems ta go their way. I wish they could be here for all this." This Thanksgiving dinner was no exception as Rance and Hadd halfheartedly responded, "Me too, Mom," to her stating.

It was a wonderful Thanksgiving as the smell of roasted turkey, stuffing and giblet gravy wafted through the house. Rance couldn't help in noticing the speed of his mother's decline – even more evident from the wider allowed gaps in her visits. Her struggles were more than her ease and adaptation; her oxygen tank's constant flow wasn't seeming to offer her relief. Yet, even with that, they could still see a glow in her being there that overwhelmed the weakness, until her being told of the need for the visit to end and her having to go back. This year, she had permission for a bonus week, as Lindy was out spending away what was left of her land money; putting it all on travel, and putting on airs. Her only thought for her mother over the holidays was how great it was that she wasn't anywhere around her and how great it was to not have her under foot while she could still have ATM access with her mother's worndown card and its well-used PIN number of 1919 – easily remembered as it was her own father's year of birth.

The bitter wind brought in a chill that wasn't seen in over a hundred years. Over ten inches of snow had fallen in a three day period. The roads throughout Clay, Archer, Foard and Hardeman counties were all but impassable, cattle were unable to graze, and the county backroads were angled with fence high drifts that were ten to fifteen feet deep. The county precincts were at full throttle to get the roads cleared, but were delayed in most areas at least a week, possibly two, from getting them open. In the meantime there were a vast amount of old boneys and newborn calves that didn't survive it. Rance and Solace went days on end rescuing cattle, putting out hay and cake and getting into places most had already given up on. Sometimes both horses were belly deep in jumping lunges; each time horse and rider not knowing if one might lead them into a snowy suffocating grave, where it would be spring before horses and riders would surface. The cell phones of the modern cowboy had helped their way through, and the two-way radios were still up and running also, so both methods of communications kept them out of much trouble and actually kept Rance and Solace busier than they wanted to be. Hank and Luddia were always checking on them both – at times just a little too much – but their concerns were welcome and their meaning of it was genuine.

That heavy winter and its unruly patterns, unusual for even the standards of the Texas plains, passed. Just another stepping-stone in the life and times of the residents who survived it. Rance and Hadd were still intertwined in the turmoil brought on by Lindy and Plover and that son of a bitch Pilfer Cage.

Both he and Hadd had confronted and stopped one of his dozers that, with orders given, began in the pushing down of their fences and force pushed a swatch of five-hundred-year-old oaks from their hard roots in the beginning build of a twenty-foot right of way, just to install his new high fence. The dozers and their operators showed up unannounced and had already overturned four of the oldest trees and twenty or more acres of younger ones splitting their fenceline in the valley of the East Fork Creek. Cage felt he could do anything he wanted just for the fact that he had accumulated all of the surrounding lands, all except for the thorny hold of Hadd and Rance. He was reaching a run of nine thousand acres and his only two holdouts were Rance and Hadd. It didn't set well with him. His big dream of buying both sides of East Fork Creek Road, and closing it for any future users, was ended by their four squares sitting smack dab in the heart of it. Rance pulled one of the dozer operators from his seat, while Hadd entered it and replicated the twenty-acre destruction of trees lost over on Cage's property. The Grand Jury called it an even draw, as hatred for the land grabber grew in the county.

Rance and Hadd were being recognized as men to be reckoned with, and revered by some, as most were busy buttering up to the obnoxious landowner. For Hadd and Rance, the some that sided and revered them were the some that mattered in their siding. Needless to say, no more fence would be pushed down, or built, without mutual approval, and only manicured precision cutting permitted if agreed by all owners involved. That final agreement of built fence that Cage put in wouldn't cost Rance or Hadd one thin dime, and it took triple the time and five times the money from slicker Cage's wallet.

Just a little before Christmas the wall of fence was up. It changed the look of the valley, and all that happened in its build would be forever there and never leaving, while leaving all that wanted through it unable to pass. Four-hundred-year-old game trails lost, as whole populations of breeding white tail deer and small game were lost to find new routes. It was life-altering in its changing, and the city dude with deep pockets was too ignorant in that knowledge to care. The East Fork Creek basin would now be home to the African addax, black buck, striped zebra and giraffe. The honor of the ranches was slowly ending. The people coming in were not the ones Rance and Hadd had respected, nor wanted to be around. They piled onto the county in droves. Bringing in what they said they were leaving behind. They came in their four wheel camo-colored trucks and wore camo gear to match, just to shoot at the tamed down, caged, animals with the broken spirits. The animals were no more than entertainment; zoo animals in a big cage. The hunters weren't even human, as Rance saw them, just shooters with no appreciation given to the animals taken. They were killers who hid it well, with boredom of life unfulfilled, searching for short-lived and different excitement for the minute; none really knowing why or how. Cage was bringing them in.

It would be a change Rance could not welcome, but he didn't have the means to escape it either. He was unable to fight it back. Rance now felt as the wild "Comanche" must have, when they too once roamed this now high fenced valley, and how it must have appeared to them, when the first covered round-wheeled wagon was seen in their world. How confining it must have been to them in its day. Rance was feeling it in its completeness; maybe it was just as fair to him as it was to them.

34

PEACE FOR A NEW ANGEL WHEN ALL THE
NIGHT FELL SILENT

Christmas came around one more time. To Lindy, it would
be just like Thanksgiving. She wanted as usual to keep the
pay coming, but rid herself of her mother. The money from
the home place sale was leaving her without notice, at an
unreplenishable rate. She and Plover – now out of the
operations picture – were gone, and Rance, Luddia, the
girls, and Hadd spent another holiday together. This time
was not in the usual way; they all were at the bedside of
grandma in the Regional Hospital of Wichita Falls. She
had been admitted for pneumonia, and dehydration, Rance
knew it was from neglect and she had been falling quite a
lot. He could see the signs, but held it inward, as the
visiting doctors went over her care. He had watched many
an old cow in his time readying themselves for death, and

his mother had all of those signs. Rance was hurting for her as well as for himself, with her glaze-eyed look, and confused responses. He watched her. The wavering motion he understood completely. He knew there was no stopping nature in its course. He held her hand, brushed her hair, and comforted her in the ways that he could, but she was failing and he knew it. The next morning she perked up and began to eat. Rance saw that as a sign and he knew it well. She would perk up and settle just enough to be released from her stay, but Rance could sense it. He could see the need for her to stay, but knew the need for her to go was much greater. Rance, Hadd, Luddia and the girls would take her home and spend out her Christmas, high on the hill in south Clay County. She watched and enjoyed the unwrapping of the gifts, but her eating had halted. The fire in the fireplace no longer held a brightness for her as before, and Rance was in doubt she even noticed it at all. He saw her loss of appetite, the wide stare coming and presenting itself out at a distance Rance could not see, and even in her forced grin giving, he felt it. It was a terrible burden on him in hiding what he knew from everyone else. He thought to himself that her time would be closer now than he ever wanted.

He covered her with a blanket. The Christmas lights lit up the room. The family elected to leave them alone as a cold wind blew smatterings of snow outside. He sat with her, while Hadd sat gazing into the hearth's fire. The pretty tree lights and the joy she had in her still there, but waning in fireblend thoughts. The fire was dying. Rance talked. They both listened. He talked about past Christmases when they were all together and things with the family weren't quite as bad. Maybe they were, maybe they weren't, but in his stories he would only allow the good to be sounded out. He held his mother close. Hadd supported them by being there, but was lost in the hearth's glow. He talked to her quietly. Luddia knew, but respected their time and ushered herself along with the girls out of the room to give the night to Rance and his brother Hadd and their faltering mother. He quietly talked to her, soothing her just enough to let her know about the coming snow. She loved it. He talked to her about seeing the joy while she watched everyone open her gifts of socks and gloves, the expected gifts she had given every year to each child and grandchild for Christmas. Rance calmed her, as he held her.

It was then that he experienced the moment felt, the exact time he knew she would not ever have the need to go back to that rotten house, with the twisted dying oak, and to the obese, abusive daughter who would spend the rest of her life alone amongst the packed junk. Rance felt the exact moment his mother would never have to hear the ignorant barking dog. She would rest there now in calm for the open range of her own house on the hill. One last time she would fall asleep, her struggle unseen with a smile from the sound of Rance's voice. This would be the best Christmas gift, given to them both; no more suffering to be had. In it, she halted only for a moment and smiled widely. From both brothers – one watching her, the other the fire – tears of sadness, tears lost for her pain no more, left to this world behind her. No more of anything. Nothing worth the worry. Was anything worth anything? Was it worth her pain or the reasons for time she had? Rance thought on it, and it saddened him even more than the never again of it all. It was the most lonesome he'd felt in all his time.

35

A CLASS FAMILY ACT TO UNRECOLLECT

A gathering would be needed to place their mother in eternal rest. How it was to be done with such a dysfunctional group was unknown. It was their mother's wish to be cremated and buried by their father. There were no complaints there by Plover or Lindy, because it would be cheaper to do it that way and they were always looking at the bottom line. The separated group made its way into the funeral home to meet the director and plan the funeral. All sat their own places, at the large round table in the center of the room. The appearance was that of the tropical sanctuary, with the Zen-like sound of water trickling from the fake molded cement fountain that seemed standard in its use for backyard gardens and funeral homes. The fountain was of a Roman-robed woman of old, pouring water from a pitcher. Artificial plants adorned the room, where mahogany-rich furniture, adorned in gold leaf of non-denominational design and neutral in other faiths, so not to allow seen the boundary lines clearly drawn that might disallow any checkbook that might need to enter and plan there. It was neutral in its design and had the quiet background of soothing music.

All of it just as annoying to Rance as was his need to sit there to plan his mother's funeral while having to put up with Plover and his aging dried-up old wife Gillian, throwing her two cents in, and Lindy putting on her air of sophistication and reserve that hid her evil being well for its course. Hadd sat the table across from Plover and Rance sat across the room, as far away from the others as possible, still within hearing range, but far enough away to be comfortable in not being too close. He watched them talk, as talk was what they'd done best. For all that anyone knew, they seemed more concerned about what was printed in the planned obituary column than about the actual care of the human being written about. It was as easy to them, in the moment, as ordering ice tea to go along with their chicken fried steak; two pretending to be heartfelt in their act in hopes of getting false sympathy from the director. Rance watched the show.

Two Oscar-worthy performances from two well-rehearsed actors. Conversations with the equally as pretentious director who, in the moment periodically, but ever so craftly, checked her watch to be sure to keep everything on track and keep on schedule with the next on-site chapel funeral that would be taking place after the one that just had been, and the scheduled meeting for the one to be planned after them. Rance looked at the dried up prune sitting beside his brother Plover, and wondered why she was there in the first place. The old bitch sat there beside the young bitch; the only difference being that Rance's mother never liked the old bitch ever since the old bag had been caught taking a pair of her shoes from her closet and keeping them as her own.

His question was answered a few minutes later, when the director asked, "What about flowers? Will you be ordering flowers to be placed, and carried down to your love ones internment?" It was then that Rance knew her true reason in being there. She was the first to speak in her mumbled, rambling way that was like fingernails to a chalkboard to Rance. "Mmm-hmmm. Flowers are a waste of money. Mmmmm. Why buy flowers? They will just die anyway. Why don't we just print at the bottom of the handout that in lieu of flowers everyone just give gifts to hospice? At least it will go where needed." "Here, here!" Lindy seconded the motion. Well, maybe not in that way, but Rance was sure in her exuberance and soft answer of "Yes that would probably be the best" words, he clearly understood their real meaning, easier rolled from her thick fat tongue than "Yes, we will purchase flowers." It was all Rance could take. "Are yew gonna give ta hospice? He hollared out. "Why doantcha just lay it out oan tha table right now, let tha director give it to em. I'd bet hospice never sees a dime a yer money!" He bellered. "If these two don't have the funds ta buy flowers, I'll buyem. Just consider yourselves off tha hook! What's she got any say in it anyhow! I don't thank she's part of tha immediate family, although she fits in real well with at least half of us." He finished as he watched the old she-devil give him the evil eye while he began grinning inwardly in just knowing he had struck a nerve. Plover sat there with a face hot red and turned to Rance, but pulling up just short in his response, knowing Rance was not one to take on in that room. The director was just now feeling the need to turn up the water sound and the tranquil music, as she was sensing the dynamics of the family before her. Rance looked over at the bloated whale of a bitch that was in the midst of comforting his brother's old marital hide with the touch of her hand, bonding in their force against the outlaw sitting in the chair across the room.

The director just sat there idle, slightly panicked in the uncertainty of what might happen next. It seemed that this family had been more different with their loss than any she had ever seen. Little did they know that she had seen just about everything up until this. She had soothed genuine feelings of loss with the family planning, having given several breaks throughout to allow time in their grieving. She had also witnessed the normal interactions of just getting the business done and over with, and had seen total absence in the preparation of it, where she would do it all. But she had never witnessed this tension felt and this total lack of regard for the departed, as a thought of the mother had never seemed to enter the picture. They discussed how the service would be performed. As his mother had never been a regular attendee at any church, it was difficult to know how the service would be performed. Rance just knew he wanted the Barnum and Bailey Greatest Show on Earth to be over with, and he was just waiting for the clowns already in the room to show up. He had said his goodbyes, and so had Hadd; it was time to end the ceremony and falseness that went along with it. The director wanted to go over the survivors list – who behind the spouses would be listed in the handout – and how the service would be performed. Hadd told the director to choose, as everyone was at an impasse at how it would be done. A non-denomination preacher was chosen, who might not have passed the scrutiny of Gillian, left unheard as she was still fanning herself from Rance's poke. The director passed that hurdle with the recommendation of a preacher she could affirm. Given her understanding of the situation, different than in her normal manner, she gave out his number to each just to guarantee someone might reach out to him.

She went over any special requests to be noted such as songs, special poems or quotes. Hadd spoke up with his request of the song "Rock of Ages," as he remembered his mother once said she liked it, and would like to have it played at some point. Not to be left out, Lindy spoke for "The Old Rugged Cross," and it was quickly written down in the directors notes. "Anything else?" As her eyes panned the table. Plover spoke up. "Do you have sumpthin by Elvis?" The director looked at him, not quite understanding what was being asked of her. "Was he making requests?" She thought to herself. The table was quiet. Rance was sitting over in his chair. "Here we go. Now the clowns are loose," he thought to himself, with inward smile contradicting his embarrassment at Plover's effort to join in. All that was overtaken by the outward blank expression of seriousness that was on his eldest brother's face. Icing on the cake. It was priceless to Rance, who was in straight line view of him. Lindy just looked pale, awkwardly thinking to herself, "This is my ally?" And the director sat with slight pause before answering, but maybe a little too long. "Elvis?" Said Hadd outloud with an equally "bumfuzzled" look on his face. The young female director sensed an outward burst from Plover toward Hadd, and, as she read it right, quickly quietly interjected, "Did she like Elvis?" "Well I don't know if she did, but I sure do." Rance erupted in laughter out at Plover, whose face was ready to explode in his hearing. The director looked as if she were going to laugh, too, especially when Hadd joined Rance. The old hide Gillian who felt the need to mother and cover the ignorance of her young spouse quickly interjected "Well he meant religious songs." Plover then perked up and said, "Yeah, do you know any religious-type songs that Elvis sings?" "I'm sure we can find something, it *is* Elvis we're talking about here," she said seriously, in order to try to calm the storm she believed was about to come. Rance and Hadd had tears in their eyes in their open roar, and even though truly mourning their mother's loss, this time it was tears of laughter toward the profound ignorance of their older brother. The young director just sat there watching the anger build in Plover while the old hide was still holding hands with Lindy, who was just about to show her true colors; the director was about to be enlightened by them. Three stood up. The old hide and the bitch, with expressions of anger all about them, stormed out of the room, as Plover shot an evil stare at Hadd on his following way behind his only mama left. The witch and the bitch still held hands in synchronized foot-stomping tantrum, while Plover followed closely behind, none ever breaking their locked-in stares at Hadd in their retreat from the peaceful Zen-like waterfall and tranquil music there, leaving Hadd and Rance experiencing a foot-stomping and knee-slapping laugh – and left both there to finalize the arrangements, and pay the bill.

...

The funeral was short, but nice, if one could say that about the type of occasion. Rance had succumbed to the sadness and felt Hadd did as well. Finally, he understood and felt a feeling of true love for his mother about the room and sensed her presence in letting go.

Lindy had made such a fuss on Facebook that a couple of her old high school friends showed for her final curtain call. Carolyn, one of her school mates, looked to be rode hard and put up wet, as most out-to-pasture mares and whores were in that part of North Texas. She made sure to give Rance the noticeable snub, showing solidarity to her horse of the same color. It was directed solely at Rance at the most opportune time to be sure Lindy would see her doing it. As far as the funeral of his mother, Carolyn didn't belong there either; it didn't provide a back car seat or a truck flat bed for her comfort. Her twin-like daughter was there as well and mimicked her mother in the snub as well. Honestly, to Rance she even looked more rode than her mother. Rance sat with Luddia. The girls wrote their goodbyes to be read by the preacher, who seemed to fumble his way through their readings, as his mind was on alotted time and his managing of the readings between the needed gaps filled by the playing of "The Old Rugged Cross" and "Rock of Ages." It didn't feel rushed, but it was a lot to pack in the time reserved. Time was overrunning, as the chapel had been reserved for the next preacher and funeral, readied to follow them.

Lindy had written a lengthy letter to be read in the finality of the service. The chapel, mostly quiet, did sit beside a busy highway where cars were stopped at every intersecting block when the red lights hanging above dictated it. At times, acceleration in their leaving could be pointedly heard through the chapel walls, but only in slight hint. In the preparation of the service the sound man hastily set up the final song to play quietly in the background for the reading of Lindy's lengthy letter – preset and ready for the pushing of the button in its start. The preacher pushed the start button and began to read. An amplified Elvis started singing "Peace in the Valley," shaking the little chapel. The preacher was ignorant to the fact he could not be heard over the song, and gave the appearance he was lip singing to it. Lindy's letter was left completely unheard. On top of that, the red light halted traffic just outside the funeral wall, and in the timing of it happened what sounded like a group of bikers, robustly sitting their Harleys behind its wait of turning green. Completely unaware of the funeral beside them, they throttled their motors in anticipation of the light turning, which vibrated the building in their stay. Everyone in the little chapel felt their presence. Rance and Hadd looked over at Lindy, who was red-faced at her letter unheard. The whole while, the preacher didn't quite notice the stir about him and never faltered in its reading. Just as Elvis was hitting a high note in the peak of the song, the light turned green. Without hesitation, both Hadd and Rance, meaning no disrespect and truly sad in the situation, could not help themselves any longer. In the need of the moment, burst out in laughter, as did everyone else sitting in the front four rows, with the exception of Plover, his old wife Gillian, and Lindy. Rance thought it, as Hadd said it out loud, "Hallelujah!" Rance pictured his vision of the moment of Elvis down on one knee with closed eyes. Closing the last verse was everything, and more, for the three stooges who had planned his second coming at their mother's funeral, when, again, the chapel crowd roared out in laughter at Hadd's response to the last line's reading of the letter. Everyone calmed, all but Lindy, Plover, and his old bitch. It finally set upon them, as both Hadd and Rance felt their mother's full loss at that moment. They were unable to look over at each other as their eyes welled up with tears. It was over.

It was time for the attendees to make their awkward pass by them all. Rance just wanted it to end. He didn't know what was going through Hadd's mind for sure, but felt that he probably wanted the same. It was a blur for Rance, but it seemed like a big party for Plover and Lindy. They were both relishing the "I'm so sorry," condolences. Rance looked at his sister and not one time did she stop her visits and look in the direction of the urn. The last passers came by Rance in their leaving. Two more were still giving their condolences to Lindy on the opposite side of the aisle. The funeral had been conducted and the files of mourners had made it out of the chapel room and to their parking lot cars, where a few talked, some smoked and others left for home or restaurant supper. It was a request made by Hadd that only immediate family be present at the gravesite.

It should have been very cold, but a break in the weather had the day calm, with temperature steadily rising above what was expected as frigid normal. Hadd managed to get the family cemetery mowed of its tall dead grass, while Rance dug the grave the day before, readying it for the afternoon service there. The crowd followed the hearse, along with the preacher, for her resting peace. There would be no Elvis, no letters, just the serenity of the ranch's own cemetery. The sky was clear and the scent of cedar filled the air, as the early melting frost rose from each individual wintergreen leaf. It all provided a pristine, crisp, feeling that had turned the site into a beautiful place. The aroma swept under the new warming day with fresh fragrance as if it were spring. The preacher just talked; nothing planned, just soothing meaningful words that fit the moment. The flowers were set by Rance, and he was glad as the winter brown grass needed its color. He could see a young cottontail sitting under one of the large green trees, in contrast to the dotted strewn out tombstones which often hid them from view. The preacher finished and the place got quiet. Only the occasional sniff of sadness could be heard from Luddia and her girls. Above them, a rustle of air under wing, as a flock of white egrets fanned low and banked just over the fresh grave. The only sound then heard was the awe of the mourners that had gathered there as they felt the significance of the white birds' flight. They seemed holy that day, especially for those who didn't know them as shit birds – birds that followed along behind grazing cattle, gleaning their waste for seeds. It was something he thought his mother would find humorous on that day she was laid to rest.

The calm of that day seemed like the only calm Rance had felt in the entirety of his adult family life. He was sorrowful and whole heartedly wished his mother there, but in her passing a huge part of dysfunction had passed with her; a dysfunction that had wasted the majority of their lifetimes

He could sense it coming, but just how it would play out he wouldn't know. Hadd walked over and joined him there at the grave. "Was Mom's life a waste?" Hadd softly asked. "Huh?" Sounded Rance, who did not answer his brother, but placed his hat upon his head and walked away from the question to his truck. His ties with Plover and Lindy not completely over, but they weren't as strong, either. The ties that left that day were Plover and Lindy's ties to the ranch. In her death, and with property sold and all money gone, Lindy's gravy train had stopped, and she would be forced out of her Wichita home. Plover's hiding shelters were gone, so his income would go to settle tax debt owed. So with that, it ended his ranch ownership as well, as Rance would soon buy out his mother's part. Hadd and Rance just had each other now to worry about, and an uphill outright fight to keep what they earned. What was left in their entanglements was the business of the divided interest of the ranch house on the hill. Each owned a quarter of the house that was surrounded by now-grown pine and one lone oak, sitting empty in the center of Rance's land. He didn't have the money to buy each of the others out of it. He felt Hadd would be okay with nothing paid for it, but he also knew that the others would soon be coming and demanding their full share.

His binding ties with the others were still there.

36

THE DAYS WERE MADE FOR THE YOUNG

Rance opened the heavy glass door of the Dairy Queen entering ahead of Solace. They both had been calving out a heifer earlier that morning and were in need of a break. They made their way in for an early dinner time burger. "Howdy Rance," the Knights sounded out in unison. "How yew boys a doin this fine day?" "Good, for old fucks!" Answered Dobber, loud enough for the car in the drive-in window to hear. A "Well! I never!" Was heard in reciprocation, as the driver rolled up her window and the wide-eyed kids in the back seat covered their mouths and snickered at the gruff old man. "Gitcha some of that fuckin coffee over there. It'll put hair not only own yer chest, but oan yer ass, too!" Dobber finished. Rance was already making his way over to it.

Solace had stopped short at the counter and was talking to Cindi Barber, the young girl working the register. She was one year younger than he and they had gotten to know each other on Solace's occasional stops there to eat. It was something Rance was seeing becoming a habit to his young partner, as sometimes he would look for an excuse to drive over, when at times it would be seventy miles out of the way. Rance ignored it, as he had done the same with Luddia, and understood the power of the draw. Cindi was a good girl. Rance had watched her grow up, and knew her father well. A prominent attorney who started out in Archer City, but now practiced in Wichita, he was also a rancher, and Rance did most of his day work when extra help was needed. It was easy, as his ranch lay just outside the city. That was how Solace had first met Cindi. She was a petite young thing, barely four feet eleven, and her eyes sparked blue every time she saw the tall, skinny and awkward boy. The two were a pair to be seen; she would stretch up to look at him and he would hunker, to do the same. The two never saw their differences, even through everyone else was quick to point it out. All Rance saw was love, pure and simple, and if he had to take a drive sixty miles out of the way under false pretense, he was sure not to let on that he knew it was.

"Hey Rance. There was a guy in here askin a boutchew earlier," Jim said from his spot at the Round Table. "Who was it?" Rance asked, after finishing pouring his cup and sitting down. "Doanno, a fancy dude. Drivin a ranch rig though," he answered. "He didn't say what he woanted?" "No an we didn tell him where yew were none, neither," Rankin spoke up. "Well why didn't yew ask him who he was or what he wanted with me?" "Weren't nunna our fuckin bizzness what the fuck he woanted!" "Yew gotta point there," said Rance. "Fuckin A. I knowd it! We figgered he might be a bill collector er sumpthin an we weren't goanna fuckin rat yew out," Dobber blasted, followed by a couple of mumbled "Yea that's right," from the others. "What was he drivin?" Rance asked. "A crew cab Dodge dually. Had a pretty little gal with him. Carried a notebook, pressed up against her and followed him like a lost puppy dog," Jim spoke up. "Yea," said Rankin. "Had some kinda green colored logo on both doors." "What?" Asked Rance. "Some kinda green fuckin sign oan tha sides a tha fuckin truck is what he said," Dobber spoke up. "Pretty little son of a bitch," he finished. "Yea, sure was," sounded out the other two. "What was?" "What?" Answered Rankin. "What was a pretty little son of a bitch?" Rance asked again. "That girl carryin tha notebook," answered Jim. "Yea. Purritee," said Rankin.

The burgers came out and that was the only time Solace made it to the table, he followed and helped Cindi bring the order. Rance didn't know how he made it to the table without running over somebody, or something, as he never took his eyes off the young Barber girl. He stood there holding Rances burger, for a good minute as Rance looked on. "Mind if ah eat boy?" "Huh?" Answered Solace. "Mind if ah eat?" He said again, pointing at his meal being held in Solace's hand. "Naugh, not at all," he said plopping the burger down in front of Rance while the boys at the Round Table enjoyed a good laugh at trance-causing love. They finished their burgers and goodbyes and headed out.

Solace's pickup had been left at the calving pasture of the Broken Spoke Ranch owned by Luddia's good neighbor Buster Murphy. The big Irishman's family had migrated into the country, along with all of the Dutchmen who founded Windhorst, early on. The Germans ran across his ancestor's caravan, lost and starving, trying to make it out to the El Paso region. They were adopted in, and even though he was more German-bred than Irish after two generations of marrying in, he still claimed his Irish heritage and wore it like a badge on his sleeve. His family even made sure the slight Irish twang still carried on down the line. The genetics of the Irish side were overpowering and he dared any man around to try to whoop him. Even in his seventies, no man would take the dare. But the big man laughed heartily and never truly angered and never met a man he didn't like, even if he had to slap him first. There was a good relationship between Luddia and Buster and he threatened to render any man harmless that didn't treat her right. He was a big man with big hands and the overpowering strength and brawn to go with it. He married the biggest raw-boned German gal there was around. Her name was Helga; aptly named and she fit the bill. Together they produced nine of the biggest boys in Young County, but they were labor-bred and took to the oil fields rather than stay with the ranch. He relied on day workers and contract help when needed to keep his ranch going. He was a farmer more than a rancher, and often bragged that he could raise a crop in a dust bowl, given one seed and a hoe to work it with. Rance pulled in at the calving pasture pickup and Solace was already anxiously grabbing at the latch to get out, when Luddia's feeder truck came racing through the gate with the brakes locked, skidded to a bone-jarring stop.

She lept from her truck, just barely taking the time to pull the shifter out of gear. She raced toward Rance with a look on her face that had the appearance of being caught between shock, disbelieving and nervous excitement, yet with no indication of whether something bad was coming of it or something was urgent that he needed to know. "What is it? What's wrong?" Rance hollered out, while the settling dust raced its way up with Luddia and draped itself around the both of them. She was holding very tightly to an opened envelope and the letter that was inside of it.

"Yer not gonna believe it! Yer just not gonna believe it Rance! She said excitedly. "What? Believe what?" "Yer just not! Sit down Rance. Sit down!" She said with breath lost in her telling. Rance took to the already down tailgate of Solace's truck and set down. "Ok, Ok, I'm sittin. What is it? Catch yer breath and tell me. What is it?" He asked. "Rance, yer not goin ta believe it! Fred. Fred Atterbury. He left you his whole ranch. His whole total operation. He left you all of it, Rance tha whole ranch in total. All of his equipment. All of his livestock, home, mineral rights, money in the bank, his investments. Everything!" She hollered, jumping up and down and doing a happy dance all over the ground around, raising her own dust cloud meeting the already hanging one around them. "Yer lyin!" "No I'm not!" "He's got a nephew and some cousins. He's leaving it ta them." "No he's not! I'm tellin yew. He left it all to you. It was going to be yew and Roy, but if one of you were not able, then it was to go to the one that was left and if that one wasn't able, it was ta go to one of his cousins, and if not them, to the Catholic Church and the Henrietta Boy Scouts. Alls I know it would be to anybody but his nephew." "What about his nephew?" Rance asked. "He set him up, too, Rance. He gave him fifty percent of the oil royalties of what's been already drilled. The other fifty goes to yew, plus a hundred percent of anything new," she screamed. "How do yew know this?" "There was this attorney driving all over the country tryin ta findja. He finally found somebody willing to tell where yew were and he wound up in our driveway. He's still there! Waiting for yew. I've been tryin to find you for halfa tha day!" She said. "Why haven't you answered my calls?" She asked. "Left the phone in the truck! How come he toldja all this?" He asked. "Because I'm yer wife, that's why! He wouldn't tell me any specifics, but he showed me a copy of this letter showing Fred's intent. He needs ya to come now. He needs yew Rance! Yew." They all jumped in their trucks, even Solace in his, and began what seemed like a race over two counties in the direction of Rance and Luddia's Young County home where sat the big white dually Dodge with the firm's company logo on each door.

The slicked up dude and the pretty little gal with the notebook were sitting there waiting for Rance to appear.

37

WHAT A CHANGE A DAY IN THE LIFE MAKES

Overnight Rance became one of the largest ranch owners in the area. The Bar Back L was his, but not without five more years of legal battles to hold onto it. Within one month of the lawyer's visit, he was already operating it, as Fred's bank accounts were unfrozen, though the production checks, still held up in legal protest, would be deposited by the second year. Something odd to Rance was how the banks then fought for his attention, and were willing to back any advance needed, when they would turn the other way before. Cindi's father, Talley, took over representing Rance, and in that second year laid the law down in no uncertain terms, making it quite clear to Fred's nephew if he pursued it any further he would "kick the chair right out from under him and Rance would own his other fifty percent." The battle stopped right then and there.

Fred's nephew would live a long easy existence with what he had, and now it looked like Rance would, too. It took another three years to just iron out the kinks, but Rance was in full mode when it came to operating. He brought in Hadd and split that portion down the middle fifty-fifty. Hadd took over living at Fred's old place.

Hadd used his money to ward off Plover and Lindy, and told them if they didn't sign their remaining ranch quarters over, he would be sure to turn his lawyers loose on them, and show the world what they were. Both, even under a first offense, would more than likely see jail time. He confronted Plover with it when the old boy had the audacity to come out and set terms that his old mother wife began to mumble out with lawsuit threats of her own toward Rance. He just looked directly in the eyes of Plover, while laying it all out for the worn out old hide and put her, for once, in her place. Plover turned red and gritted his teeth, but again thought better of taking on Hadd anytime, much less at his own place – finalizing once and for all the ranch house high on the hill, with its single lone oak surrounded by the ponderosa pine, for him and Rance. Plover and the fat bitch from Wichita were both forever gone – just like the ones that had been weeded out from the solid stock that had migrated in on the East Fork Creek Basin of the Little Wichita River a little over a hundred years before. It was now up to Rance and Hadd to prove their worth and carry on – theirs, completely, to prove out on their own.

As for Cage and his high-fence game ranch, he did eventually buy out the neighboring properties at one end of the road, but that still left Hadd and Rance's scrub bush basin not for sale in that bottom. Rance took a bit of that inherited money and opened a twenty-four-hour-a-day gun range on three sides of it, free to the public as such. When he didn't have patrons there to shoot, he hired people to do just that. He also paid others to play loud music, shoot off fireworks, and generally party like there was no tomorrow. He was sued, but for Cage there wasn't a thing he could do about it. It was far from any city limits, and how could you keep somebody from shooting on their own land, when you're doing the same on yours? He had more to lose there with clients lost and ibex and giraffe bills to pay. So retaliation was completely out of the question. He would soon agree to deal with Rance and Hadd, and they soon would be buying back both lost quarters that Cage had acquired from Plover and Lindy – and one thousand acres more just to insure a clear property line. Rance insisted on full mineral rights for all acreage bought in with the deal. And the seller, Cage, would build the new fence on the boundary line where no one crossed at the new border, with the old high fence torn out at his expense. He succumbed, as long as Rance agreed to shut the shooting range and the all night party goers down. He happily did so. He, Luddia and Hadd now operated a little over eighteen thousand acres in three counties of North Texas and he was proving his worth in the gain.

Rance watched out over the land, taking his stewardship once more. Seasons were again tilting in their favor; it had been five years from the day Rance and Luddia said their "I do's." Welcome changes and now a new horizon welcomed and looked forward to. It was a beautiful May as the storms were light and the rainfall above average. Rance had made his rounds in the same old beat up flatbed Ford that he once just put up with, but now enjoyed for the pleasure it had given him. He no longer had the worry of repairing it, as there was plenty there to do it with, and he had no desire to buy new. It was as good a friend as any and carried him when he had nothing. His old ways were still with him. He would not flaunt his means; he never felt comfortable, anyhow, in his way of what he gained and how much he had. His life had always been simple and he wanted to keep it that way. If walked up on while farming or working the stock, an outsider wouldn't have been able to distinguish him being boss from that of a hired hand. He liked it just that way; working an honest day like the rest.

The wild tickseeds were starting their blooms, along with the Indian paintbrush that were a little earlier than usual. The Texas lupine patches, in their deep blues, rolled like blankets in big squares along the hillside, leaving the rocky edges and mesas for the paintbrush orange and the tick seed yellow, with their orange dot centers, painting the soft grass spring pastures in vibrant beauty. The lime green budding of the mesquite shown out in brilliant contrast as the young Chinaberry growths shown in a different, even brighter, light lime green in their glimmer, while tufts of tall brown blue stem grass stood raised from their still winter's nap.

Rance parked his truck on the hill. He shut the engine off and the quietness of it surrounded him. Caught up in it, he sat overlooking the valley of the Pease below. The stream bed was full and the water was clear and flowing. Ripples started outwardly, eventually ending in their reaching of its snaking white sand curves. He listened to the quietness of it. In its slow sweeping, he believed he could hear its life. There was no other movement or sound anywhere in the distance; just the wave of the rise and fall of a lost soft breeze as it would pick up and wane in its short speed, and filter out in its dropping rest. Not a soul in sight. No where. Even off in the distance, and even farther. This was Rance – his whole being.

Fort Worth and all of its uncivilized quirks was moving in, but maybe it would be a lifetime before it would reach him here. Despite his wishes never to be in the reality just one hundred and fifteen miles away, they were coming and changing his world. But he was no better than they, and no worse than those of his own kind that had come and changed the free spirit of the Comanches that had watched the wild tickseed and paintbrush before him. He was feeling what the last great Comanche War Chief, Quanah Parker, might have felt as he once might have sat the same hill. Rance was sensing, now, what he must have felt when the change of the white man took it all in, as he had, and claimed it, as he had, from another. Its toll on his heart and his people's hearts would have been no different than that of Rance's and no different than the toll others would take with the newcomers 115 miles away. Rance felt that now. He never thought it before; in earlier life he never thought about them at all, nor had the Comanche. It had felt to have been his always. His as if it had been generated by ancestors' hands and not of Gods. Now, like Natives past, he resented the contradiction of them coming, as if it was not his kind that had done the same to the tribes that claimed it the same and resented the loss the same. It wasn't fair and equal thought and he didn't wrestle much with it. He resented them coming and now felt a brotherhood with Quanah that, in truth, wasn't at all. But resent them he did.

To the east a second wave was moving, and bought with fast money every loose piece of soil found in their escape from the confining boundaries of the big cities. The rough work had already been done by forgotten settlers that left it to those the fast money buys from. They buy it with the ease of not wishing to know or learn the history of the land bought, with most that *would* know it long gone from it. Without regard, they would plow it, and fence it, and grade over the Comanche graves unknowing. They would shut off and dam up anything that was there to be dammed, by damn. Rance, even knowing the truth of the forever change that they were bringing, also knew it would be too late for them. Too late for Cage, as he was one, with more money than he knew what to do with. He wanted the title of it, but hadn't earned its course. He wanted to be big, look big, and impress the rest, but Rance saw him as small, very small, in his dealings. Rance saw the old ways; the need to partner with his neighbor and not purposely do anything that would hinder their process, their programs, and their lives in the doing. The new buyers were ignorant to that way. This was the difference for Rance, as he and Hadd were surrounded by one of the bad kind; Cage was of the new, who had no feeling for the ones he encompassed. To the contrary, it was easy for ones like him to run roughshod and run personal projects over any worry about the side effects cast in his doing it. Rance had seen his like come and go, but their agreement would stand, and by it the current peace would hold.

Luddia was surrounded by the good for now, but many were old. Who would know how, why, or when that dam would break, but for now, it seemed, her neighbors had heirs who were content in the work they had grown up in; heirs willing to carry on hard-earned tradition with humble ambitions to take the lifestyle and traditions in stride, and not abuse the privilege.

Now Rance and Hadd were surrounded in a new fight, cornered like the last free band of Quanah's tribe in time-lost-land on the noble Pease. Their ranch was now bordered by three ranchers contemplating selling out. But theirs now was a vast spread and it would take a total buyout of all three to cause them grief. And there was enough oil coming from the ground to insure a larger portion purchased out further west to get away, if that would become the need to be. Rance thought on that for a moment; in his possible leaving and driving westward into those newer places for him – but older for those there first -.would he be seen as he saw those who came from the cities? His thought was short lived. He was not like them.

He was ranch-raised, and he would adapt without overreaching. He would assimilate naturally, as his ways were their ways, too. Like them, he had also come from an ancient background – the same ways and type of background – so Rance would be accepted, as he was descended from those who had assimilated with the Comanche. The same ways in background, so Rance would be accepted as he would be accepting of his kind. He thought of the look of the land. Would it always look this way? What change would come, even here? And how long would it take?

He thought about his buddy Hank, and the new house built in the place of the little green one, on West Walnut. Rance moved the original out to the center of the home place spread, being a bit sentimental. The new house was a delayed, but special, wedding present for him and Merna, and greatly appreciated by his old friend that had always been there for Rance or Luddia when times were different. Hank was always there and never once let him down. Rance met him at the diner off and on. Things did change for them both with the introduction of spouses between the daywork they both enjoyed, and morning gatherings with the Knights at the Dairy Queen. Hank would have the sole contracts of cattle hauling from the different sites of Rances Backed ЯB. Rance had also given his friend a section of land for his own; a place he always mentioned to Rance as a good place in Foard County, where it overlooked the Pease. That would be its name on the shingle that swung over its entry gate: "A Good Place." It had plenty of bees, as Hank enjoyed his new hobby with the hives.

Rance had been set up, just as anyone who had stuck by him in the hard times would be. Just as Fred had done, he made sure the Meals on Wheels kept plenty of food in its pantry for the old folks of Archer and Clay County. He also supported the old hands that found it difficult to retire and make ends meet. He and Hadd humbled in their spoken names over the loud speakers for the first time as sponsors for the annual Archer County Rodeo; and their brands recognized for all to hear. They even enjoyed a ride in the parade inside the white Cadillac convertible that carried only the county's finest for their greetings of recognition once a year in the rodeo parade. The Cadillacs had longhorn steer horns attached to heavy chromed mounting collars, and cut to lay just one inch outside the front width of each Caddy's hood. The cars, polished with mirror finish, had plush red velvet interiors, chrome hub caps, and memorable cow-bell-sounding horns – some even bellowed when passing the parade crowds. Patrons made greetings of hoots and forced pitched whistles in their passing, unable to admit that, deep down, they always wished they could ride behind those same long mounted horns. Rance and Hadd were recognized, but didn't let it affect their ways. Both stayed secure in their grounding, greeting anybody and everybody, just like they had before.

Hadd was happy, too, and had found a woman of his own – one that he had hired originally to keep his house in order. She was a very quiet and studious woman with a welcoming way, and a name that befit her beauty. Her name was Ha'ng, meaning "Angel in the Full Moon," with the last name of Tao. She was the same age as Hadd, of Vietnamese heritage, and spoke decent, but slightly broken English, Unbeknownst to Rance, until their meeting, Hadd was well-versed in her native tongue. Something he had not used in a long, long time, and never around his younger brother. Rance couldn't ask, but thought she might have reminded him of a time that he needed to forget, but also needed to remember. Maybe she was his understanding when nothing else was, because of it. A hurtful time of the Mekong Delta, but a life in common they both once shared.

They were a good fit and a good pair. Rance could see his older brother was finally at ease in just knowing her. She had brought out a peace to him only the two could relate to, even though Rance would tease him at times with his warning to sleep with one eye open.

They settled together into the Atterbury ranch home and he and Ha'ng changed a few things about it to make it more relatable for her. Hadd added a small greenhouse at one end for Ha'ng to raise the plants and spices for her Asian cuisine that weren't readily available at Kings. It made her happy and Hadd was happy to do it for her. They truly loved each other, and, while most didn't understand his choice, Rance did. He welcomed her in with open arms.

Solace and Cindi dated for about two years, then married. Although he was offered a position on the Talley's Broke Spoke, he felt he and Cindi needed a start of their own, close enough, but far enough away from Talley to be comfortable. Talley respected Solace even more with the decision, and Solace would begin to run things for him, while continuing his day work partnering with Rance. They would trade out assistance on both ranches – a change they all needed. Rance would never be able to find another top hand like Solace and Solace never a partner like Rance. So Rance, after talking it over with Hadd, agreed for Solace and Cindi to stay in the ranch house surrounded by the ponderosa pines and the one lone oak that sat high on the hill in South Clay County. It would be a place far away from the old shack start of Rance's memory. A better way for them both until they would decide where they would need to be. Rance figured his mother would be at peace with the decision made.

38

ABERNATHY'S CONTINUATION OF THE BRAND

The year was 2018, the month was May. Rance sat the driver's seat of his old truck, centered on that old road he loved to sit, high above everything else on the hill overlooking the Valley of Foard County below. He sat, viewing the Pease River flow below him. The quiet in the moment was priceless. The clouds changed shape before him, never settling, always in their quest. He watched the buzzards lift and fall, bank and rise with speed, then, slowing, halt and circle over the river valley below. The corner of his eye caught the movement, as the slow slide of a lone diamond back rattler would break its hiding cover and forcibly cross the road just in front of him. In the distance a lightning strike pounded the dry dirt plain with no response from the high building cloud that it fired from, fifteen miles out. The heavy darkness ever chasing in its rise, as the storm unleashed its wave upon the calm below it. The rest of the sky was clear and quiet all around him, and to his right as far as he could see was the same. A bobwhite quail hopped up to the top of an old cedar corner post, ruffled himself out, then took stance as solid as an orchestra conductor. He quickly settled himself and started his call.

"What's that Daddy?" "It's a bobwhite quail, son." Rance answered the young boy beside him happily sitting atop Rance's folded down arm rest in the center of his old truck's seat. "It is?" "Yes, Son it is. Ain't it beautiful?" "Shore is Daddy. Kin I hode it?" Rance laughed at the four-year-old's question. "No Son. He's singin now tryin ta find his family. If we hold him he'll probly stop and they might git lost. Do yew still woant ta hold it?" "No Daddy. I don't woant his family ta git lost." "I don't woant em to neither. Once someone loses their family they're always lost." Rance said, while looking at the storm wind down in front of him and the sky's beginning clear. "Am I ever goanna be lost, Daddy?" "No, Son, I guarantee yew woant. Me and yer Uncle Hadd are goin ta make sure a that." Rance said. "Yer appreciated Son, an loved just like tha rest a yer family. I love yew, yer sisters, yer mama and yer Uncle Hadd, an yew remember that." "Ok, Daddy. Yew thank that Bobby quail loves him's family too?" The young boy asked while leaning up and into the window to get a closer look. "I know he does. That's why he's fightin so hard ta call out to em." "Daddy?" "Yes son." "I love mommy, Kaylee, Taylor and Uncle Hadd, too. And Hank and Merna, too." "I know ya do son." Rance answered, as he watched out in the distance, caught up in the moment of several layers of geese all trying for the same goal yet at different levels and speeds – just like the folks down below them, all in their way trying to find true north. Their white bellies contrasted brightly in their passing of the still dark clouds of the breaking storm.

The two-way radio keyed in the voice behind it, settling all around the insides of Rance's old truck. "How are yawl doin out there?" It was Luddia. She must have caught some skip from the storm bouncing the signal their way, as they were some distance out to be getting her call. "Good, Honey." "Hi Mommy!" Then Rance said "Over." "Baby is that yew?" Luddia keyed out as Rance keyed in for his boy's response. "Yes, Mommy it's me." "Are yew havin fun?" "Yes." "Did Daddy git yew sumpthin ta eat?" "Yes." "What did he get yew?" "A hot dog at the store an sum chocolate milk." "That sounds really good Baby. I hope yer havin fun." "I am Mommy. Daddy showed me a Bobby quail. He woants him's mama and family." "He does?" "Yep." "I love you Mommy. Daddy does too. So does Kaylee and Taylor and Uncle Hadd and Aunt Ha'ng and Hank and Merna." "I love you, too, Paul." "Thanks Mommy, bye." "Yew be good now." Luddia laughed at her little boy's talk. "Sounds like a little Rance there in the making." "Ah doan't thank so, Luddia." Rance said, then keyed in again and added, "He's good like yew." "Yer a good man, Rance. Don'tchew ever forgit it. I love yew. And, as yer son says, so does he and Kaylee and Taylor and Uncle Hadd and Aunt Ha'ng and Hank and Merna. Yew comin home soon, Rance?" "Oan our way Luddia. Me'n Paul will be woantin supper when we git there. Over and out." Rance said, as he patted the next in line on his leg, and began their long drive down every less traveled dirt and gravel road they could find on their way back toward the ranch in Young County, and home.

39

RELATIVE EVOLUTION FOR RANCE;
SETTLEMENT AND UNDERSTANDING PEACE

Still 2018, early summer setting in as Rance made his way through the cow pen gate, leading his big roan gelding in a cooling walk, before allowing him to water. There the big round trough lie, splitting the fence of the holding pen and the feed barn lot. Water flowed over its sides endlessly, while the windmill spun slowly under the mid-day breeze. He patted his gelding's lathered neck in his restraint to letting him drink, as he needed to cool down a might. Rance stood in wait with him, even being as dry as the worn out waiting cow horse. A grasshopper made its fluttering hop from a stalk of barnyard Johnson grass, over into the open top stock tank, where normally it would be its end. "Not taday, little feller," Rance said, as he scooped it up with his hand and back out onto the hot Texas dirt. It had been time enough, so Rance loosened the girth, led Yank over to the trough and dropped the reins. The old roan sucked in the cool water in long sucking gulps as did Rance, only his came from the flow pipe that filled the tank. A lonely yellow jacket wasp swept in, agitated by Rance taking his spot. Rance looked up at the winged creature, realizing it was only protecting its nest, so he backed off and let it calm, he would finish his own drink later. Rance was feeling wiser about his shortcomings, and with age he was readily backing off from conflict, as he understood the tradeoff of his limit in time there, for the wisdom he had gained in the process. He wiped the sweat that was coming down his leathery face with a single bare forearm swipe, leaving a streak of mud upon him, mixed of sweat and the West Texas dirt that had accumulated in his behind-hoof driving of his cattle to the pens. "What a beautiful end," he said aloud, causing the still drinking roan, water dripping from his quivering lower lip, to look up at him with slight pause, then return for his finishing drink. Rance once again looked over the windblown scrub short growth trees, that only he would understand and said, "Beautiful." He was a survivor that his descendants would now hold high in regard. He stood and listened. Again it was quiet. A different kind of quiet to him, with the rustle of the penned cattle, along with the stomping of Yank's hooves, trying to shake another horse fly from his hide.

Rance stopped there, completely silent in thought. "How did it git this way?" He said quietly to himself, while looking out over the top rail of the pipe lot fence toward the green pasture grass beyond it. A group of Rio Grande toms walked slowly out in the rise before him, without even the slightest bit of fear of the rancher or his penned cattle. They had learned a long time ago that he was no threat to their being. He wasn't alone anymore and he felt it. He looked over at his very old friend Bingo, and asked, "Well howyew bin ole boy taday? I shore missed yew oan tha drive," as he reached down and gave his worn out old dog a pat on the head. He was a friend to Rance that had been there no matter what. He never judged him, as so many had. Now Rance wouldn't pass his interminable companion without noticing him and showing kindness at his worth. He thought about the pat, then, realizing it wasn't enough, began to briskly rub the old dog's shoulders with both hands. Rance could see the smile form on his old friend's face in acceptance of Rance's added attention and gesture. He looked at his old dog. Seeing the glazed over blind eye dancing in is socket, he recognized that now the other was doing the same. "Good ole boy, aintcha?" Rance asked him, knowing his time was limited as they both were in the waning years of their lives. Rance no longer needed his mirrored reflection to know he was getting there. He felt the changes, but was still in the transition where he noticed and recognized the experiences. He pulled up the reins and led the old horse back to the waiting stock trailer, loaded him and tossed in a bucket full of oats to the forward deck feed trough. He placed an old four-wheeler ramp to the back of his truck and watched the old dog, with his help, limp up it and curl himself at his place under the tapered feeder box shade, readying himself for the ride.

Rance looked around in his surveying of the ranch. He caught sight of the old ranch house, lonely no more as Cindi was busy hanging out wash clothes on the line. With her wave at him, he knew he'd done right in giving that old house that sat on the ridge overlooking the valley to her and Solace, after his dealing it back from Cage. It wouldn't be long that another would be added on that hill, with the old oak lots, the again-used garden plot, with the new-mowed grass, and the rebuilt chicken coop that sat beside it. It was in good hands now and under new management for the first time in a hundred years – given by choice of Hadd and Rance of the Backed ЯB of Clay County.

...

Rance stood and watched Hadd's white Ford pickup move its way up the long white gravel dusty road, and the mile it took in its making its way to its spot beside him. Rance, never turning his head, stood still looking down at the old ranch home that sat below them, beyond the new house drive high on the hill. The opening squawk and followed slam of Hadd's pickup door was the only thing that silenced the momentary singing of the mockingbird that sat in the lone oak tree yard. It would be the only resident of the house on the hill surrounded by the ponderosa pines that stood behind both brothers. "How's it goin little brother?" Hadd asked. Rance, not intentionally ignoring, stood quietly looking down at the old ranch yard out in the distance, at his hanging tree of boyhood long past, and concentrating inwardly while gazing still upon Cindi, lost in thought of its meaning. "Well?" Hadd again asked. "Oh. Fine, Hadd. Just fine," Rance answered.

"Ya know Hadd I never answered ya that day, but the answer is 'No.'" "What?" Asked Hadd, while Rance continued. "She wasn't a waste. Not a waste at all, a matter a fact. She done tha best thang she knew how. That's all." In slight puzzlement to his brother's randomness, it slowly dawned on Hadd his meaning. He remembered his question to Rance that cool winter's end – left unanswered. Hadd put his arm around the shoulder of his brother as he often had done throughout their long years spent together and both looked out over the old house with the surrounding oaks on the ridge that had long passed them both. Then the quieted mockingbird broke the silence. After some pause Hadd did as well. "Ya know Rance, I guess yer right about that, she wasn't no waste, but she coulda done a lot better. But yer right, she just done the best she knowed how that's all," Hadd finished. Rance just shrugged his shoulders, turned back toward the house surrounded with ponderosa pine and the single mockingbird-filled oak high on the hill in south Clay County and answered his old brother quietly. "I reckon Hadd, I reckon."

THE END

Jonna Parr Photo

Roger Browning is a successful North Texas rancher. He has hand-written hundreds of books, showing them to no one, and throwing them away out of a belief that they could not possibly be any good. Over the thirty-some years he has been putting the stories from his mind onto paper, he has never allowed anyone to see them or know of them.

For some reason, he decided to take a chance and read one page from one of the thirty or so spiral notebooks perched on the dash of his old Ford Bronco to an outdoor columnist/small publisher from Washington State and that man's son-in-law. Stunned at how they found themselves standing alongside the protagonist on that first read page, the two quickly disabused Browning of his attitude toward his writing.

This first published Roger Browning novel is that story – Rance's story.